Dancing in the Dark

Dancing in the Dark

Donald Thomas

St. Martin's Press
New York

Library of Congress Cataloging-in-Publication Data

Thomas, Donald Serrell.
    Dancing in the dark / Donald Thomas.
        p.   cm.
    "A Thomas Dunne book."
    ISBN 0-312-10447-2
    1. Crime—England—London—History—20th century—
Fiction. 2. London (England)—History—1800-1950—Fiction.
3. Criminals—England—London—Fiction. I. Title.
PR6070.H6D36   1994
823′.914—dc20   93-37004
                                                         CIP

First published in Great Britain by Macmillan London Limited.

First U.S. Edition: January 1994
10 9 8 7 6 5 4 3 2 1

FOR MICHAEL THOMAS

Dancing in the Dark

1

STARLIGHT RENDEZVOUS

1

Sidney Royce, also known as 'Roller', stared at the shadowless brilliance of the green baize. His eye measured the table-top distance between the black ball and the top right-hand pocket. Smoke curled blue and sinuous into the overhead whiteness of the pool-room light.

'Watch this, my son,' he said quietly.

He chalked the cue, leant forward and snicked the white ball, the movement of his eyes following its sleek hiss across the green nap of billiard cloth, as though he would lose control of its direction if he straightened up. It cut the black ball with a click light as a finger-snap, dropping it hard and straight. Only when it thudded into the netted pouch did Royce stand upright. He looked across at the thin man with the drawn face and narrow moustache who watched from the far end of the table.

'Never bet against a sure thing, Tonto. Never do that.'

The thin man wore a slender black tie and narrow trousers, like an old-fashioned clerk. The shoulders of his jacket were padded into high narrow peaks. His black hair was Brylcreemed into a single conch-like wave above his pale forehead. He grinned and then shrugged amiably at his own ineptitude. Instead of answering Royce, he turned and made a quiet comment to an older man standing in the shadows beyond the pale glare of the downlights.

Royce put his cue away, clipping it into the rack, and pulled on his jacket. He was wearing an evening suit and smoking the squat remainder of a cigar. There are men on whom the most expensively tailored evening dress still suggests cinema management or fight promotion. Sidney Royce was one of that class.

5

Buttoning the jacket, he went across and took two five-pound notes from the nearest of three men sitting on the bench which ran along the dark plank-panelling of the wall. The pool room, like the noisy bar adjoining it, was hung with prints of forgotten Derby winners and long-dead boxing champions. Above them was a laurelled photograph of the last Prince of Wales, who had been briefly Edward VIII before his abdication ten years earlier.

Royce looked at his watch and went out into the street. His dove-grey Humber Pullman was parked by the far pavement, where a high blank wall ran opposite the length of the terrace known as Tips Tenements. Beyond the wall, with its rusting tin-plate advertisements for Ogden's Guinea Gold Tobacco and Virol Tonic, was a world of docks, gas works, and ship yards. Here and there, between posters on the patched concrete, were the last stencilled traces of 'Your Duty Now is War Work!'

As he turned to walk round a long dark car parked at the nearer kerb, the bulk of a man standing against the light blocked his way. Royce moved aside to pass round him and the man moved to block him again. On the plate-iron bridge that crossed the empty street lower down, a line of shunted rail wagons jangled and clattered. Royce glared in the dark, never doubting that it was an attempt by Tonto's friends to take back the ten pounds. He was a little drunk and now regretted that his head was not clearer. The large man kept his back to the street light and it was hard to see much beyond his height, his hat, and his coat. The cheapness of the trick moved Royce's contempt.

'Who the hell d'you think you are?'

'I'm this,' the stranger said. He held a heavy automatic pistol to one side so that Royce could see it in the street light. From the size of it and the wooden stock, Royce guessed that it was a 9 mm Mauser, pre-war issue and built like a cannon.

'Very clever!' he said scornfully. 'You're not going to start loosing off artillery like that in the middle of the street. You know it. I know it. So bugger off while you can still walk!'

'Best not make this more difficult than it need be, Mr Royce,' the man said quietly.

Royce felt strength from his growing anger. But while he was being brave about the Mauser, there was a sound from the dark car beside him. It was scarcely more than an old man spitting in the gutter, the crack of a small target-automatic at close range. Its flame was subdued as a table lighter. Royce stood quite still,

6

as though listening to a far-off sound. The concealed gun spat twice more. He sank to his knees on the damp paving, swayed and fell without another word. By the time that he lay motionless, the man with the Mauser was back in the car and the dark shape of the vehicle had moved off smoothly down the length of the dockland street, past the narrow terrace of Tips Tenements and the baker's shop at its corner. The dark-haired man, Tonto, with the Brylcreemed wave, was the only one to emerge from the doorway of the shabby pub. He had ample time to step outside the pool room, draw the wallet from Royce's pocket, and extract the two banknotes. The serial numbers of five-pound notes were still routinely listed by the issuing banks. Best not leave them lying about. He walked unhurriedly away from Tips Tenements and turned the far corner.

2

Latifa Noon, dark haired and almond eyed, drew the green velvet of the curtains across the long windows that looked over the park trees towards Baker Street. It was quiet now on the carriageway below, only the intermittent traffic of buses and taxis swishing past to Camden Town, as though the tarmac was still wet from the morning's rain. The apartment had been furnished with carpeting in dark green, walnut shelving, and tear-drop light-pendants. Its radiogram was the size of a small sideboard. She balanced a record of Eileen Joyce playing the *Warsaw Concerto* on the turntable, touched the needle to the edge, and closed the lid.

Tom Foster, stripped of his jacket and waistcoat, eased the wide square knot of his red tie. He sighed with contentment and lay back splay-legged in his wing chair, watching the girl. She had all the natural eroticism of the Levant, heightened by aids to Western beauty. And she had everything to gain from pleasing him. The lids of her almond eyes were made up white and the lashes darkened. The tall brow, the sharp nose, and the weaker chin of her profile seemed accentuated by the beehive of dark hair. The narrow-waisted bow-thighed figure in the flared red dress was lithe and exquisite.

'You go first,' she said.

Foster got up and kissed her. 'Mix us a drink, then.' He felt an excitement in treating her as a servant. Her submission to him in little things was the great aphrodisiac of their love-making. 'Mix us a cocktail. Then come in and take your clothes off where I can see you.'

He went into the bedroom alone, listening to the sound of glasses and the chords of the piano. Taking off his heavy gold Rolex wristwatch he shed his clothes and presently walked dressing-gowned to the bathroom. Hot water tumbled into the wide lime-green tub, obliterating the long chords of the mood music for *Dangerous Moonlight*. Foster stepped from the shantung dressing-gown and then felt in its pocket for the slim silver oblong of his cigarette case. A moment later he lay back in the warmth of scented water and touched the lighter flame to his Churchman's No. 1.

Latifa Noon turned up the volume of the radiogram and carried the tray of glasses into the bedroom. Foster exhaled a long breath and waited for several minutes, watching the ash of the cigarette. Then he paused and frowned. There was a smell, perhaps a perfume or an aroma, that was out of place. He thought it was not truly a perfume. It was sickly sweet, reminding him of hospitals and operating theatres.

All the same, he smiled as the bathroom door was pushed open, anticipating the slither of the dress, the provocative half-clad look in expensive underwear, and then the absolute pale gold nudity which he had commanded. But the girl was not there. A stranger stood in the open doorway of the bathroom, a big man in an overcoat, soft trilby hat, and gloves. Almost concealed behind him there was a second man in coat and hat, slightly built and moustached. They came in without speaking to him. Words would do nothing to help Foster. The two men were professionals and knew that it was kinder to their victim to have the thing done quickly, before the pleading could begin. Foster took the cigarette from his mouth and shouted the girl's name, knowing there would be no answer. Trapped by the unforgiving logic of false confidence, he felt the particular terror of being naked before his killers. Had he known of his friend, he would have envied 'Roller' Royce his last moments.

As the two men came towards him, there was no time to pull himself from the bath. He snatched the heavy glass ashtray and threw it. But it went wide, bouncing unbroken against the tiled wall. Then he seemed helpless as in a dream. His courage went even before the big man with a towel wrapped round his hands seized Foster's ankles in a powerful grip and pulled them upright. Foster went back and down in a churning wash of water, hands scrabbling for a hold on the smooth edges of the wide bath. The struggle seemed longer than it was. The upper half of Foster's body was immersed in two feet of water. Like a large pale fish, he threshed from the waist up. Several times he managed to get his head above the water. Each time, the smaller man who braced himself against the bath thrust him back under the surface, careful to use only the little force that was necessary. The battle had been lost early when Foster, caught by surprise and about to reason with his killers, had inhaled a scorching lungful of water before he could close his air-tracts against it. Twice he lunged hard enough to slop water on to the bathroom floor. At last, the man who was holding the ankles high felt the body go slack. The face was open-mouthed and pop-eyed under the water, like a sea gargoyle. As the two strangers watched, there was a spasm of some kind and a cloud stained the water a faint rusty red, diffused like tobacco smoke from the lungs.

The heavily built man switched the light off as he left the bathroom. Before Latifa Noon had carried the tray into the bedroom, she had turned the record over on the radiogram. Foster's last moments had been so brief that the *Warsaw Concerto* played for a little longer. The girl herself was lying fully clothed on the bed, the hem of the dress drawn high enough to show a band of warm ivory skin above the top of one stocking. With a sense of decorum, the tall man pulled the dress straight. Then he raised her over his shoulder in a fireman's lift, her head drooping down his back, unconscious but still alive.

3

'Seems a waste,' the smaller man said, glancing at the back seat of the car in his driving mirror, 'a looker like her.'

The smaller man was driving while his companion sat with Latifa Noon in the back. Those who heard something of this double act, not even certain that they were the same men, called them 'Stan and Ollie' with a wry facetiousness reserved for death and pain. The large man took out a slim gold-grained cigarette case and lit a Capstan for himself. On the far ridge of the Surrey downs a headlight beam or a dry flicker from an electric storm lit the dark line of horizon trees. The driver regretted his first remark and changed the topic.

'One thing,' he said, 'there won't be tears shed for Tom Foster. He always was a slippery sod.'

'Best all round,' said the large man with a self-conscious laugh. 'How's the car?'

'Drives like silk,' the smaller man said. 'Foster always treated himself to the best. Good of old Tonto to fix us up with it. Nice touch.'

'Dab hand with motors, Tonto is,' the large man said, stubbing out his cigarette in the arm-rest ashtray. They drove on in silence for a while.

'Hot enough for a cloudburst,' the little man tried again. 'It'll look better if it rains. She could've easy skidded.'

Beyond Guildford, the car turned off towards Haslemere and then turned again on to a minor road.

'Put your foot down,' the tall man said, 'she's beginning to move.'

He reached in the pocket of his overcoat and pulled out a smooth silvered flask, unscrewing the top. He poured whisky for the girl in the little cup and touched it to her open lips.

'You had a bad turn, darling,' he said. 'You need a bit of a pick-me-up.'

The lights of an oncoming lorry caught the tight-lidded beauty of her almond eyes, the long slope of brow and nose. Though conscious, she was still confused by the effects of the chloroform.

The big man held the metal cup firmly. 'Chin-chin,' he said, 'there's a good girl. Doctor's orders.'

Latifa Noon protested a little but tried to drink so that she should not choke. When he filled it again, she refused. He put his arm round her. She twisted her head away but he held her firmly. It was the firmness with which a child or an animal is held for some prescribed act of treatment or punishment. The driver kept his eyes on the road, knowing that there are certain things which it is best not to witness. Like the soundtrack of a movie melodrama, he heard the little sounds from the rear seat of the car. The girl's pursed protests and refusals, her enforced obedience, the slight gurgling or choking noises, and the big man's quiet encouragement. Presently there was a frantic burst of coughing and the smell of whisky that ran down her dress. The driver glanced in his mirror and had time to see the edge of a blade that seemed brighter for its sharpness. He looked away quickly before the big man saw him. The girl gave a grunting gasp of surprise, as if she had been winded. One of her hands moved up to her breast and then fell back as she lay against the panelled leather of the seat. The large man took his arm away.

'If she'd stayed under, we could have saved that. Still, by the time they find her, there won't be nothing to be seen. They'll find drink in her, if that much.'

They stopped at the crest beyond Gibbet Hill, where it was wooded and there were no houses. The large man was still wearing his gloves as he took a spanner from the toolkit. He raised the bonnet and made one or two adjustments to the carburettor. The two men lifted the girl's body into the driving seat, released the handbrake, and closed the doors. The long dark car began to roll forward slowly on the slope even before they added their strength to it. It gathered speed, the engine dead and the tyres crunching fragments of stone. Almost two hundred yards on, it failed to take the corner and plunged into the trees. There was a shudder and a bright puff of flame. The two men had begun to walk after it as if to put a finishing touch to the drama. Now they saw that it would not be needed. Without speaking, they walked back towards a telephone box at a junction on the Guildford road.

4

A thunder and echo of breakers on firm sand rose from the undercliff to the black marble facing and chrome handles on the balcony of the third-floor apartment. Their guests gone, Sonny Tarrant and the old woman sat side by side in the opening of the sliding doors, snuggling into their two voluminous and padded chairs. In the hour after midnight, they looked as content as a pair of mice in an old glove.

The old woman's eyes were closed but she was not asleep. Tarrant glanced to make sure of that before returning his attention to the view below them. In the lamplight he could make out the zig-zag path down the cliff to the lower promenade, winding through a mass of wind-slashed veronica. By day, the old woman sat here, dozing before the warm view of a quiet tide stretching to the Isle of Wight from the flowering shrubs of the twin promenades. In the long afternoons the wash of breakers was overlaid by a dance tune on the radio and the twang of tennis racquets in the communal enclosure of Scotch pines. Now, at the day's end, the mirrored sideboard of the apartment was strewn with glasses containing the dregs of Sidecars, Tom Collins, Egg Flips, and Manhattans. Mrs Tarrant's girl would clear them next morning. The Tarrants had had guests that evening, including their lawyer and a justice of the peace.

'Sonny Boy' Tarrant got up, stretched, and walked to the balcony rail, leaning his forearms upon it. He was a tall man with a long intelligent face. The grey-blond hair piled naturally on his head with a suggestion of a Pompadour wig. His speech and manner betrayed him as something baser but the look of equine intelligence was no illusion. At a glance, there was the promise of amiability in the beginning of a smile on his lips. The smile never came. It was the natural line of his mouth which gave Tarrant a false look of joviality. He leant on the rail staring at the phosphorescent rim of the incoming tide. Beyond the gardens, the white modern front of the Palace Hotel was flushed with blue neon and he caught a snatch of trombones in the shuffling beat of big-band swing.

On a mirror-glass table in the room behind him the phone rang. Tarrant listened without moving. It rang six times and stopped.

'Not for us, Mum,' he said to the old woman. His voice sounded prematurely aged, as if he might have been her husband rather than her son. It had a hard-earned south London gentility, a manner of dropping a final 'g' in imitation of polite society, an old-fashioned way of pronouncing 'roof' to rhyme with 'woof' and taking 'room' half-way to 'rum'. When he said 'ain't', it sounded like flashy and sporting aristocratic use.

The phone rang again. Mrs Tarrant sighed.

'Answer it, Sonny. Do.'

He walked slowly to the table, picked up the receiver, and listened.

'No,' he said, 'I hadn't heard. Is that so? All happened tonight? Well, I got nothin' I can say. Mind you, Latifa Noon was in pictures. Other two is just names, for all I got to say to you. No, my friend, I can't think why and I got nothin' else to add.'

When he put the phone down, Sonny Tarrant turned towards the balcony again and thought of the consequences. Sid Royce would count for nothing. Perhaps a column in the east London press and a couple of inches in an evening edition. Foster might be an unreported coroner's inquest. Latifa Noon had been in pictures, a minor part as a harem glamour-girl in a Jack La Rue and Monte Blue comedy released early in the war. Her career as an actress had not prospered, though there was a film for which Tarrant himself had put up a little money, an entertainment shown privately in clubs and at parties. All the same, she had once been on the screens of Odeons and Gaumonts, Regents and Ritzes, up and down the country. As a starlet, she might even have her death mentioned on the radio. Not that Tarrant himself wanted association with publicity. He was a man who worked quietly and with secret purpose. He sat down next to the old woman again and took her hand.

'That young lady Latifa Noon been in an accident, Ma. The one that was Tom Foster's friend. Seems to have been one or two accidents tonight, accordin' to the phone.'

'Bad, was it?'

'Seems so. And Tom Foster. And old "Roller" Royce that used to work the Streatham garage for us and then the Luxor picture house. Remember him?'

The old woman stared at the night sky, her gaze gentle but vacant.

'You got a lot to be grateful for, son,' she said at last. 'You got so many friends.'

'Tom Foster was one of the firm in the old days, Ma. I always took care of him, like the rest. Not none of them never wanted for nothin'. There was a time I don't know how I'd have got on without a man for bookwork like old Tom. Still, p'raps someone thought he was gettin' a bit too clever for his own good. They're good lads, most of 'em, most of the time. But they aren't family, Ma. None of 'em. That's you and me, and Wen' and Pat. And that's what counts in the end. That's what you got to remember, Ma, if anythin' was ever to happen to me. There's nothin' like family. You forget 'em all and go to Wen' down in Essex.'

She pulled against his hand impatiently. 'There's nothing going to happen to you, son. Don't you talk so silly.'

He smiled at her and drew his hand away. 'I don't suppose it will, Ma. I'll live to draw a pension yet.'

They sat in silence until Tarrant returned to an idea which had been in his mind since the phone call.

'I'm wonderin', darlin'. I'd best go back to town for a few days. I feel a bit responsible for this girl that had the accident, me

13

havin' put her in the pictures once or twice. Best see it settled without anythin' nasty bein' said. You got Vi to look after you here and you could have Mrs Gerrish and one or two others down to see you.'

She shifted towards him. 'I thought you was staying, Sonny. I thought you'd be here a week or two.'

He took her hand.

'That phone, Ma. Press ringin' up. They're some right little guttersnipes, they are. I don't want nothin' mucky bein' said about you or me or the girls. Nothin' that might upset you. I never had anythin' else to do with that Latifa Noon but you can't tell what that voice on the phone might make of it.'

'Make up stories?' she said.

Tarrant watched the wind in the curtain at the open veranda door. 'Mind you, that reporter will be carryin' his nose home in his hanky, if I catch him at it, Ma. I won't have you upset by any of them.'

'Sonny, don't!' But there was a glimmer of pride in her reproof.

'And with Tom Foster gone, there's business needs lookin' at,' he said. 'I'll be back here before you know it. Only I got the picture house as well as the garages to think of now. Staff is apt to skive when there's no one in charge of 'em. No proper guv'nor. A flyin' visit from me might make all the difference.'

'And I don't suppose it's a girl that's taking you away, is it?' Mrs Tarrant enquired with a private smile. 'You won't be back this side of Christmas.'

He held her hand a little tighter. 'You're my girl, Ma, you know that. You're worth more than the lot of 'em put together. Anyhow, I'll be back in the week. If I'm not, I'll send the motor to bring you up to Temple Court. You'll see.'

It was part of the understanding between them that girls and Sonny's healthy appetite for them, even in middle age, sometimes took him away from home. Mother and son understood that he was a rip but with no real harm in him. If she thought about this, which she rarely did, Mrs Tarrant also knew that she had seldom learnt who these girls were or what her son did with them. The old woman had long ceased to be her son's adviser. She now preferred that there were things about which she would never be told.

Tarrant got up and went to the phone again. The old woman heard his voice.

14

'Hello, Foxy. It's me. Wake you up, did I? Never mind. I need one of the motors down here tomorrow to take me back to town. Ma's got Vi to look after her but I'd appreciate young Rodney comin' down for a bit. He could bring the motor back again and drive it here as required. Be nice for him down by the sea this time of year. Say about lunchtime tomorrow, then. Thanks, Foxy.'

He put the phone down again and went to his bureau, unlocking a drawer and taking out its contents. Turning away, he stooped to kiss the old woman and went back to the balcony rail, staring at the dark sea with the banknotes rolled in his fist. Most of the education he received as a child had left him at a loss. But there were certain stories and certain men that had impressed him. Some were unlikely to be remembered by a boy of his kind and he had forgotten the names of the minor figures. But he had been absorbed by legends of men who held power through bold and sudden decisions. There were Roman emperors who transformed a triumvirate into a single imperial rule by the blade of a knife. Then they removed their rivals, as other men prepared their knives for the supreme solitary ruler. He supposed that his feelings as he gazed across the shrubs and paths of Bournemouth's central gardens were much the same as those forgotten heroes must have known when their lieutenants fell to the enemy.

Then the firmness of his long aquiline face was disturbed by a look of concern. He hoped, after all, that Latifa Noon would get a mention in the press, on the radio particularly. It was her misfortune that she had been mixed up with Tom Foster. He wanted to see her get the tribute that she deserved.

When he sat down beside Mrs Tarrant again, his unclenched hand revealed the wad of twenty or thirty five-pound notes.

'You have Mrs Gerrish or one of the others down for a few days, Ma. Have 'em all, if you like. Spend out a bit. Not as though we can't afford it now, is it?'

'That'd be nice,' she said, reassuring him with a smile that deepened the crazed wrinkling of her face. He pushed the money into her hand, like an indulgent lover.

'You go out with Vi or one of 'em and get what you like,' he said encouragingly. 'You have anythin' you want.'

2

EASY STREET

1

The cry came distantly through warm afternoon air like the remote call of a night-jar. It rose within the ivory-tiled block of the Temple Court service apartments, ruffling the carpeted silence of empty corridors and steel-latticed elevators whose air was perfumed with a thick sweetness of orange blossom. Two elderly women sat in conversation on a shaded veranda of their first-floor suite, mohair stoles discarded on the backs of wicker chairs. The one who had been speaking paused and glanced up at the sound. Then she resumed her thread of gossip, staring into the blue heat of the west London sky beyond the white-painted rail.

The cry was not quite a scream. There was defiance in it but neither panic nor unbridled pain. Echoes of its brief anger dwindled in the heat above Paris-style café tables set out by the little shops at the Belgrave Square end of Pont Street. In the mellow tea-time sunlight, men in Chelsea slacks and sports-jackets talked and smiled among girls in tailored suits and wide-brimmed hats. Beyond the dark pink cherry blossom in the communal gardens along Sloane Street a saxophone from an open window sobbed along with the crooner who wanted red roses for a blue lady, send them to her Mr Florist, please. Behind a café window, two cylinders were grinding coffee beans with an occasional pop of flame. A toasted richness of Brazil overlaid the afternoon warmth. Then the other sounds of the metropolitan spring asserted themselves and the shrillness of the woman's protest was extinguished above the white candles of the chestnut trees.

Heat and stillness settled again on the angular lines of the Temple Court. The Egyptian modernism of its pre-war design, the frieze of coloured hieroglyphs and the potted palm trees in the chrome-railed entrance, would have been as much in keeping with Miami or Cairo as with Belgravia. After six years of wartime neglect, the white tiles had been darkened to ivory by city soot. Across the street, cups and saucers rattled on the tables of the café paving, talk intermittently lost among the groan of traffic as the junction lights changed. The hot paving of Pont Street echoed to the rapid clockwork beat of high heels while the saxophone and crooner raised their lament again for blue ladies and red roses.

Billy Blake crossed Sloane Street at the lights and turned a corner. The midnight-blue Chrysler, a 1939 Airflow saloon with sleek aerodynamic lines, was fifty yards out of sight of the Temple Court. McIver had drawn it up by the central gardens of Cadogan Square, where the arcaded mansions in Victorian terracotta brick rose tall and turreted. They seemed like a land-locked quarter of Amsterdam, though their Gothic ornament suggested a world of girls with Pre-Raphaelite hair, stolen moments among the magnolia trees and lilac bowers in the garden.

Blake stopped with his arm resting on the roof of the Airflow and looked in at the driver's window. With its white-walled tyres and the low sweep of its windows the Chrysler might have been a Mafia battle-wagon. The man who sat at the wheel was tall and blazered. The strong jaw and narrowed blue eyes, unblemished skin, and slicked fair hair were impeccably those of a matinée idol. The profile too might have been a stage-lit portrait, framed for a theatre foyer and a new Terence Rattigan run. But John Patrick McIver was not quite a matinée idol. Somewhere in its making the handsome face had been flawed. It was the mouth that betrayed him. The compression and the thin underlip suggested impatience and egotism. Perhaps the eyes smiled a little too easily, the charmer's flesh-wrinkles at their corners tightening too precisely in the devil-may-care mockery of his wartime pilot's reputation as Johnny Zero.

'Chocks away, Johnny,' Blake said brightly, 'they won't be long now, by the sound of it. I'd say that Sonny Boy Tarrant must have had a real West End performance from the Moke and Solitaire.'

McIver nodded without looking up. He was frowning a little with concentration as he sat at the wheel. Between his hands lay a puzzle, a shallow glass-topped box about three inches square with six silver ball bearings. The floor of the box was pasted with a miniature map of Europe from London to Berlin, notched by cut-out holes for the ball bearings to rest in on their marked route. A little ack-ack gun spouted flame over the Dutch coast. ME109s dived with cannon flaming over the Rühr. Last of the six cut-out holes was a bombed emblem of Berlin itself. Roddy Hallam, a slightly built and dark-haired young man, was the occupant of the passenger seat, his medium blue pin-stripe suit matched by a dark blue shirt and canary-yellow tie. He watched a silver ball bearing miss its hole and run to the corner of the box. Then he returned to his own pastime. Holding a pair of card-framed lenses before his eyes, one red and one green, he looked like an ophthalmic surgeon inspecting a patient's retina. But the subject on his knee was an unfocused page of photogravure, pink and pale green. *Folies Bergère in 3D.* In his private world, Hallam's goddess stepped towards him smiling from the page in elastic-tight underwear.

Unable to make out anything but a blurred outline in Hallam's magazine, Billy Blake watched McIver attack Berlin.

'You have to do it in the right order,' he said patiently through the open window, as McIver tilted the little box gently between his hands. 'Bombs away comes last.'

'Do dry up, Billy, there's a good fellow.' McIver lost interest as Blake saw him cheating. Reaching out, he took the folded evening paper from under Blake's arm and handed him the puzzle. 'Let's see you do better, you sanctimonious old bugger.' While the three men waited, the afternoon sun played patterns of light and shade on the central gardens of the Victorian mansions, the creamy magnolia cups nodding in a light breeze and the purple lilac beginning to darken.

Of the three men at the car, it was Hallam who seemed out of place. McIver had the slick good looks and Billy Blake's was the good nature of an oversized tail-wagging mongrel. With his hacking jacket and pilot's moustache Blake had a suggestion of doggy companionship in pre-war clubs or in airfield mess-rooms during the years of combat. Hallam was a slighter and more intense figure with the tight dark waves of his hair, his small neat moustache and the worry lines of his forehead. He was old enough to have been an assistant stage manager in a repertory company for two years before being called up for war service. A quiet worried little man, Blake thought him. But it was Roddy Hallam who had introduced Solitaire to John McIver. That was something to be grateful for.

Blake kept his elbow on the roof of the car, rested a polished brown toe-cap on the running-board and tried his hand at the puzzle while McIver opened the early edition of the *Evening News*. There was a long report of the previous day's victory parade in the Mall and a photograph taken from Admiralty Arch. The grey newsprint showed a ghostly King George VI in field marshal's uniform, saluting his blurred regiments of men and women. A rival column offered the puckish face of Tommy Handley kissing the swimsuited winner of a beauty contest at Parliament Hill Lido. McIver turned a page and glanced at the crime reports. The last of the small fry who had broadcast to England from Berlin were being sentenced to prison terms. Now that Lord Haw-Haw and their leaders had been hanged, the remaining British Fascists rated only half an inside column. A foreign report announced the execution of the Nazi puppet ruler who had been premier of Romania. A good many scores were being settled. Like most of those who had seen action, McIver felt no enthusiasm for the process of civilian vengeance. The smug politicians and lawyers, their words dutifully echoed by radio and newsreel commentators, inspired only his contempt. Small wonder that the letters BBC were irreverently said by his RAF unit to stand for 'Bloody Baptist Cant'.

In any case, McIver cared little about world news. It was the paper's vision of ease and promise that warmed him. He studied the Piccadilly and Berkeley Square showroom pictures of the new Hillman Minx and Rover Saloon, the smiling and well-dressed men and women who smoked Craven-A for their throats' sake or assured him that Players Please, against a background of evening dresses and elegant dance floors. For six years McIver, Blake, Hallam, and their comrades in arms had been told that there was a good time coming. Never was so much owed by so many to so few. McIver grinned at the thought. High time that the debt should be paid.

As they waited at the car, the streets beyond the quiet enclave of Cadogan Square were bright with summer dresses and the parks were strewn with sunbathers. He watched a crocodile of little girls from one of the expensive day-schools near Sloane Street moving quietly as nuns under the eye of their mistress. It reassured him to see the future provided for. Turning back to the paper, he ran his finger down a list of weekend trains for the seaside. Brighton with its super cinemas, moonlight on the pier, and popsies in the sun. Palm trees and big-band swing at

Bournemouth. 'My dreams are getting better all the time.' The sleek flanks of a Coronation Year locomotive with the air washing away to either side sped towards him on the page. He glanced briefly at the latest scores in the county cricket and folded the paper again.

'Silence in the ranks!' Billy Blake said suddenly. 'Here she comes. Can't say the old girl looks exactly pleased with life.'

Roddy Hallam yawned. 'She's a tart, Billy. If you want tarts to look cheerful, you have to pay them first.'

'Chuck it, Rods,' Blake said quietly. 'She's doing this for all of us.'

'I'm a realist, for God's sake,' Hallam said. 'That's all. I'm the one that camps in her little knocking-shop at night. It smells of tart and punter.'

McIver put away his paper and looked up. A tall young woman had crossed Sloane Street and was rounding the corner. Solitaire. It was absurd to think that she had been born with any other name than this. There was glamour in it and her profession, after all, was to be glamorous. The waves of her collar-length auburn hair shone in the sun and the complexion of her beauty was flawless as a face-cream advertisement. She walked quickly towards the car, the swagger-jacket buttoned and the metallic blue dress tugging at her knees a little in its tightness. The head-piece was a coquettish elaboration of a cloche hat, angled a little, with a light veil which might have covered the upper half of her face but which was now put aside. As usual, the green eyes were wide and the glossy lips parted slightly as if in exertion or anticipation. McIver was not surprised that the face had been seen several times in advertisements for soaps and cosmetics. But there was no money in that, less than in the brief 'supernumerary' crowd scenes when she had appeared before the movie cameras at Pinewood or Denham. Still, at twenty-six, the line and agility of her figure would have been the envy of most girls ten years younger. She moved with an actressy manner, brisk and correct. Yet the authority of her manner was no more than skin deep.

Blake was humming to himself, as he watched her. 'I'd say Mr Sandman sent you a dream, Johnny . . . Made her complexion like peaches and cream too . . .' He sighed. 'Talk about melt in your mouth. You're a lucky old sod, McIver. You really are.'

He took his foot off the running-board, opened the door, and watched as the young woman stooped into the rear of the car. He walked round the back of the Airflow and got in beside her.

Solitaire propped her black patent leather handbag against the side of the seat, unpinned her hat and shook her hair free along her shoulders. From the bag, she took a flat gold case, angular and smooth, and drew from it a cigarette gilt-stamped with the monogram of a Bond Street tobacconist. The case had been untidily filled, as though she might have replenished it hastily from the silver table-box in Tarrant's flat. Her finger-nail, varnished immaculately blood red, stroked the wheel of a matching lighter. Flame spurted briefly and she exhaled smoke with a sound of relief.

'See anything interesting?' McIver enquired, but Solitaire ignored him. With her hat removed, her face was tense and her green eyes bright with determination.

'Next time any of you pick a partner for someone's little lunch party, I want to see him first,' she said, 'Mr Hallam's friend the Moke has the bedroom manners of the Gestapo.'

McIver turned and grinned at her, like a decent but reckless schoolboy. 'Not had the pleasure of his acquaintance,' he said casually. 'And don't tell us the rest. We know. He's a brute. Don't worry, old girl. You'll soon train him.'

'Brute?' she said, letting out another breath of smoke. 'He's practising to be a bloody sadist. It was deliberate. Believe me. Next time, Mr Hallam, find me someone who knows what he's doing!'

Drawing up the hem of the electric-blue skirt, she detached an elastic suspender-strap and tried to examine the skin above the top of her stocking. McIver watched her in the mirror. There appeared to be no mark.

'You could take it as a tribute,' McIver said, 'I don't suppose the poor old Moke meant to play rough. How was the audience?'

'Creepy,' she said with fastidious elocution. 'Only Mr Tarrant. That's weird.'

'Made you blush, did he?'

She shook her head and the sheen of auburn hair whispered along the shoulders of the dress. 'I don't blush,' she said impatiently, 'and as a rule, it's rather good with people watching. But when it's just one man like that, it's downright creepy.'

'No cameras?'

She shook her head again. 'Not part of the deal. Mind you, I wouldn't put it past him to have one hidden somewhere. Still, he wasn't actually holding it in his lap.'

McIver gave her a grin and a wink. 'We'll get Roddy to have

a word with the Moke. Get him to take dancing lessons. You didn't happen to see anything worthwhile at Mr Tarrant's, I suppose?'

Solitaire ignored the question again. 'It's going to be a bruise,' she said sadly, 'I can't work with a bruise and there's going to be one. And these nylons were new this morning.'

McIver shrugged. 'You'll get work,' he said cheerfully. 'Tarrant has friends who could put you into the movies, properly this time. If you still want that.'

'Like Latifa Noon?'

'Did Tarrant tell you he had her chopped? She was his investment.'

'It's the assumption everyone's working on.'

McIver looked at her in the driving mirror and shook his head. Then he turned the ignition key and watched the sluggish movement of the fuel gauge. They waited for it to reach its maximum. Hallam said, 'Better park this crate somewhere for a while, Johnny. There's hardly enough juice to move the needle. You don't want to run dry where there's law around waiting to be helpful. I reckon we might be on their visiting list.'

McIver tapped the glass of the gauge and watched the needle budge a little.

'There's plenty of juice, old son, if you know where to find it. Best not hang about here. Anyone might come by. Even Tarrant himself, taking his old woman's dog for a walk.'

Billy Blake looked in the mirror. 'Don't want to break bad news,' he said, 'but there's a car back there with two blokes in it. Been parked there quite a while. Might be a bit of interest from the law. Folks in the square complaining of burglaries and all that.'

'Right,' McIver said, 'let's head for home.'

He started the engine and they slid forwards towards Knightsbridge. At the corner, he gestured towards the long window of the Sloane Street Furriers.

'Be a good girl and see what you get,' he said to Solitaire in the driving mirror. 'If this little number clicks, you could go into that store and buy everything in their display. That must be worth something. Anyone behind us now, is there, Billy?'

Blake looked back. 'Nope. They could've been waiting to hoist some other poor sod. Unless they wondered what three of us were waiting for in a car. Those places get burgled by the dozen.'

'We wouldn't dream of it,' McIver said virtuously. 'Two of them were done last week. 'Fair's fair. Spread the agony a bit.'

Between the tall Edwardian palaces of the department stores, their pavement blinds pulled out against the sun, there was a glimpse of beech trees in the park. McIver followed a slow trail of buses and cars. The washed marble and art-nouveau grilles of Harvey Nichols' window displays promised good things to come. Like bronze and silken beauty in a conqueror's triumph, the prizes adorned a frieze of slim wax mannequins, slave-girls of a returning warrior.

McIver felt a sense of well-being at the sight of such opulence. Not that he could do much about the present offering, having bounced a couple of cheques off them already. He wondered if they were still looking for 'Wing Commander John Walker' and 'Lieutenant-Colonel Richard Linton'. If they looked long enough, they'd find Walker among the 'killed in action' files and McIver felt quite sorry he'd had to use the name. Still, doing a brother officer a good turn wouldn't hurt Walker himself, wherever he might be. Colonel Linton, on the other hand, had been president of McIver's court-martial. The old boy had even tried to be decent about it, as he thought. It seemed to Johnny McIver that the little matter of the cheque couldn't have happened to a nicer person.

The traffic lights changed to green and the Chrysler moved forward.

'What you have to remember,' McIver said, 'is that there can't be trouble this time. Taking money from a man who's not supposed to have it in the first place is part of the game. I don't suppose old Tarrant has seen an income tax form in his life. All's fair . . .'

'In love and war,' Solitaire said coldly. 'Don't tell me about war. That beast has left a thumb mark.'

'Shouldn't go on about it, old girl,' said Roddy Hallam quietly, 'there's a sport.'

McIver followed a long circuit into Knightsbridge, absent-mindedly humming the notes of red roses for a blue lady. At Hyde Park Corner the winged victory rose black against the sky of the summer afternoon, like an avenging angel. They stopped again at the westbound traffic lights. Beside them, the newspaper seller's board proclaimed: HALF-BROTHER OF PEER ON BIGAMY CHARGE.

'You know,' said McIver thoughtfully, 'I wouldn't mind if that was me. Bigamy isn't what it was. He'll get off light – and rich. Might even manage to keep both popsies happy. Lucky old sod.'

Sergeant Frank Brodie got up from the café table where he sat alone with a drained coffee cup and a paid bill. Across his broad dark-haired scalp greyness and baldness were in close competition. Baldness seemed likely to win. He walked across to the shallow half-moon steps of the Temple Court with their potted palms and went from sunlight into the lobby darkness. The marble foyer of the apartments was laid out like a hotel with a public call-box to one side. Brodie pushed into it and glanced at the desk clerk who sat with the secrets of his profession in the cubby-hole office of the foyer. In the past two years, to Brodie's knowledge, the metal filing-cabinet had accumulated details of dishonoured cheques, petty thefts, two deaths from natural causes, and a suicide by an overdose of sodium amytal. It was an average level of incident in such a place as this. From the telephone box in the lobby, Brodie had a wide view towards the mahogany sweep of the reception counter, across the glass-tiled modernism of the square pillars and the sleek beige marble of the broad steps leading to the double elevators. Beyond the dwarf palms in their brass urns, he could see that the Temple Court barber's shop remained empty. The little kiosk that sold tobacco and flowers was shuttered for tea. A service door swung open and there was a rattle of china.

He glanced round again, as if to make sure that he was not overheard. Then he folded his copy of the *Evening Standard* which had concealed him at the café table and reached for the phone. When a young woman's voice answered he said, 'Frank Brodie. I'm in the Temple Court apartments. I have something for Inspector Jack Rutter, if he's there.'

'I'm sorry, Mr Brodie. Special Duty reports should be made to the relevant divisional CID. That's the agreed procedure.'

'This can't wait for the divisions.'

'I'll see what I can do.'

'That's my girl,' Brodie said encouragingly.

There was a pause. Then a voice that sounded as if it might have been relaxing in a deck-chair said, 'Hello, Frankie boy. What've you got for me, then?'

'A bit of news from Sloane Street, Jack,' Brodie said cautiously. 'You want to hear about it now?'

'For what it matters,' Rutter said, 'just so long as you weren't breaking rules to get young Suzanne to put you across her knee. What's happening in the Temple precincts, then?'

'Our friend had a visitor,' Brodie said. 'Just left. I take it he's still our closest friend, is he?'

'So they tell me,' Rutter said wearily. 'Presumably his mum's still out, is she?'

'The word is she's down at the seaside on holiday, more or less permanently, staying in their place down there.'

'So Sonny's alone and being a naughty boy, is he?'

Brodie looked across the sunlit marble of the lobby. The florist's shutter was raised again. An elderly man in oatmeal tweeds was writing a cheque for tulips in a cellophane sheath. His face was mottled and thin-blooded in the early summer warmth.

'He had this visitor just now,' Brodie said softly into the mouthpiece of the phone. 'Stayed about an hour. Auburn hair. Legs to make you dizzy when she moves. Been up there about an hour. Just before she left, she yelled as if she really meant it.'

Rutter sighed. 'P'raps she'd been a bad girl,' he said wearily, 'you know how our friend is about that. Still, if she left in one piece and she's not complaining, I don't see where that gets us. Unless, of course, she did our friend with a hat-pin to even up the score. Have a look at some photographs when you get back. See if she matches.'

'Solitaire,' Brodie said. 'Known less romantically as Sally Brown. I don't need photos. The last time I saw her, to my knowledge, she was in the company of our lad Johnny Mac.'

'Now that's interesting,' Rutter said. There was a pause. 'So what do you think, Jack?'

'What I think, Frankie, is that our friend is too big a man for a small-time artist like Pretty Boy McIver to go and see on his own. His girlfriend could be another matter. According to the form book, the lady is still doubling as a dancer and as a high-class tart. Place in Shepherd Market. Johnny could easily be running her, of course. If he is, she's presumably performing a delivery service for the clients. The rich and lonely wouldn't mind an afternoon visit from her but they aren't to be seen going upstairs in Shepherd Market. All right?'

'You think that's all there is?'

There was another pause and a sigh, long and luxurious.

'No,' said Rutter wearily. 'Young McIver is a lad that always did overestimate his own ability. If he does it with our friend, he's going to be in serious and permanent trouble.'

'So what do you want, then?' Brodie asked him.

'The big one's my concern, Frankie, the little one isn't. I've got several of Tarrant's friends on my visiting list today, for what good it'll do. I'm seeing a grocer south of the river who's fiddling tinned food by the ton on his points ration and selling it to the clubs. He's got a mate who's knocked off so many ration books that the price has gone down nearly half in three months. Some of the big stores have stopped even noticing the dud clothing coupons. There's enough US Army petrol on the black market in this city to start an oil-field in Hyde Park. If it's a question of Sonny Boy smacking the lovely Solitaire, I don't want to hear about it. What she does for a living is her business. She can either hit him back, move on, or put the price up.'

'Just thought you'd like to know the score, Jack.'

'I do, Frank. No two ways. I'll pass it on to our leader. And there's a nod and a smile down the drinker for you, if you're in the World's End about half-seven tomorrow night.'

'And where does that leave our friend?'

Rutter chuckled. 'Come on, Frankie! I don't want to get the nudge for naming names like this on the phone. Worse still, we could both end up directing traffic in tall hats. See you tonight.'

3

A hot afternoon light across the park was filtered by the pale scooped lace of the curtains so that it filled the hotel bedroom with a gleam that was cool and neutral as water. The filtered sun broke in prism-colours on the pendants of the lamps and the bevelled surrounds of the mirrors. Lozenges of green and violet, blue and red dappled the warm pearl silk of the hangings.

McIver drew at his cigarette as he lay back and watched her. The blue dress was on its hanger now and the auburn hair lay across bare shoulders. Between the lace pants and the stocking-tops the skin where a bruise might be detected was bare. McIver could see no bruise. He frowned at the ceiling, concentrating upon a smoke-ring.

'No keys, then?'

'Not yet,' she said, turning towards him. 'If they're in the wall-safe, I wouldn't have seen them. I found out where that is, though, and it's not behind a painting nor in the bedroom.'

'It never is except in the movies,' McIver blew a perfect ring. 'First place anyone would look.' His eyes moved down, photographing in his mind the silk-cupped breasts, the bare midriff, the lace pants, and the bare flesh of thighs above stockinged elegance. *'La Vie Parisienne* or *Vogue* even. That's where we'll try the pictures next time. With you like that and a room like this, they'd be a knock-out.'

'It's in the kitchen,' she said. 'The back of the stove above the hot-plates folds forward. There's a dial . . .'

'It's a Mosler,' McIver said. 'Roddy found that out from one of his mates in Tarrant's car business. Tarrant was boasting about it one day when this ear was listening. Hundred-figure dial. Once to the right, once to the left, second time right, second time left. You could have fifty million possible combinations, give or take a few, if you want to be pedantic about it.'

She walked across and sat on the bed. 'So how do you open it?'

The flesh crinkled at the corners of McIver's eyes. His hand fell lightly on her bare thigh.

'You leave it to me, old girl. I'll have it open.'

Solitaire put her hand on his. 'I didn't stand too close. When he started, it was pointing somewhere to the centre.'

'He'd have to start dead centre, if it's the sort I think it is.'

'First he turned it right. I couldn't tell exactly how far but almost all the way. Then he turned it up but not very far. Then right down again and then up by only one or two. Then up to about twenty. Then right up to somewhere about eighty or ninety. Altogether it was four very low numbers, one about twenty and the one near the top. I couldn't stand close enough to see much more and the dial isn't marked with numbers anyway.'

McIver's hand fell more firmly and possessively above the stocking-top. 'You're a bloody wonder,' he said. 'The pick of the bunch.'

Solitaire wrinkled her forehead. 'Does that help?'

'Ask me later,' McIver said with a grin.

He pulled her down to kiss him and watched the auburn hair slide back across the pearl sleekness of her shoulders. Solitaire stood up and walked away, peach-coloured silk diaphanous against the window-light, outlining the grace of her shadow-figure. McIver chuckled. There had been a number at the Copacabana where the dancers moved naked in silhouette against a fluorescent screen, entirely legal since they wore body-stockings. The image of it was like an icon in his memory. Solitaire looked at him in the dressing-table mirror, her finger testing the smoothness of the lipstick. McIver drew at his cigarette, winked at her and tapped ash into the small frosted shape of the Lalique ashtray on the bedside table. He picked the ashtray up.

'This,' he said, lifting the frosted leaf of glass, 'is pleading to go with us when we leave.'

She sat on the padded boudoir stool and drew off her stockings. 'What's the good of seeing the safe?' she said, the tumble of hair hiding her face as she looked down. 'There could be a million combinations to that lock.'

McIver watched the pale nudity of her hips on the padded silk. 'About fifty million. Don't worry. There's always a way.'

Solitaire turned and came over to him, sitting on the edge of the bed. The green eyes looked down, serious and direct, while McIver's hand moved on the satin pallor where the tops of her stockings had been.

'Your friends,' she said slowly, 'you're sure they're right for this?'

He smiled at the question. 'Billy's a good type. We were on the same camp for about eight months. Why?'

'He seems a bit of a clown,' she said. 'And Roddy . . .'

'You've known Roddy longer than I have.'

'Only because he was moving props at the clubs. He's never going to get a part in his life. There's something there, Johnny. Billy probably dreams of a society lady in high heels taking him walkies on a lead. Roddy's different . . .'

'I'd hope so!' McIver said with a laugh. 'How about a penny for his thoughts?'

Solitaire stared at the scooped Nottingham lace of the curtains. 'Something to do with shame and humiliation, I should think,' she said carefully. 'But he's acting all the time. Just now he's playing a gangster, so it's dark blue shirts and yellow ties with a dark suit. He's all front.'

She got up and went back to the boudoir stool.

'Leave them to me, sweetie,' McIver said. 'They're good blokes. Billy would do anything for anyone and Roddy's sharp with a car even if he's got no talent for the stage. It'll be OK. You do your bit and leave the rest to me.'

'Nothing worries you,' she said, as if with curiosity. 'Does it?' She stood up, looking across at the chromium-banded wardrobe, and studied her naked figure in its long mirror.

'Tarrant doesn't worry me, if that's what you mean,' McIver said. 'He's past his best. His world ended with the war. All that garbage about East End pals and carving the faces of people he didn't like.'

She turned, lodging her behind against the edge of the leather-inset dressing-table. 'I'd like to know, McIver, out of curiosity. What would get you really worried?'

The matinée-idol face was angled as if for a publicity portrait. He blew smoke at the ceiling and smiled.

'Having to work for money. Getting up in the morning and going to the office for eight hours a day. Not being able to walk home from a night-club at dawn with the birds chattering. Not being able to go to bed with a woman at tea-time in a swank hotel. Things like that. Better off dead.'

'Nothing big? Nothing that would wake you at night?'

He thought for a moment. 'Used to be afraid of climbing and falling. But that was a long time ago.'

She came over and sat on the edge of the bed again, McIver's hand relaxing on her knees this time. 'I thought you had a head for heights, rooftops and window-ledges.'

McIver shook his head. 'It was a long time ago. We had a house, when I was a kid. The bedroom had a door that opened on to a long balcony with a drop of about thirty feet to a paved terrace. When I was about nine or ten, I used to put myself to sleep by thinking of things you might do before you woke up and knew nothing about them. Sleep-walking and so on. You might even murder someone and go back to bed and wake up and find you'd done it.'

'Dreams!' she said scornfully, getting up again.

'I used to have an idea that while I was asleep, I'd get up without waking. Sleep-walking. I'd open the door and walk on to the balcony. I'd get on the rail and walk along it, balancing. On and on, the rail running out as I got closer to the end. I'd keep on walking, still asleep, until I stepped into space. Then, I'd wake too late, already falling. Couldn't go to sleep without thinking of it. And I really used to wake with that sense of falling you get and I'd yell before I realized I'd been in bed all the time.'

'You never told anyone?'

'Nope. I used to think out ideas. You could put a bell on the balcony door that would ring when you opened it – but you'd told yourself that it wouldn't wake you. You could lock the door – but in your sleep you'd take the key and open it. You could hide the key – but in your sleep you'd remember where. You could give the key to someone – but you might go looking and find it.'

'I might believe you,' she said to his reflection in the dressing-room mirror.

McIver laughed. 'I woke one night. I was half-way between the bed and the door. I was scared as hell for a moment. Then I knew what to do. Whatever scares you, the only cure is go ahead and do it. So I used to go climbing like a fool, up and over anything. I walked along that rail, at night, except that I did it when I was awake. No more fear of falling, even after I'd come a cropper a time or two in other places. I grew out of being scared. I know what Tarrant can do to people. If I thought about it long enough, I might be scared. But either way, I'd have to go ahead.'

She was standing against the light again, the underclothes and stockings shed about her as she turned towards the bathroom of peach-blossom marble, pearl nudity against its warmer tone. She was a damn sight too good for Tarrant or any of them, McIver thought. Good enough as the stationary naked goddess at the rear of a Windmill Theatre dance, the huntress drawing a bow. If it was true that she had a husband and a child somewhere miles from London, nothing in the lines of her figure suggested that experience.

'So what scares you?' he asked.

Solitaire frowned at him, trying to recall. 'Not being free,' she said at last. 'But not the way you mean it. I hated the idea of being locked in a room. I couldn't bear games where you were held or tied up. Not even clothes that were tight and you couldn't get out of them easily. I still couldn't. It's about the only thing that might make me panic. I can't do it.'

'Not even in grown-up games?' McIver watched her with casual intent.

'No,' she said, turning away, 'I don't play games like that. Certainly not for Tarrant.'

'And how many hard-earned Oscars did you collect this afternoon for not playing games?'

'Mind your own business,' she said, half-smiling at him.

'It's our business,' McIver said seriously, 'I've got to pay old Champion for the passport. We'll need to be on our way sharp once the job's done. We're short at the moment. How much?'

She stood motionless and naked on the threshold of the bathroom.

'Ten,' she said quietly, 'it's in the handbag. You'd better take it, if you need it for Champion.'

She went across to her cream swagger-jacket on its hanger and took the notes from a pocket. McIver grinned.

'Ten quid? He must think a lot of you. Still, Tarrant's the type that pays for laddering a lady's stockings. And don't be rude about Mr Champion. The old boy's bought three sets of your photographs for his customers. We'll try him again soon.'

He levered himself up and patted her as she slipped away to the bath. Then he looked round the room for her purse but there was no sign of it. It was his habit to check the purse for other money she might have and for evidence of any other life that she concealed from him. Soundlessly, he drew open one or two of the more likely drawers. There was nothing. It was probably in the bathroom with her, concealed there when they came in. He gave up and began to unfold a clean shirt, calling towards the drifts of perfumed steam beyond the half-open door.

'I'm going out presently. I'll see you down the Copacabana about seven.'

She said something which was indistinct among the rumbling of the water from the taps but her tone suggested that she had understood. McIver buttoned the shirt and adjusted a red tie in a square Windsor knot. So far as he had any political interest, he had been for Edward VIII in the Abdication crisis ten years earlier. Threading a belt through the loops of his grey slacks, he pulled them on and then took a Harris tweed sports jacket from a hanger. Finally, he stood before the mirror, combed his hair slickly into place and imparted a final gloss with violet oil on both hands.

The water was still running in the bathroom. With as much care as if he had still been hunting her purse, he opened a drawer by the bed and took out a stiff envelope which had contained photographic paper. Inside were twelve black and white prints. She appeared in them all, usually naked and sometimes almost so. There was a man in several of them, seen with his head turned away. A slip of paper contained three strips of negatives. McIver slid the envelope into a pigskin briefcase. The case was an unwitting present from Colonel Linton to the Lieutenant McIver whom he had cashiered in 1941. McIver snapped the lock shut, picked the case up, and went downstairs. He walked out under the rounded overhang of the hotel front, a sleek and debonair figure crossing the sunlit expanse of Knightsbridge.

31

4

Beyond the park, the hot and unswept little streets round Paddington still carried the fading insignia of war. The shabby brickwork of their walls was daubed with yellow and black directions, pointing to communal air-raid shelters, stirrup-pumps and static water-tanks. Scuffed white paint on the corners of walls and kerbstones outlined the hazards of the blackout. In the central gardens of Norfolk Square the brick shelter with its slab-concrete roof and blast walls was a treacherous and rat-infested playground for ragged children.

McIver's destination was a corner shop that might have suited a local grocer or newsagent. Its windows contained out of date glamour magazines, a few second-hand copies of *Blighty* and *Lilliput* turning acid-yellow in the sun. Paper-covered copies of *White Slaves in a Piccadilly Flat* or *The Road to Buenos Aires* showed men in evening dress with cigars, their female subjects in flimsy chiffon. He pushed open the door, whose little bell jangled on its thin strip of metal.

'Hello, old son,' said Mr Champion cheerfully. 'Brought some good news, I hope?'

Mr Champion was tall and amiable with the look of a wind-ruffled sheep. There was an air of gruff decency about him which suggested a military man fallen on hard times or perhaps a master from a good school who had left for undisclosed reasons. The slum tenements and the street market had been his habitat for the past dozen years.

'Come on through,' he said bravely, bolting the shop door and opening the way to an inner room. As McIver followed him into the back room, Mr Champion set two wooden chairs at the plain table and lit the gas-ring under the kettle. From where it had fallen on the floor, he picked up a Paris-printed volume of *Nights in a Moorish Harem*. They sat down by the shelf which held tea and sugar in picnic jars, a pre-war copy of *Feathers in the Bed*, and a leather-backed *Coral Island* stamped in gilt as a school prize.

McIver opened a rolled silver case from his breast pocket with his thumbnail. One side was filled with flat oval cigarettes, the other was empty. 'Abdullah,' he said, 'if you don't object to Turkish. Best I could find.'

'Don't mind if I do,' Mr Champion said. He inhaled and

breathed out again with a checked cough that was like a groan. 'First things first,' he said. He opened a table drawer at his side and took out a brown envelope. From this he drew the hard dark blue shape of a passport. 'At forty pounds,' Mr Champion said, 'I'd call it a bargain.'

He opened it for his visitor to see. McIver's photograph appeared over the name of John Guy Walker.

'Not bad,' he said casually. 'Not a bargain, though.'

Mr Champion puffed at his cigarette as if in pain. 'Not bad? This is the real thing, my dear boy, if your name happened to be John Guy Walker. Your passport photographs were signed by a real solicitor, a poor old devil now so senile he'll put his name to anything our friend the nurse lays in front of him. He thinks she's a secretary, when he thinks at all. And here's your birth certificate back – or rather the late Mr Walker's that you kindly obtained from Somerset House.'

'Wing Commander, actually,' McIver said with quiet respect. 'He was an equerry to the Prince of Wales before the war. Copped it flying a sea-plane on the Lisbon run.'

'I'm sure he wouldn't mind being of service now,' Mr Champion said philosophically. Behind the old man's shoulder, on the narrow mantelpiece of the black-leaded grate, a photograph of an officer in the Royal Flying Corps uniform of a previous war was set in an offcut of a wooden propellor-blade. Among his back-room stock of Paris-printed novels, histories of punishment, lesbian romances, and sets of photographs in cellophane packets, he talked of service and sacrifice in the tone of a headmaster before the boys and their parents.

'You could go anywhere in the world with that passport,' he said wistfully. 'That is a genuine article issued by HMG. You'd pay almost as much for one of those back-street jobs botched up with rubber type.'

'Oh, well . . .' McIver said. He reached into his pocket and took out the wallet, unfolding the thin crisp paper of five-pound notes. 'No chance of making it thirty-five? I'd like something left.'

Mr Champion gave a short schoolmasterly sigh and tucked the money away. 'The people who produce these items would find me very tiresome if I discounted goods on their behalf. The full price, I fear. And I do hope that those fivers are all they seem. Numbers can be traced so easily these days. Now then, do I see an envelope of photographic plates? I believe I do.'

'You'll like these,' McIver said, sliding them from the envelope. 'The best so far. I was half-thinking of trying some of them on one of the new pin-up mags.'

Mr Champion took the dozen plates of Solitaire and spread the images of bare flesh on the table like playing cards.

'Good,' he said. 'Nice technique your cameraman has with natural light through the window. Flashlight never looks erotic. Pity it's the same young lady.'

McIver smiled. 'You know what they say. Can't have too much of a good thing.'

'Do they? Do they say that?' Mr Champion poured from the kettle. 'I fear they may be wrong.'

McIver reached for a cup and laughed. 'With this one? She's a Windmill girl. Star of the show at the Revuedeville. Take a run down to Piccadilly and see for yourself. She could be on the silver screen in a few months. One of Mr J. Arthur Rank's starlets.'

Mr Champion made tea and clicked his tongue philosophically. 'Trouble is, Johnny McIver, I'm not Mr Rank nor the Windmill. I can only tell you what my clientele has to say. They're not fools, you see. I get people from business who look in on the way to catch a train home to Reading or Maidenhead. After they've seen a girl for a bit, they want a change. I'm not saying that if it was a bit heavier in terms of subject I might not know of someone. But this one of yours sounds as if she's a class above that. Mr Rank and the Windmill.'

'Take the negatives and call it a tenner,' McIver suggested. 'I'll put it to her about the other stuff. She might not mind something stronger. I think she might be rather good at it. Between you and me, she enjoys the work. A born exhibitionist.'

They argued a little more.

'Tell you what,' Mr Champion said at last, 'leave the one lot of prints and the negs with me. I'll see what I can do. If people want a set, I'll have copies made as they buy.'

'Ten quid for the negs and prints,' McIver said.

'Five,' said Mr Champion gently. 'More to come if more's called for.'

There was no moving him. Mr Champion took a well-used wallet from his pocket and found five folded notes. 'I won't hand you back one of your fivers, Johnny. Those are for the passport wallahs. A place for everything and everything in its place.'

McIver looked at his teacup. 'How many five-pound notes could you change for me, supposing I could bring you the genuine article?'

The steam of the tea made Mr Champion's eyes water a little. 'All at once?'

'More or less.'

The teacup went down. 'I don't know, Johnny. As a rule, five pounds would get you three. If it's a lot of money at once, then the trade reckons it must have come from somewhere undesirable. You could still change it but you'd have to tempt their taste buds. Five pounds might only get you one or two, not even that if they read that some poor devil's been shot in a robbery.'

McIver shook his head. 'Nothing like that. Banknotes from doing business. They wouldn't all be fivers but the numbers on the fivers would need careful handling.'

Mr Champion read his tealeaves. 'Suppose you should have money to change for its own sake, you might do worse than call in here. There's a connection of mine, a bookie with race meetings all over the country. Catterick, Aintree, Lincoln, Plumpton, Fontmell, Ayr . . . He pays out notes as winnings and keeps the ones he takes in. In less than a week, a bundle of fivers might be scattered from Land's End to John o' Groats. Numbered or not, they won't be easily traced after that. Even if one turns up, the trail's likely to be cold long before.'

He stood up as McIver put the wallet away and slid the wrapped passport into his pigskin case. The old man followed him out through the shop. A passing bus rattled the glass panel of the door.

'Come and see me when you've got something like that to talk about,' Mr Champion said.

McIver patted his briefcase. 'I'll remember all right. Could be sooner than you think.'

'But one thing,' the old man said.

'What's that?'

'You're a handsome lad, Johnny McIver. Don't outgrow your strength. Some very unpleasant people have come out of this war. Worse than last time. Don't try to get too big too fast.'

McIver laughed. 'You read too many books, Mr C.'

But Mr Champion looked serious. 'Word to the wise, old son.'

The shop door jangled as Mr Champion closed it and slid the bolt across again.

5

McIver turned away and walked up past the gaunt structure of the mainline railway station, towards Paddington Green and Maida Vale. A group of children from Canal Street were playing in the fire-blackened cavity of a bomb site. They turned and chanted at him as he passed, recognizing and hailing him, half in homage and half in mockery, running after him at a distance down the cracked uneven paving.

'Johnny got a Zero! . . . Johnny Zero! . . . Johnny Zero! . . . Johnny Zero! . . .'

He grinned at them and waved his hand in a dismissive salute as he walked on. The moment of his national fame was not one that he had ever chosen to hide. Belatedly, on his return from the Far East, he had heard his name accompanying a cinema newsreel, shown to him by courtesy of Gaumont-British News. McIver had seen the newsreel once, in a private projection-room in Wardour Street. The words of the gritty tough-chinned commentator were incised in his mind. Sometimes he still felt a thrill as he rehearsed them but increasingly he felt that they were written for a stranger.

As he walked on, he saw in his mind the booming wings and fuselages of the projected image. 'Japanese fighters from forward airfields again attacked Allied positions at Imphal on the Burma frontier. But this time three Zero pilots got more than they bargained for. Before the attack began, Flight Sergeant Johnny McIver was airborne in his Hawker Hurricane. Ignoring the usual advice "never dogfight a Zero", Flight Sergeant McIver intercepted the attack alone. In a breathtaking display of aerobatics, he shot down the leading Zero A6M and damaged a second of the Japanese planes. The damaged Zero and its companion broke off the engagement and turned for home. As any man on the ground at Imphal will tell you, Johnny got a Zero and Johnny is a hero today.'

McIver smiled again, warmed by the memory and by the voices of the local children following him down the shabby little street, the salute to his brief heroism dimly in his mind as he turned the corner and went up the house steps, their dusty edges still showing a ghost of white paint as an aid to navigation in the blackout.

Glory and gratitude were perishable goods, he thought. Ten more years and the brave little chant would be as meaningless as the tunes of Waterloo or Blenheim. He stopped at Mrs Doyle's front door, brown varnish peeling from its solid Victorian panels. McIver listened carefully at the door and then gently slid his key into the lock. There was no sound of movement from the cool hallway with its threadbare linoleum and the dim light through the panels of coloured glass beyond the stairs. He stood in the dank air, among its scents of boiled cabbage and washing. With hardly a sound he went up the carpeted stairs and into his room on the second floor. He had been meaning to make a move for some time. Mr Champion's advice merely hastened his departure.

From under the bed he drew a bulky old-fashioned suitcase. Opening it, he tipped in the contents of several drawers and stuffed clothes from the worm-eaten wardrobe on top. His chalk-stripe demob suit and the rest of his belongings were in the hotel bedroom. There was nothing here worth keeping.

Twenty minutes later he was ready, the swollen suitcase in one hand and the pigskin briefcase in the other. The air was dusty with late sunlight. Listening for any other sound of movement, he heard only a radio in the sour cabbage-steamed air of Mrs Doyle's kitchen, a soubrette voice out-singing a Palm Court orchestra.

> Walking in the Zoo!
> Walking in the Zoo!
> The OK thing on Sunday
> Is walking in the Zoo!

Moving down the stairs again, he still listened for sounds of a door opening, for a voice or footsteps. The sun, slanting lower, caught the dust haze from the summer street. As he opened the front door and lodged the suitcase on the step, the girl's voice sang imperiously.

> Oh, walking in the Zoo!
> Walking in the Zoo!
> How the monkeys make us blush,
> Walking in the Zoo!

He closed the door, went down the steps, and moved off along the street, walking more awkwardly with his burden. He chose the other direction now, towards Maida Vale and Warwick Avenue.

McIver continued until he came to the canal bridge where the tow-path dipped down along the bank opposite Clifton Gardens. No one seemed to notice him as he went down opposite the cream-washed terrace with its balustrades and ornaments in a long sequence of the late-Georgian terrace. McIver still remembered the area of Maida Vale and St John's Wood from ten years ago, the last summers before Hitler's war, when he had once come this way to watch cricket at Lords. A prime minister with his comic umbrella and a promise of peace in our time. Now it seemed remote as something remembered from a school history lesson. Hutton scoring 364 against Australia at the Oval was the real thing.

He walked along the bank a little towards Regent's Park, the house-backs crowding more closely but the tow-path still deserted. The only narrow-boats moored on this stretch looked as if they had remained abandoned since 1939 and the outbreak of hostilities.

Looking back quickly to see that the path was still empty, he stood quietly on the bank, the weed-green water slopping by at his feet. It was no more than five or six feet deep just here – but deep enough. He put down the pigskin briefcase and held the toughened canvas of the suitcase as far out as he could. Then he launched it with all his strength and let it go. It fell with a flat splash about six feet from the bank, floated for a moment, and then subsided into the silted water, stirring bubbles of pond gas as it came to rest on the bottom of the canal. No one had seen him, he thought. Even if they had heard the splash, the suitcase and all that could be identified of John Patrick McIver would have disappeared into the silt before anyone had a chance to look.

He turned away with his briefcase in his right hand and walked quickly back along the tow-path opposite the Georgian windows and verandas of Clifton Gardens. The radio was still playing but his mind was full of other things. The career of Johnny Zero had begun. As he walked energetically towards the dark green paintwork of the wrought-iron bridge, where the tow-path came up to the road again, he was humming to himself. Johnny Zero and Solitaire, the perfect team, with Billy Blake and Roddy Hallam as their supporting cast. Long ago, during his Borstal training, the boy prisoners had been trained to believe they could do anything by will and effort. There was nothing he could not do now, if he tried.

3

BLUE HEAVEN

1

The flickering darkness of the News Theatre was scented with California Poppy. Rutter sat at the end of a row, where a subdued flush of electric light mapped the way towards the stalls exit. He glanced at the green-lit electric clock to one side of the screen and saw that it was half-past five. Almost time to go. Pathé News had completed its summary of world events. The skipping inconsequential music of the soundtrack now prepared its audience for fun at home. Rutter coughed and stubbed out his cigarette, as the adenoidal baritone voice jollied him along.

'The Odeon Leicester Square was the scene last week for the first charity première since the war in aid of the London Children's Appeal. Famous faces were there and so were the crowds to greet them. Almost twenty thousand pounds was raised towards the Duke of York's fund for children's playgrounds and youth clubs in the East End, as well as country and seaside holidays for less fortunate youngsters. Personalities from the worlds of entertainment and sport were on hand to ensure a record success for this year's appeal. The crowds who had waited patiently outside the theatre were rewarded by glimpses and autographs of the stars. But it was left to the two princesses to make this a truly royal occasion . . .'

The music surged again and Rutter, looking up at the screen, studied a row of monochrome figures in their Leicester Square seats. One or two he recognized from minor parts in films. The rest were anonymous producers and promoters, proprietors and entrepreneurs, whose donations had bought them an invitation. Grey-haired, and almost birdlike with emaciation, Evelyn Tarrant sat close to the far end of the row. Next to her, Rutter saw the curled lip and tall head of Sonny Boy Tarrant himself. With a professional interest he watched his prey. Tarrant sat with the look of a man whose mind is far away. During the four or five seconds when the camera was on him he showed no awareness of his surroundings at all. Rutter waited for the newsreel to end and for the apricot flush of light to illuminate the curtains across the screen. Then he got up and went out into the frosted glass and black marble of the tiled foyer. Dazzled by the evening sunlight of Trafalgar Square, he turned down Whitehall towards the Palace of Westminster and the river.

The members of the 'Ghost Squad', created in the aftermath of war, had inherited the Special Branch offices used during hostilities. Located at the foot of the stone stairs to the basement, their doors and interiors resembled prison cells rather than offices. They were the only offices at the Yard whose occupants could lock them up and take away the key. Entering the foyer, Rutter flashed his identity card at the duty sergeant and went down the stairs to a corridor of painted brick with caged light-bulbs in the ceiling arch. He pushed open the first of the iron-braced doors, stepping into the light and conversation of the outer office.

'Mr Gould waiting to see Mr Rutter,' the girl at the desk said, without looking up from her copy of *Woman's Journal*. 'Good film, was it?'

'I'd call it instructive,' Rutter said. 'How's the story?'

He looked over her shoulder at the magazine. Suzanne turned and laughed at him. She laughed a lot with instinctive self-defence in a world where she was the only pretty woman among a dozen men. She was the girl of the day with sharply outlined breasts under her sweater and mobile hips under a tight pencil skirt, rather fluffy blond curls, and a pretty face. Rutter supposed she needed protection.

He tapped on the door and went into the inner office where Chief Inspector Harold Gould was waiting. One wall of the room was covered by photographs and documents on a pin-board. Among them was Sidney Royce, a head like the Emperor Nero on a barrel-chested torso. Tom Foster, a big bland globe of a face and a frizz of fair hair, was looking slightly away from the camera, smiling into the distance. Latifa Noon was the only one in colour. She was modelling a bare-limbed and elastic-tight water suit, the devil-mask of her beauty turning over her shoulder, the blood-painted nails drawn self-caressingly up one smooth-clad hip. Last in the row was the tall-domed, sharp-nosed profile of Sonny Tarrant, the straight underlip worrying against its partner's curve.

'I had a look at Tarrant on the newsreel,' Rutter said, sitting down across the desk from Gould. 'No one with him but his mother. There's nothing in it for us. But Frank Brodie reckons it was John McIver's woman he saw leaving the Temple Court apartments about three yesterday afternoon. A flashy young con-man known in the trade as "Pretty Boy" McIver and two of his friends were waiting to pick her up beyond Sloane Street. Driving a Chrysler Airflow saloon. We're checking the details but it seems the car is genuine.'

Gould sipped his tea, staring towards the sunset. The bruise-coloured bags under his eyes had been there for several months past. DCI Gould now looked chronically sick. 'I don't know McIver,' he said. 'Should I?'

Rutter stretched his legs from the broken-down leather arm-chair. He lit a cigarette and dropped the match into a brown Bakelite ashtray, compliments of Imperial Airways.

'McIver's not in the major league but he could be a bloody nuisance. He's not Tarrant's friend, of that I'm sure. And he's not a match for Tarrant. Of that I am dead certain. If McIver mixes it with Tarrant, we'll all live to feel sorry for ourselves.'

Chief Inspector Gould turned round and put his teacup on the desk. He was a clerkly looking man with horn-rimmed glasses and tight black hair almost grey.

'What do I need to know about McIver?'

Rutter frowned at the paper in his hand. 'Born Wimbledon, 1916. Educated at a minor public school. Left rather suddenly. Warehouse clerk, 1932. Employment terminated after eight months. Royal Air Force officer cadet, 1935. Pilot officer with wings, 1935. Flying officer, 1936. Cashiered for petty theft, 1936. Probation for taking and driving a motor vehicle without the owner's consent, 1938. Sentenced to two years Borstal Training for burglary, 1939. Released for war service, 1940. Private, Royal Army Service Corps, 1940. Commissioned, second lieutenant, 1941. Cashiered after court martial at Cairo for being absent without leave and holding a second pay-book, 1941. Absconded when the troop ship bringing him home round the Cape docked at Port Elizabeth. In 1942, a certain "Jimmy Cunningham" turned up in India with a story about having applied as a trainee pilot in

South Africa. This was when every RAF squadron in India was being transferred from tribal patrol duty in the north-west to stop the Japanese in the south-east. They tried his aptitude as a pilot and, not surprisingly, thought he was damn good at it. They didn't commission him but he was sergeant pilot, then a flight sergeant. To top it all, he got mentioned on the news for shooting down a Zero over Imphal. Johnny Zero. Some twat even got up in the House of Commons to complain that McIver had been refused a medal because he was only a non-commissioned officer.'

'So they knew he was John McIver by then?'

'His name came to light at the time of the Johnny Zero business. By then he was good propaganda value. And they were desperate for anyone who could fly and shoot. Mind you, the RAF were careful never to give him another commission or let him get his hands near the mess funds after what happened in 1936. He was demobilized, September 1945. Convicted and fined by the Bow Street magistrates in November for wearing a uniform and decorations to which he was not entitled. In this case, as Group Captain the Honourable Alistair Trumpington, DSO, MC. The bloody fool took the name from a novel. For the last six months, there's nothing against him. At least, not in the records.'

Gould closed a folder on his desk. 'And what's he doing running a girl who visits Tarrant in the Temple Court apartments?'

Rutter shrugged. 'You tell me, Harry. He's a lad with the girls. There's likely to be a bit of pimping but I'm not proposing to pull him for that. Where McIver's concerned it's only high-class tarts like this one. Calls herself Solitaire, born Sally Brown. Married but separated. You wouldn't get much out of her and not enough to stick an immoral earnings charge on him. He's got a camera and a hand in the shady side of the pin-up trade. I'm not pulling him for that either. It's not illegal to take photographs, unless you retail them. He's a supplier, not a retailer. If he's got a habitat, it's hotels round Knightsbridge and Chelsea, clubs like the Copacabana in South Kensington. He's driving a Chrysler Airflow, ex-US Army from Ruislip, sprayed midnight-blue with white-walled tyres. The tyres he must have picked up for himself. Might be interesting to know where he gets the petrol from. There's one other thing I could get him for. Seems he's sold his ration-book to a grocer in Southwark. Doesn't eat at home often enough to make it worth having one.'

Gould opened his drawer and slid the folder into it, politely but purposefully getting ready to leave for the day. 'Anything else?'

'Not much,' Rutter said. 'I've got a whisper that McIver and his friends have smart ideas. "T" Division had about a dozen robberies on their patch in February and March, anywhere between Hyde Park and the river but Sloane Square and Belgravia for preference. All of them from apartment blocks and all but two from wall-safes. Divisional CID put McIver close to four of them. They tell me he fancies himself as a cat-burglar.'

'No chance of putting McIver away for a while until we get Tarrant?'

Rutter shook his head. 'Not on what we've got. I just hope McIver doesn't kid himself that he can take on the big boys and win.'

Gould puffed out his cheeks and patted the folder on his desk. 'I'm getting stick from upstairs, Jack, and earache on the phone. A couple of weeks more and Customs and Excise reckon they could have had Tom Foster. There was a small fortune in Scotch whisky under bond for export. No duty payable. All the documentation was right, all the moves were right. But that whisky was being drunk here, in London. Either it never left the country or it came back, unnoticed, in short order.'

'What was Foster doing?'

Gould chuckled at the neatness of it. 'He was cooking the books to *cordon bleu* standard. They reckon he was buying in the whisky as a wholesaler through a bent company of his own making. The supplier would invoice him for £10,000 and there it was in the books, full payment. He'd actually pay them, say, £5,000 and pocket the difference from the till. Customs and Excise reckon they could have had him in a fortnight more. He was Tarrant's bookkeeper as well. Would you reckon Tarrant was involved in this racket?'

Rutter shrugged. 'Ask Customs and Excise.'

'They don't know, Jack. I'd say Tarrant was far enough in to want Foster out of the way for safety's sake.'

'And Royce?'

'Royce?' Gould shook his head. 'Perhaps Tarrant was making a clean sweep. Divisional CID were watching Royce. More important, they were asking questions about his past. Quite a few people south of the river suffered grievous bodily harm from the late Sidney Royce. The day he was picked up for that, he might save

43

himself by shopping Tarrant. He was knuckle-dusting and carving on Tarrant's behalf. Mr Tarrant's going straight now, Jack. Charity shows at the Odeon Leicester Square with the two princesses. If Foster had to go, Royce might as well be tidied away at the same time.'

Rutter knocked off cigarette ash against the brown Bakelite of the Imperial Airways ashtray.

'No one's telling that story on the streets, Harry. The reckoning is that someone as big as Tarrant aims to put him out of business. Wipe out two of his most important men and leave him isolated. No one he can trust. Either he talks terms or he's the next to go. Or else we've got a couple of complete newcomers prepared to shoot their way to the top of Tarrant's empire.'

'McIver?'

Rutter laughed. 'Not McIver. At least, I hope not. McIver's a pisspot. He'd wouldn't go two rounds against Tarrant. If Tarrant ever thinks he's trying it on, then God help McIver. The story is that someone bigger is having a go at Tarrant and he knows it. I think it's just talk, Harold. This isn't Chicago.'

'No one has a go while I'm sitting in this office, Jack. If Tarrant gets the chop, it won't be a nice easy succession. Every hard man from Stepney to Hammersmith and from Islington down to south of the river is going to want his chance. It won't be the old days either, with a bit of razoring to show who's boss. All those clowns have got guns now. Paddington Green pulled in three Mark IV Sten guns from a dealer last week. Five hundred rounds a minute and an effective range of two hundred yards. You could sit here and wipe out people across the road who never even knew you existed.'

Rutter smiled. 'I used a few of those,' he said. 'Grip a Sten gun the wrong way round and it takes your fingers off as it fires.'

'I want Tarrant,' Gould said softly, 'that's what we're here for. Until you can show me otherwise, Royce and Foster and Latifa Noon are chalked on his slate. But I'm not going to stop with him. When he goes down the steps, he takes the rest with him. Including McIver, if I have anything to do with it.'

Rutter glanced at his wristwatch. 'I'm meeting Frank Brodie in an hour or so. We'll see what else Sonny Boy Tarrant has been up to.'

2

Rutter went home to change. He crossed the Bayswater Road just before seven o'clock as the sun began to go down like a molten disc above the trees of Kensington Gardens. Flashes of fire caught the upper windows of houses and hotels along Park Lane. A solitary Truscott-trained nanny was wheeling a hooded pram towards Lancaster Gate while the last regimental selection from the bandstand carried the overture to *The Count of Luxembourg* across freshly mown turf.

Rutter's grey chalk-stripe was regulation demob suiting, inconspicuous among thousands of its kind. His war had ended eighteen months before with a return to duty in the CID. In the world of the black marketeer and the post-war gunman, as Scotland Yard created its first 'Ghost Squad', Rutter was destined to be part of it for as long as this tour of duty lasted. Now he turned across Kensington Gardens and strode towards the Knightsbridge trees. To his left lay the glass moons of the lamps among dark evergreens, the sunset outlines of Edwardian balustrades and wrought iron. Between the trees, a violet stretch of the Serpentine lay warm and calm as an Italian lake.

Traffic was busy along Knightsbridge as he came out of the park again and walked towards the welcome refuge of the World's End. In the narrow mews where the plain little houses were occupied by plumbers or bakers, the public house was no more than the parlour and adjoining rooms of a coachman's lodging. With the creeper covering its Georgian cottage front, the purple clematis and yellow roses on its narrow ledges, it had an air of provincial France. Rutter stepped into an interior of old-fashioned frosted glass, dark mahogany panels, and the coloured bottles lining the little bar. Its cramped and cosy room suggested the easy comfort of a family ale-house. The white stucco of the dado was darkened to creamy brown by the companionable pall of smoke which never seemed to clear.

He paused to duck his head under a beam and shook a clean white Senior Service from a crisp new packet. He lit it and drew the smooth toasted fragrance of tobacco soothingly into his lungs, letting it trail out at leisure through his nostrils. Framed and signed theatrical photographs dimmed by time covered one wall, while on a radio behind the bar Noël Coward urged Mrs Worthington not to put her daughter on the stage. Rutter pulled at the white smoothness of the cigarette again as he moved between several groups of drinkers and touched Frank Brodie's shoulder at the counter of the bar.

'What's it to be then, Frankie?'

'I thought I heard something about pre-war Scotch,' Brodie said hopefully. 'Not much beer here to speak of. You catch that newsreel all right?'

'You're right,' Rutter said grimly, 'he's on it. Him and his mother. They shot it almost two weeks ago, before his seaside holiday with his mum.'

By contrast with the thin and nervous figure of Rutter, Brodie was rubicund and relaxed. The burr of his voice suggested agricultural fairs and country markets, the long afternoons of county cricket. It was a simple and open face that smiled easily. A good many criminals had misjudged its amiability and now considered their mistake at leisure in His Majesty's prisons. Rutter watched the barman fill two glasses and then motioned Brodie to a table at the other end of the room, away from the drinkers.

'We'll take these two out the back, Charlie, if that's all right with you.'

The barman, hand on the beer-pump, looked back over his shoulder. 'You can have it all to yourself out there, Mr Rutter. Nice and quiet now till dinner's over.'

Rutter picked up the glasses and led the way down a dark passage, through a back room and into the walled yard which served as a garden to the mews house. There were two folding chairs either side of a weather-stained table. Brodie sat down with a long comfortable sigh.

'What've we got then, Jack?'

'Grief,' Rutter said. 'The three funerals were officially passed to us last week. Two employees of Sonny Boy Tarrant and one of their women. All three of 'em wiped out the same evening. Sid Royce, that managed the Streatham garage and then the cinema near Croydon, shot dead down Tips Tenements. I ask you, Frankie! Three bullets fired in a quiet street at night. But not a head looks out of a window and not a nose peeps round a door.'

'Seeing the last of old Roller Royce won't exactly be a blow,' Brodie said philosophically.

'Wait!' Rutter said. 'An hour later, at most, Tom Foster drowns in his bath. So much for Customs and Excise trying to find out how bond whisky for export winds up on tables in half a dozen London clubs. They'd put six months' hard labour into that.'

'Customs and Excise should sniff about their own home,' Brodie said. 'That's where the real smell's coming from.'

'Tarrant's two senior men wiped out in the hour. Another hour and Latifa Noon dies in a car crash in Surrey, having provided Tom Foster's creature comforts for the past few weeks. According to divisional intelligence, she was Tarrant's playmate before he passed her on to Foster. That's three in one evening! The people who did this don't really expect anyone to believe that Foster drowned accidentally in his bath and Latifa Noon was so cut up that she went straight off and topped herself by driving the car off the road.'

Brodie squeezed the butt of a cigarette to his lips and drew the last comforting breath of tobacco smoke from it.

'How you don't burn your lip doing that I will never know,' Rutter said sternly.

He took a sheet of paper from his breast pocket and unfolded it. 'That's the last word from forensic. It was Foster's car and the coachwork went up like a torch. What they found of Latifa Noon looked more like a log from the remains of a bonfire. But the autopsy still got quite clever. No sign of smoke in the thorax. No carbon monoxide in the blood from fractured pipes. In other words, she stopped breathing before that car crashed – with someone's assistance. And then a lot of things under the bonnet didn't burn – and the rest burnt so fast there wasn't time for the metal to melt. That includes the junction nut on the fuel pipe, leading from the tank to the carburettor. Forensic found that it was loose. They used to say that a brass junction nut would sometimes loosen with expansion during the fire. It wasn't likely but it might happen. In the course of other modifications, Rover changed the alloy of the nut so that if fire ever reached the pipe, at least the petrol wouldn't leak. The monkeys who killed Latifa Noon didn't know this. They knew just enough to loosen the nut.'

'And Foster in his bath?'

Rutter gave a snort of derision. 'Amateurs. No fingerprints on the bathroom-door handle. There should have been his but their gloves wiped them off. There'd been hot water all over the bathroom tiles, even though it had dried off. He didn't just slip away and drown. But they didn't really care, Frankie. Why should they bother if we know it's murder, so long as we can't tie it to them?

They couldn't care less. Look how they shot Royce and left his body in the street for the dust-cart to clear away. Three bullets from a .22 target automatic. Close range by an expert. With something that small, you have to be accurate. This was spot-on. From behind and to one side. Not six feet away. So far as forensic can tell, this gun had never been used before and by now it's probably at the bottom of the Thames.'

In the warm evening a vanilla-cream sweetness filled the yard from the mauve flowers of the montana clematis.

'Sonny Tarrant's in town,' Brodie said helpfully.

'But not on the night in question,' Rutter said. 'He was on holiday at Ma Tarrant's in Bournemouth. While Royce was being shot and Foster was being drowned, Sonny Boy and Ma Tarrant were entertaining guests, including one magistrate and one member of the local police authority.'

'He's got to be in it, hasn't he?'

'Only if you believe old Harry Gould,' Rutter said. 'He reckons Royce was topped because he'd been talking where he shouldn't, almost enough to incriminate Tarrant. Tom Foster had to go because sooner or later Customs and Excise would crack him wide open and find the way to Tarrant.'

'The girl?' Brodie prompted.

'Latifa Noon just had bad luck. She was in the wrong place at the wrong time. The net result leaves Tarrant owning a cinema and three garages south of the river and a string of operations north of it. It also puts the investigation back to the start again.'

'What's his other connections?'

'Just Ma Tarrant,' Rutter said. 'God knows what she thinks of him. I doubt if she could tell you who his father was. Ma Tarrant reckons she was a Gibson Girl. A high-class high-kicker before the first war. London and Paris. The story was that she'd several times been screwed by the king – Edward VII – before he was king. Another version was that she was one of the girls hired to teach bedroom manners to the royal sons. All in all, Evelyn Tarrant wasn't the quavering old ghost that she looks like now. Not that the good time lasted long. When the first war ended, she was living off favours from old men who hadn't noticed how they'd all got old together. By then, Sonny Boy Tarrant was sharpening his first razor and learning to count money.'

'His father could have been famous.'

Rutter glared at the idea.

Brodie leant back and yawned at the evening sky. 'Did Mr Gould say how much longer we might be kept on the job?'

'Nope.'

'Because,' Brodie said, 'this living-out allowance or whatever it is doesn't nearly cover the cost. It's something the federation ought to take up. No one could live on it.'

Without paying much attention, Rutter listened to Frank Brodie's complaint and spoke the appropriate monosyllables. His chair gave him a view of the intimate bar through its window. He wondered how he must look from the other side. A man in a grey trilby and a chalk-stripe grey suit, the thin face lined by too many drinks with men like Frank Brodie in too many bars.

'So what's next?' Brodie asked.

Rutter stubbed out his cigarette. 'I'm going to go back to Harry Gould tomorrow and have a chat. What we're chasing is a complete waste of time. Divisional CID and everyone else is thinking exactly what the other side want them to think. They're convinced Tarrant hired two professional gunmen to get rid of his two men next in line and the girl. Bollocks, Frankie. The more I look at this, my son, the more I'm sure Tarrant had nothing to do with it. He's a bastard. Everyone likes to think a man who's that big a bastard must be behind a triple murder. Tarrant's more likely on the receiving end.'

'You think it could be McIver and his friends?'

Rutter gave a helpless shrug. 'McIver's a dreamer. Small time. We're looking for someone bigger, Frankie. Whoever he is, I reckon Tarrant's the next on his list. If Tarrant had wiped out a couple of his own men, that might be serious. If there's some mystery guest about to make a bid for Tarrant's empire, then there's likely to be blood coming down like rain.'

Brodie narrowed his eyes.

'You reckon it's that way round?'

'What else, Frankie? You tell me anything else that makes sense. If Tarrant wanted to get rid of Royce, he'd drop him in the river, not leave him lying in the street with enough evidence to hang someone. Same goes for Foster.'

'But Tarrant didn't do it himself. He was too far away.'

'That's another thing, Frankie. This notion that he hired a couple of killers to do it for him. You think about where that leaves him. Whatever Tarrant had hanging over him, he's not going to prefer a triple-murder charge instead. And, as I keep saying, if anyone would listen, Tarrant himself was a hundred miles away when those three died. We're all chasing our tails, Frankie. It was Tarrant who was on the receiving end this time. And Harry Gould still can't see it.'

3

McIver watched the waiter, a tray balanced on either hand, negotiating the evening crowd on the floor of the Copacabana like a tightrope walker. The chromium bar and the oval mirrors, the white and green swirls of wall mosaic, were lit through panels of fused glass. The miniature dance floor at one end was balanced by a small stage at the other. A woman in coatee and matador pants crossed to the bar. McIver watched her. Billy Blake watched McIver watching her.

'Tell you what, Johnny,' Blake said philosophically, 'the day you die, there's parts of you they'll have to beat to death with a stick.'

'Just jealous,' McIver said. 'You think that's something, you get an eyeful of Solitaire now.'

They paused while the waiter unloaded the first tray. McIver smiled and gave the man a coin for himself. There was utter frankness and decency in the smile. 'This one's to go on our crime sheet, old boy. I'll catch the cashier later on.'

There was a drum roll and a chord that suggested Latin passion. With the lights dimmed and the impetuous rhythm of 'Lady of Spain' rebounding from the walls, Solitaire was doing her first fan dance of the evening. Her auburn hair was drawn back in an elegant bun with a cardinal-red rose at its side. She assumed an expression of pride and magnificence. The body make-up darkened her nudity to Andalusian warmth.

Solitaire twirled on her toes, curving one fanned ostrich feather across her torso while the other formed an arc above her head. In perfect time to the drumming rhythm, she turned and curved, revealing the nudity of elegant legs and graceful arms, bare back with its light-muscled beauty perfectly etched. The timing was immaculate as each secret of breasts or loins was promised and then concealed. McIver glanced round. All conversation had stopped. Every man and woman in the place, barman and waiters, watched the display. She was superb. He grinned and thought that Tarrant could never have had a chance.

The legs were like a moving advertisement for the finest silk stockings. The curve of the back and shoulders made McIver dream of liners' dance floors on tropical voyages, a world of expensive night clubs in Paris, Madrid, Manhattan, Singapore . . . Until the end of the dance, he left his glass untouched. In the final drum roll, Solitaire stepped up on to her pedestal before the cyclorama. The lights died leaving only the pale blue flush of the screen against which, as she stretched the ostrich plumes wide, her nudity appeared in perfect silhouette.

McIver kept his cigarette clipped between his lips, eyes narrowed against the smoke, and held both hands high as he joined in the applause.

'Fan-bloody-tastic!' he said at last.

Blake turned his chair back to the table. 'You think she's as good on locks?'

McIver grinned at him. 'No, old bean. But then you wouldn't pay to see me do a fan dance. I'll manage the lock. I reckon I'm good enough for both of us.'

'Did she get the combination?'

'No,' said McIver thoughtfully, 'but I reckon she got enough. She doesn't quite realize what she's found out. I'd rather keep it that way. Let's face it, Billy. She's a good little scout but she might talk in her sleep.'

'You'd have heard her by now,' Blake said coolly. 'So what did she see?'

McIver looked round with a genial smile as if to make sure that there was no one in earshot. 'She saw him open the wall-safe in the kitchen. If his keys to the Luxor office and the main safe aren't there, they aren't anywhere. The lock in the kitchen wall-safe of the apartment is a Mosler combination. He picked out six consecutive numbers on a hundred-digit dial.'

'That could be bloody millions unless she got the numbers,' Blake said.

McIver looked at him with a fierce exasperation. 'It could be, Billy, but it won't be. She saw him pick four numbers low on the dial, less than ten, moving the knob left to right. OK? Then he went up to somewhere round twenty, then somewhere up about ninety. That opened it.'

The lights were dimmed again. The voice of a torch singer in her black evening-gown was husky with smoke, as she delivered a letter from a lady in love.

'It's still a hell of a lot of possible numbers to try, especially

51

with Tarrant or his stone-faces likely to walk in any minute,' Blake said.

McIver leant forward, elbows on the table and chin propped on his hands. He smiled patiently.

'Billy, old son. Do you know how people pick numbers for combination locks or anything else of the kind? You really think they pick them out of the blue?'

'If I knew that,' Blake said, 'I'd be out making a fortune.'

'How would you do it? It's a number you've got to be able to remember for certain and quickly. So how would you do it?'

'Car number, perhaps.'

'Too few numbers and anyway you'd change your car. And also people know your car number. Might put two and two together.'

'You tell me,' Blake said wearily. 'National Insurance number? Identity card number?'

McIver laughed. 'How many people could remember those in a hurry?'

'All right,' Blake said, 'I give up.'

McIver leant forward, elbows on the table. 'I knew a cove while I was His Majesty's guest in Borstal. He'd worked as a locksmith for a big firm, until they caught him. He reckoned a lot of people would either just pick 1–2–3–4. Or they might use a phone number, if it could be made to fit. They were more scared of forgetting the number themselves than of someone else finding it out. Tarrant's no different. In fact, he's got better reason than most for needing to open up quickly.'

'So what's the answer?'

'Birthdays are top of the list,' McIver said. 'This chap reckoned that far and away the most common number was a birthday. You don't forget it and you can stretch it to eight figures if you need to. If you were born on 20 October 1922, let's say, that gives you 20–10–1922 and you're not going to forget it. But no thief is going to put 20101922 together from guesswork. I suppose you could even reverse it and have 22910102. Point is, you'd know it straight off.'

'You reckon it's Tarrant's birthday?'

McIver grinned and shook his head. 'It could be, but it's not the most likely. Too many people know it. Too risky. No. What you need is a birthday you'll never forget. One you can work out any time. Tarrant's wouldn't do. There's a high number at the end of the combination, according to Solitaire. But Tarrant was born in 1904. No good.'

Blake grinned at him. 'How the hell do you know when he was born?'

'Roddy Hallam got a copy of Tarrant's birth certificate,' McIver said. 'Courtesy of Somerset House. Costs you half a quid. Nothing to stop you getting any birth certificate you like and the party concerned knowing nothing of it. Tarrant's was a waste of ten bob. Mrs Tarrant was a different matter. Apart from his own birthday, who's the one Tarrant will never forget? Not likely to be his father. Seems he never had one.'

'I'll bet,' Blake said.

'Roddy Hallam also found out that Ma Tarrant's birthday is 1 March 1883. It gives you 01031883. Four low numbers left to right. That's 0–1–0–3. A number near twenty, in this case eighteen. A number between eighty and ninety, in this case eighty-three. Think about it. Suppose anything was to happen to Tarrant. He's got no one except the old woman – no one he'd want opening the safe. All she's got to do is remember her birthday. Even if she forgets it, someone can tell her the date.'

'I'm thinking,' Blake said, 'what I'm thinking is they might deliberately jinx it by altering one number.'

'They might,' McIver said, 'but they don't. They'd rather have a certain sure number than muck about with one digit and then forget in a crisis which one it is. There's times when the old bird is at Temple Court and Tarrant isn't. There could be a crisis then. Would you want Ma Tarrant having to remember which number's been altered? You wouldn't. It's that simple.'

'But you don't know for certain that it's Ma Tarrant.'

'It doesn't have to be certain, old son. We can have as many as we like. All I'm saying is that this one ought to be first on the list. That sound all right to you, does it, Billy?'

'Of course it does.'

'Then that's it. We'll have a list of the most likely numbers with her at the head of it. If the first one doesn't work, we keep going down the list. How else do you think it's done? Any way you look at it, I reckon Ma Tarrant has to come at the top. Tarrant needs to know he could phone her in an emergency and say, "Open the safe, Ma, and shift whatever happens to be in there." I reckon I'm right, Billy. No two ways.'

The torch singer in her black gown had yielded to applause and now began 'Black Magic'.

McIver waited for Solitaire. Heads turned as she appeared in the blue-lightning sheath of her silk dress.

'You were bloody marvellous, old girl,' he said, 'took the entire staff to prevent the punters storming on stage.'

He kissed her and steered her on to the dance floor, utterly content in the glances of the other men and women at the tables who envied Johnny Zero and his girl.

4

The seamed leather of the Austin's passenger seat was hot from sunlight against Rutter's back as he pressed against it. 'Inquest's not until next week,' he said in answer to Brodie's question. 'They released the body to get this part of it over. Something to please the ghouls.'

The bow-windowed and green-tiled houses of pre-war suburbs were screened by privet and yew from the cemetery gates. A few sightseers, most of them women with shopping-bags, waited by the entrance where two uniformed policemen were on duty. Latifa Noon had become more famous in death as a film star than she had ever been during her life.

'Forensic get any more on that fuel-pipe, did they?' Brodie enquired.

Rutter shook his head. 'Someone certainly had a spanner on it not long ago. The marks were quite new. But that could have been in the course of maintaining the car. And Tom Foster's not here any more to tell us.'

The high square shape of the hearse was approaching, its roof massed with bright spring flowers, the cortège moving slowly past the hedged gardens of the suburban houses with several cars following.

'Another thing,' Rutter said, 'the spanner that fitted the nut hadn't any fingerprints on. It was in the tool box, which survived the fire more or less intact. How many mechanics do you know who work with gloves on, Frankie?'

Brodie wound the driver's window down a little more in the heat. 'So we get an inquest verdict of persons unknown, do we?'

'Wait a minute!' Rutter said as the cars moved slowly between the open gates into the avenue of monkey-puzzle and holly trees. 'Tarrant's here! He's with a woman in the third car.'

'Ma Tarrant, by any chance?'

'Could be. I think there's more than one of 'em.'

'Bit cheeky,' Brodie said. 'On the other hand, you keep saying that he was a hundred miles away when she died. There's a dozen witnesses saying much the same.'

The hearse had drawn up by the narrow Gothic porch of the mortuary chapel. Rutter opened the door of the squad car and got out.

'You're not going in, Jack?'

'No,' Rutter said, 'I'm going across to see who comes out again. I want Tarrant to notice me. I want him to know that he's got our company. See what that does to him.'

He walked across between the trees, reaching the porch of the chapel as the last of the mourners entered. Outside the gates, the sightseers waited, impassive and unblinking, for the mourners to return. A small van was parked there with a movie cameraman on its roof, winding his spool. Rutter breathed the warm resinous perfume of pine trees and scowled at the quiet lawns. Latifa Noon's last moment of fame was brief enough. At the end of fifteen minutes the chapel doors opened and the mourners began to file out into the sunlight.

Brodie had been right about Tarrant's companions. The hunched figure of Mrs Tarrant in a mauve summer dress and a hat with a veil seemed dwarflike beside her son. The old woman's fingers were encumbered by rings and the brooch on her dress was a gold salamander set with diamonds. Mother and son displayed the same heavy vulgarity. On the far side of Tarrant, Rutter saw a tall girl with auburn hair, professionalism in the poise of her figure and the composure of her face. He let out a shallow breath. Frank Brodie had seen McIver's girl at the Temple Court apartments. Surely her contract with Tarrant, whatever it might be, did not extend to funerals.

Rutter stood back a little and watched the thirty men and women as they waited to take their places in the cars again. Tarrant was talking to two dark-haired women and Solitaire was standing back slightly, as if to indicate that she was there in her own right and not as his guest. Tarrant turned away momentarily from the other two to say something to her. It was then that Rutter saw a flash of anger in the girl's face and heard her say:

'Because if it hadn't been for you, she'd still be alive!'

Tarrant's lips moved, the sneer not quite becoming a smile. He put out a hand, as if this would restrain the girl's anger. Though he managed to catch hold of her arm, Solitaire contrived to bow backwards and break free from him.

'Let me go! Leave me alone, will you?'

She turned, stumbled a little on her black high heels, recovered her balance and ducked into the first car. The other mourners were still standing in the grove of sunlit trees as she sat alone in the rear of the car like a little girl in disgrace.

'Someone needs a smack!' said old Mrs Tarrant bitterly.

Rutter judged it time to walk forward. Tarrant turned and saw him coming. 'Mr Rutter? I do apologize for not havin' a word before. Not knowin' you would be here but I quite see why. Sad circumstances to meet under, all the same. You know Mrs Tarrant, I expect. This is Mr Jack Rutter, Ma. Inspector down the Yard.'

Rutter inclined his head in the old woman's direction. Mrs Tarrant smiled below the hem of her veil.

'Everything all right, is it, Mr Tarrant?' Rutter asked.

Tarrant stepped aside towards the first line of tombstones. 'All in order, Mr Rutter. Latifa Noon was one of my protégées. She had two small parts in pictures that I helped to finance. No one to take care of matters after she died. I took upon myself to see that everythin' should be done decently today. It was a nice little service, just now. Very nice. Done with feelin'. There's refreshment at the Argyll presently. Private room there. If your duties permit, you'd be welcome.'

'I'll have to disappoint you this time,' Rutter said politely.

Tarrant smiled as if he understood. 'It's a sad time, Mr Rutter. I'm afraid Latifa's young friend got a bit overwrought just now. Best for the ladies to sit quiet in the cars on occasions like this. Nothin' you can say about your investigations, I suppose?'

Rutter felt a chill at the reptilian look in Tarrant's eyes and the movement of the lip towards a snarl. 'They're making progress, Mr Tarrant.'

'Not an accident, then, the car crash?'

Rutter smiled. 'I leave that to the experts and the inquest.'

Tarrant glanced round him as the mourners began to move towards the cars. Then he looked fiercely at Rutter.

'Only, supposin' it's no accident, Mr Rutter, then I'd like to burn the bastard that did it, same as he burnt that little girl. And I'd do it slow for the satisfaction of hearin' him scream long and high.'

Without waiting for a reply, he turned round and picked his way among the graves, the ends of his dark blue cashmere top-coat adrift, and took his place in the car behind the hearse. The

56

cortège moved slowly on the long parkland avenue towards the destination of the open grave.

5

'Your girl was in the graveyard with Tarrant,' Billy Blake said, 'when they saw off Latifa Noon. Roddy Hallam's been keeping a bit of watch on her, making sure his own back's covered. He reckons your gorgeous Solitaire could be a bit closer to old Tarrant than we asked for.'

McIver buttoned the case of the camera. 'She was friends with Latifa Noon,' he said, 'close friends.'

'You reckon they were both a bit ambidextrous?' Blake suggested.

'Could be. Actresses together.'

'That'd be a show worth seeing. Anyway, Hallam's slanging her because she was with Tarrant at the funeral and nothing was said to us about it. What you have to ask yourself, Johnny, is why Hallam's stirring it. She could be undressing and performing for Tarrant without complaining about it, even taking a smack or two off him perhaps, because she wants to see him pay for Latifa and to give us the chance to break him. You have to ask yourself, Johnny, whether a girl like Solitaire would actually do those things for a man like Tarrant otherwise, hating him that much. Only thing is, if she did it, if she was willing to be screwed by him if he could have done it, would she still hate him?'

'I've known some women who would,' McIver said, 'and Tarrant's not the one she goes to bed with. He just sits and watches. Hallam provides her with this dancing partner, Jimmy Maxton the Moke. Tarrant doesn't take the floor himself.'

'The Moke!' said Blake scornfully. 'Whoever the hell he is, his sort is half cut most of the time. Couldn't tell you who he was in bed with nor when, nor what happened. Tarrant could have had her a dozen times without the Moke even waking up. Face it, Johnny, you don't have enough to be certain about Hallam, the Moke, or anyone.'

Blake stared at the ranks of house-roofs to Thornton Heath and Croydon, their slates sleek and dark as sealskin with light rain. On the far side of the busy arterial road stood the Luxor Palace, the only movie house not leased out by Tarrant Rents to another operator. Bought cheaply from a bankrupt firm eight years earlier, the Luxor Palace was a modern monument. Above the black glass pillars and canopy of the entrance, the wide, streamlined façade of white tiling was banded with green neon. A central window recess with decorative ironwork in a Greek-key design blazed light from the circle lounge through the darkening air of the storm. Above the grillework, the words 'Luxor Palace' glared in square-cut neon lettering.

'They keep it on all night,' Blake said, 'they light the foyer and the front. Not the back. That way they just need a night watchman, some old boy that used to work on the door till his feet gave out. I found out about that. The fire escape from the projection box is round the left-hand side. There's no tiles there, just an enormous plain brick wall. It's easy to get about forty feet up the iron ladder. Then there's a gap. They keep a hinged stretch of the walk chained up. That means you're on your own for about six feet across the wall to the last bit of ladder that goes up to the fire escape door. Rather you than me.'

McIver grinned. 'That's why I'm going up, old son. The good news is there's nothing underneath but the railway coal yard. No lights, except very dim ones on the barbed wire at the top of the fence to stop the neighbours thieving the nutty slack. And the big wall is painted black. I'll be about as visible as a cat in a cellar.'

'Watch it!' Blake said.

There was a man near by, at the edge of the pavement, staring at the car. A uniformed policeman, to whom the man had been talking, was looking in the same direction. The man in plain clothes had a large face with a round fair-haired freshness, a match for his bulk in the grey suit and soft brown trilby. The hard dry look of the blue eyes had seen a great deal of others' misfortune.

'That's twice!' Blake said urgently. 'The law watching in Cadogan Square, and now these two. I tell you, Johnny, this whole thing is beginning to smell. It's all been a bit too easy. We should have kept clear of here, anyway.'

'You don't know the fat one is law,' McIver said easily.

'If he's Tarrant's lot, that's no better. Hell's teeth, Johnny, he's been watching long enough to see you taking photographs of the place.'

The uniformed policeman was walking towards the driver's window.

'No parking here,' he said firmly. 'No stopping neither. Case you hadn't seen.'

McIver gave him the quick smile of a decent chap in a fix. 'Sorry,' he said quickly. 'Just finding our map of the Brighton road.'

'Straight on!' The policeman moved away, unconvinced.

'They'll know us again,' Blake said, as McIver started the engine.

'There's no law against photographing a building, Billy. I've seen all I want now.'

Just north of Croydon centre he turned into a side road with a long view to the squat concrete cooling towers by Mitcham Common.

'No chance he could follow now without showing himself, Billy.'

'There's still too much that smells wrong,' Blake said. 'Are you sure about the girl? I don't like Roddy saying she's just a tart. She's a class above that. But are you sure that she's yours and not Tarrant's? You've only got her word for it that she had the hots for Latifa Noon or whatever it was. She knows what you're setting up. Does Tarrant know it by now?'

McIver shook his head. 'I've thought of all that. I reckon I can trust her but I don't depend on it. She thinks I'm still just dreaming how to clean out his safe in the Temple Court. She doesn't know I could do it any time. And she doesn't know that I only need to open the safe to get to something bigger. This weekend, Tarrant's going to take the old woman back to Bournemouth. This weekend, there'll be a few days' takings in the Luxor safe, waiting for the bank on Monday. And those takings are nothing compared with the money that no one's supposed to know about.'

'This weekend?'

McIver nodded again. 'This weekend. While the lovely Solitaire thinks we're still making plans, she'll find it's all over. If she really is doing Tarrant a favour, I wouldn't like to be wearing her skin when he finds out he's been stung.'

Blake turned with his arm on the back of the seat. 'What about Roddy?'

'Let's tell him afterwards,' McIver said. 'Let's make it a real surprise for him.'

6

Harold Gould slapped at a sheet of paper on his desk. 'I've just saved your backside from a thundering good kicking higher up the line, Jack. What in hell were you thinking of, walking up to Tarrant at that funeral? This is surveillance, not a recruiting drive.'

Rutter sighed. On the wall beyond the desk, the photographs of Sid Royce, Tom Foster, and Latifa Noon on the pin-board had begun to seem remote as eighteenth-century caricatures. 'Surveillance was what I was doing, Harry. Tarrant must have known we'd be there for the girl's funeral. That's the form. No point disguising it. If we're going to be there anyway, why not get as much as possible of him, close up? What I saw was a man who was genuinely and nastily angry about what happened to Latifa Noon.'

'What you saw was a man who was responsible for the girl's death putting on an act at the graveside,' Gould said swiftly.

'That's not right, Harry,' Rutter said coolly, 'it's not right – and you know it. What we've got here is a balls-up in the making.'

Gould's eyes scarcely moved. He relit his pipe and stirred the match into the debris of the Imperial Airways ashtray. The bruise-coloured bags under the eyes looked swollen this morning and the skin was a little tighter over the cheek bones, tighter and waxy. Looking at him and waiting for a response, Rutter knew that the DCI wasn't merely a case of fatigue. He was ill, perhaps mortally so. For the first time in his CID career, Rutter wondered what happened if the commander of an operation died during the course of it. Worse still, what happened during the process of his dying?

'Tarrant,' said Gould slowly, 'it's got the marks of him on it. It's what he does with his lieutenants. Builds 'em up, uses 'em, cuts 'em down. When he was tried for complicity in Charlie Armstrong's shooting before the war, he'd have been hanged if he hadn't had Birkett as his defence counsel.'

Rutter paused and tapped the folder with his index finger. 'Tarrant's got the two Brandon garages in Streatham and Bromley. For show, he's got the Luxor Palace and a stake in someone's production company. All the actors and actresses he needs for his private bedroom theatricals. In the last eight months he's bought six bomb sites across south London, while they were still going cheap. A couple of weeks work and he could have petrol pumps and a prefabricated showroom. The sites come cheap enough. He's hardly touched his money. Now, you ask any business analyst about the future. In the next five years, the motor trade and retail petrol is going to be one of the biggest mushrooms that ever sprouted. And Tarrant is going to be sitting right on top.'

Gould blinked sharply. By God, the poor old boy looked rough, Rutter thought. 'Listen, Harry,' he said gently. 'Tarrant's set up to be a multi-millionaire. He could afford to pay Royce and Foster to keep them happy. Even if they were in jail he could see them all right when they came out.'

'I remember Tarrant,' said Gould quietly. 'When I was a skipper in Lambeth before the war. Only thing wrong with a razor, he used to say, you can't get enough strength behind it. Always carve with a knife. That's him, Jack. My lot are scared of me, he used to say. Know why? Never treat 'em the same way twice. Keep 'em on their toes.'

They sat in the tobacco-hazed air of the office where so much spent breath over the years had fogged the uncleaned interior of the basement windows.

'But this is London, not Chicago, Harold,' said Rutter quietly. 'Killers get caught and hanged. I don't think this lot loved Tarrant so much they'd kill three people for him. Money's no good when the warders move the cupboard aside and you see that the rope's been coiled up waiting just a dozen feet from where you slept your last night. I don't believe in hit-men and contract killings. Not in this case. Royce and Foster were Tarrant's men. Latifa Noon was his girl, in a way.'

Gould seemed tired of it all. He bowed his head and Rutter saw, for the first time, how thin the grey hair had become. 'So what do I tell the commander, Jack?'

'Put it down to me,' Rutter said softly. 'A year from now, Tarrant could be legitimate. Until then, his empire could be taken over by some other gangster who could go legitimate in short order. With Royce and Foster gone, Tarrant's there alone. The sky's likely to get black with vultures.'

'What about the other girl, Sally Brown – Solitaire – and Pretty Boy McIver?'

Rutter shook his head. 'McIver's a small-time crook. Officer and gentleman gone bad. All he knows about gangsters is what he's read in Crime Club stories. He'll loot and cheat but he's not going to run a gang. Billy Blake's not the stuff of crime. Nothing on him in Criminal Intelligence. Roddy Hallam's been arrested once, just about a year ago. He was driving a car that had been reported stolen, a pre-war Rover. A squad car picked it up, chased it, couldn't hold it. They rammed it at the traffic lights near Earls Court station to stop it going out of control and probably killing someone. There was a passenger. Guess who? Miss Sally Brown, alias, Solitaire. They let her go. The case against Hallam was dropped. The owner of the car decided that it had all been a misunderstanding.'

'Which owner?'

'Mrs Wendy Worth, somewhere in Essex. Whoever was running vehicle theft decided that Hallam was probably her bit of gorgeous. End of story.'

Gould took a diary from his breast pocket and made a note in it with his pencil. 'The commander had better know, if we change direction,' he said philosophically, 'and I'll need to tell him something about who we think the two killers were.'

Rutter gave a faint groan. 'One large and one small. That's about all we've got so far. If I'm right, it's not surprising that we've got no further.'

Detective Chief Inspector Harold Gould managed a brave smile. 'Let's hope you're right, Jack. Let's hope so.'

On his way out, Rutter paused by the desk where Suzanne with the fluffy blonde curls sat in her snug sweater and pencil skirt. The door to Gould's office was closed again.

'How is he?' Rutter asked quietly. 'He looks very tired.'

She gave him a quick, brittle smile.

'Oh, he's fine. He says he feels more perky than he's been for a long time. And you'll be pleased to hear that we've got an extra pair of hands next week to put the archives straight.'

'That's nice,' Rutter said. He went out into the sunshine and traffic noises of Northumberland Avenue, the sky glittering above the summer river and the Embankment trees. He recalled the last time he had been told by such a bright young voice that a colleague was fine and perky. That voice had belonged to a ward sister. When he went back next day, the bed was empty and the man was dead.

4

JOHNNY ZERO

1

Johnny McIver hung by his fingers in the starlight like a thin black spider. There was no trick to it this time, only nerve. A crescent moon, veiled in a light gauze mist, was suspended like a theatrical ornament of the summer night somewhere beyond Belgrave Square. His hopes were up there with the moon, above the chestnut trees and the dance music, rather than in the dank shaft on to which Tarrant's kitchen window looked. The Temple Court was big enough to take up half a street. Behind its ivory-tiled front, the walls that could not be seen from the gardens were of plain modern brick. They ran round interior wells, the metal-framed windows with frosted glass panes leaving the central shaft of the building blind and blank.

For twenty minutes, McIver had worked his way up from the service yard until he now looked down into this interior crevasse. Sixty or seventy feet below him were the skylights of a basement area, housing the boilers of the central heating system. A fall on to the pitched glass and concrete would probably splinter every bone in his body and sever a few arteries for good measure. Death was so certain and sudden that if it came in those circumstances it seemed scarcely worth worrying about. Even easier than flying a one-way op in a Lancaster bomber. But McIver knew that he was not going to fall. It was a matter of faith with him.

The well was formed by the rear of the apartments on four sides, the frosted glass and metal frames of casement windows in kitchens and bathrooms with grey-painted pipework. By this time of night, there were only half a dozen lights illuminating their blind glass. No one would see him, in his black trousers and sweater with a balaclava covering his head and his lower face. There was only one opening, a gap in the fortress wall of apartments on the far side. It gave access to the shaft and also showed McIver a stretch of Pont Street, where Blake had parked the Airflow. Billy Blake had a flat electric torch, a boys' adventure toy. Its top slid to and fro, turning the white light of the bulb red at one extreme and green at the other. The light was too feeble to carry far on its own. They had experimented by shining it into a mirror-glass bowl, using that as a reflector. By this means, when Blake turned the torch on in the driver's seat of the car, McIver would see red or green, dimly, from his perch at the rear of Tarrant's own apartment.

McIver looked back over his shoulder, across the dark gulf below him. A faint green flush lit the interior of the Airflow. Blake, watching the approaches to the Temple Court apartments, would signal, every minute on the minute. Red for danger. Green for all clear. McIver waited. Green again.

The climb had been straightforward. From the well below, McIver had gone up a corner drainpipe to the level of the flat roof. He had worked his way along until he was above the rear windows of Tarrant's apartment, three floors below him. Now it was the descent that brought whatever danger there might be. McIver's reconnaissance had shown nothing to which a rope might be tied. The windows of the apartments were directly under one another, a downpipe to one side. He knew better than to try moving sideways from pipe to window-ledge at this height. There was a band of stone above each window and a ledge below it. The safest descent was window by window, his right hand on the pipe when there was no ledge within his reach.

Silent as a spider on its web, he had lowered himself with his back to the drop, until the first window-ledge was under his feet. His right hand moved aside and down to the pipe, feeling it firm and strong. His left hand pressed the rough brick of the embrasure for balance. Using the lower edge of the facing-stone as a pivot for his thighs and hips, he slid his legs into space, straight and together. His body passed down between his hand-holds until his arms were above his head and he felt a narrow toe-hold of dressed stone above the next window. But then it was easier, knowing that the next drop was to the safety of an eight-inch ledge at the window's base. He reached it, his fingers now hooked over the band of dressed stone that ran above the recess. He worked his fingers to ease the slight cramp that had come with subconscious tension. Lean and light-boned as a child, he seemed clamped like a limpet high on the surface of the tall apartment block. He looked back once more to see the faint green reflection from the Chrysler Airflow. In doing so, his fingers dislodged crumbled mortar that had gathered on the ledge. McIver froze and heard, after a pause, the far-off rattle of the fragments on the dark basement skylight below. He drew a deep breath in the summer night and was surprised how cold it felt in his lungs.

Two more to go. Again the hand to one side and downwards on the pipe, the other on the rough brickwork to brace him. Just then there was a gurgle of water down the pipe from the upper apartment. McIver waited until the tumbling water ceased. Then his legs slid down until the ledge of the window above Tarrant's was under his toes. The night breeze would be stirring the beech trees in the park and it seemed to him he could almost hear them from where he was. At his back there was a view across the gardens to Sloane Square and the fairy-lit outline of Chelsea Bridge. A blue neon sign above a block of shops near Victoria assured him that Players Please. A car horn sounded somewhere in the direction of Hyde Park Corner. As he looked back once more, the interior of the Chrysler showed a pale green flush.

One to go. McIver eased himself down, right hand still on the firm pipe and left hand braced for balance. He stood on the window ledge of Tarrant's kitchen. Solitaire had done her stuff, he thought. The lay-out was as she had described it. The window space was between two and three feet high, about four feet across. The metal frame was in three main sections, those at either end opening on a casement handle. What's it made of, this handle? Brass, he thought she had said. McIver smiled. Perhaps not brass, but a soft alloy at the worst.

The left-hand casement window consisted of eighteen small metal-framed lights, six rows of three. McIver took a pencil-torch from his inside pocket, shone it through the frosted glass and saw the shape of the handle at the mid-point of the frame. He put the torch back and drew out his glass-cutter in its little leather sheath. Even Tarrant would be content with builder's glass here, given the sheer drop and the lock that held the window-handle anyway. McIver ran the diamond edge up and down, side to side, working quietly. A sink inside the window, she had said. So let it fall inwards this time. He felt it yield and fall with a sound no greater than a milk bottle being put out in the next street.

His gloved left hand went through the gap. The brass handle

was there, needing only to be turned through an inch of its downward circle to free the window. A small steel locking-bolt, fastened to the main frame with headless screws, blocked its path. McIver smiled. A mental tip of the chapeau to Tarrant, he thought. The old boy must have felt so sure of himself with a contraption like this. But then, Tarrant had been a fence, a swindler, a beater of men and women, sometimes a killer. Housebreaking was not something he had time for.

A steel brace from the inner pocket this time, something like a bicycle tyre-lever. He slid it under the brass handle where its pivot was bolted to its metal flange. Letting go of the drainpipe, he leaned in against the window with all his weight. One hand on either end of the steel lever, he bent the brass handle away from the steel bolt that blocked its movement. It gave slowly but evenly under this pressure. McIver felt the window budge as the handle was twisted inwards, clear of the bolt.

Only the bar with its three holes, at the base of the window's interior, was holding it now. There would be no lock on that. He slid the lever in and down, the length of his forearm. He felt it catch the hook of the bar and move it clear. McIver let out a long breath. Drawing aside a little, he opened the window outwards and eased himself in, sliding his legs over the sink to the kitchen floor.

The little pane of frosted glass had fallen into the sink without breaking. That was good. He took its wrapped replacement from his pocket. For the next fifteen minutes, McIver worked neatly and meticulously by the light through the window and with his own pencil torch. Easing out glass fragments from the metal frame, he puttied in the new piece of frosted glass. To his own eye, it seemed blatantly new. He guessed no one else would see it. Then he closed the window and bent the handle back until it was level with the lock.

The kitchen was modern in the most ice-cool style of the new apartments. He went out past the Frigidaire and the electric cooker, noticing the clean swept and uncluttered look, the absence of debris, newspapers, or bottles, which was a sure signal that no one was at home. Tarrant was with the old woman in Bournemouth. Solitaire had been right about that too.

McIver opened the door from the kitchen to the dining-room. The worst was over. From now on it would either work or it wouldn't. But it was going to work. No two ways about that. His next move was to inspect the lock on the door of the apartment, just to check that it operated in the way Solitaire had described. The movement of his pencil-torch showed him a sitting-room that was fussy and old-maidish, antimacassars on the backs of stuffed chairs, swagged curtains of ivory silk tasselled on the floors. It was an old woman's apartment, McIver thought. Would that be Mrs Tarrant or Sonny?

In the hallway of the apartment he confronted the main door. She was right again. The lock was built in. From the outside, it could be used as a deadlock. On the inside, it could be opened at any time without a key. It made sense. Sonny Tarrant had envisaged the danger of the confused old woman looking desperately for a key to let herself out as fire spread or some other disaster overtook her. McIver gave him marks for that. The inside handle would override the dead lock. The door could be left on the latch, so that it would open from outside without a key. It was getting easier all the time.

McIver went back to the kitchen and stood before the white-metal modernism of the electric cooker. General Electric Company, 1938. Clean and efficient. He folded down the back panel across the hot-plates. The sleek and bulbous steel door of the barrel-safe faced him. It was like a shell-casing or the hatch of a submarine. Billy Blake and Roddy Hallam had both at various times hinted their distrust of Solitaire. Blake and Hallam had even said things about one another, Hallam regarding Blake as a fool and Blake calling Hallam a born twister. McIver smiled at the safe. They were all right, Blake and Hallam. Good blokes. But the stars of this show were Johnny Zero and Solitaire.

He pulled his gloves on tighter and smoother. It was time to put Roddy Hallam to the test. Ma Tarrant's birthday. Hallam had been to the national registry of births, marriages, and deaths at Somerset House to ferret out Mrs Tarrant's birthday. 1 March 1883. 00–01–00–03–18–83. Six numbers on the dial of the Mosler safe. Back to centre between each number. McIver licked his lips. It was not fear that made his hand tremble a little and his heart beat faster. Just excitement. Excitement and expectation. He spread his fingertips round the dial. With a slow dry clicking, he turned it to nought. Then back to centre again. The slow turn back to one, making sure that it was spot-on. Back to centre. Down to nought again. Back to centre. Down to three. Back to centre. His blood was moving so fast that he had to open his mouth and draw a long breath.

Now. Down to eighteen. McIver listened to see if he could hear any sound of metal digits engaging. There was nothing to tell him whether he was on the right path or not. No clue. Back to centre. Last of all. Up to eighty-three. McIver counted the dry ticks of the dial. Back to centre.

Nothing. No sign. He took the cold metal lever of the handle. It was ice-smooth and he felt the sweat of his palm upon it. He pressed down, felt it move and heard the bolt slide back. The round door of the barrel wall-safe opened without a sound and as if it had no weight. McIver stared, hardly able to believe that he could have done it. Thank God for Roddy Hallam.

It crossed his mind that the whole thing was too easy. But if it was a trap, they would never have let him get this far. Tarrant or his menials would have stopped him at the kitchen-window or, more probably, dropped him to the yard below.

There were several envelopes inside, which he ignored. Further back he saw a tin, reached for it, and found that it was a small unlocked cash-box. Inside it there were three keys on a ring. Two of them were far too small to open an office safe. McIver slipped them all into his pocket, replaced the cash-box and closed the safe. He folded the back of the cooker against it, slipped his pencil torch into his pocket and went to the main door.

With the lock held back by its catch, he opened the door a little and looked out into the corridor. It was dimly illuminated by a low-power night light. He went out, pulled the door to behind him and walked silently towards the service stairs. It was possible that someone went round last thing at night, testing the doors of unoccupied apartments. Even that was unlikely. There was no reason whatever for regular patrols. Even if Tarrant's door was found unlocked, no one who went in would see anything amiss in the apartment. McIver conceded to himself that such things could go wrong – but not this time. It was almost half-past one. The whole thing was going to be over before three.

He found the service stairs at the far end of the corridor, where Solitaire had described them. Pushing through the doorway, he went down a dozen levels and came to the door that opened into the yard. The lock was an ordinary Yale. He pushed it up on its catch, slipped out and pushed it to behind him without letting the lock close. Dark in the shadows, McIver moved towards the gap in the building. He paused and waited. After twenty seconds or so, he saw the faint green light in the Chrysler. There was no one in sight as he slipped out, crossed Pont Street, and opened the passenger door of the car.

'Step on it, old son,' he said to Billy Blake, 'we'll need to be down there and back in an hour and a half at the most.'

Blake was breathless but relieved. 'Was it OK?'

'Piece of cake,' McIver said, pulling off the balaclava. 'Solitaire did her stuff down to the last detail. And Roddy Hallam was spot on. The old girl's birthday number opened that safe easier than any I've known.'

Blake took Sloane Street and Chelsea Bridge, the streets deserted, the neon dead and unlit.

'Come on!' McIver said.

'Don't be a silly sod, Johnny. We don't want to get stopped for speeding now. You sure that key's going to work?'

'Why wouldn't it?' McIver said. 'Everything else has gone like a dream.'

Moonlit views of Battersea, Wandsworth, and Streatham passed like ghosts across McIver's vision.

'It must be the one,' he said, touching the outline of it in his pocket. 'What else is it for?'

Blake brushed his moustache on the edge of his hand and shrugged. 'We'll know soon enough.'

They drove through Streatham, the shops and cinemas dark, paper blowing along the pavements in the night wind.

'Turn off the main road,' McIver said presently. 'There's no sense in parking too close. A few minutes' walk won't hurt.'

'You don't want signals?'

'I wouldn't see them from up there. If there's trouble, it'd be at Temple Court. No one's got any reason to think we'd be here.'

Blake turned and stopped the car. Once again the cooling towers of Mitcham Common were topped by ghost clouds against the night-glow of city sky.

'Wait here,' McIver said. 'Keep your head down. If I'm not back in half an hour, take a quick look at what's going on. Scarper, if there's any doubt.'

Blake nodded. It seemed that he tried to find words to wish McIver luck, then checked himself as if bad luck might balance it.

But this was the easy part. McIver walked back to the main road and saw the Luxor Palace about three hundred yards ahead. Blake was right. The foyer was lit and the building looked occupied. There was a clank of iron buffers as wagons were shunted in the sidings beyond the coal yard.

The wall of the coal yard was the worst, though it was in shadow from the alleyway. Its outward iron braces with their barbed wire were a relic from the need to keep out pilferers in a time of wartime austerity. With the end of air-raids and the black-out, the coal company had trusted to perimeter lights. Now even those had been abandoned. It was cheaper to lose what little coal was still taken.

He reached up and held the barbed wire with his gloved hands. It was rusted and rotten, trailing down in places, the iron braces themselves loose in their mortar after several years of neglect. The strand nearest the wall came away from the braces, leaving a gap for him to climb up against the brickwork. A schoolboy could have done it. McIver jumped, held the top, doubled up his legs with feet planted against the brick, shoved hard, and levered himself up so that he was draped over the top of the wall. He swung his legs round, hung, and dropped clear. An engine hooted softly, somewhere in the railway sidings towards West Croydon. Wagons bumped and jangled. There was no one in sight.

He crossed to the blank side wall of the Luxor Palace. It rose about fifty feet, pierced only by the little fire escape door of the projection box some forty feet up. An iron escape ladder was clamped to the wall. It stopped about six feet short of the small railed platform outside the high door. A hinged section of ladder was chained up so that it could be lowered to join the main escape section. Without it, the fire escape was a one-way route.

The wall of yellow brick had a diagonal scar. A high-explosive bomb, missing the railway, had landed in the coal yard and blown in the lower wall. The rebuilt section was painted black. Until he was a few feet from the top of the main section of the iron ladder, McIver climbed black on black.

The horizontal section of iron walk, now chained back against the wall, was designed to rest horizontally across the gap. It was supported by the main ladder and also by an iron strut bolted into the brickwork along its side. The strut offered a three-inch-wide toe-hold across the six-foot gap. In McIver's view, it was as wide as a cross-bar in a school gymnasium with the added advantage of a wall to save him on one side. He stepped out on to it. Six feet. Four careful steps at most. He looked down at the drop to the coal yard. Never look down, they said. It hadn't bothered him. Thirty or forty feet. Being a pilot and looking down into incalculable depths cured a man of such phobias. One . . . two . . . three . . . four. Across the gap. Easy as falling.

The projection box door was like the small kitchen-door of a terraced house. He tried it and was not surprised to find it unlocked. Fire regulations required that escape doors should open quickly and easily. The pencil torch again. He was in the warm space just below the flat roof of the building. There were two automatic British Thomson-Houston projectors angled at the wall slits. They were splendid matte-steel monsters, like some form of modernist sculpture with their enclosed spools and the pregnant swell of their steel-cased workings. Stacked to one side were leather cases with black reels of film. This week's offerings. *Odd Man Out* and *It Always Rains on Sunday*.

McIver opened the door above the projection box stairs. Immediately below him was a floor of offices and stores. Below that was the grand circle and restaurant, from which light showed. Below that again were the stalls, pay-box, and street entrance. The office level was in darkness. He heard nothing of Tarrant's night watchman. If Roddy Hallam was right again, the watchman slept most of his shift in one of the seats at the rear of the circle.

McIver went down to the office level, silent on the thick carpeting. On the next floor, which was fully lit, he could see down the stairs with their sweeping chromium rail to a wall hung with coloured portraits of the stars, thick peach-yellow carpet and a pillar faced in mirror-glass. The office door was locked. It was a Yale again. He tried one of the three keys on his ring and opened it. That left one for the safe and a much smaller one. Probably the desk. Though prepared to pick or force the door lock, it pleased him that it should be found undamaged and its levers unmarked. Everything in the plan would point to one of Tarrant's associates having carried out the robbery.

He flicked on the pencil-torch again. The desk was there, as he had expected. The safe was behind it, an impressive steel cube some four feet high and three feet wide. McIver guessed its weight at about half a ton and the thickness of its steel skin at almost two inches. No wonder Tarrant felt secure. To move it was impossible. To blow it would have brought down half the building.

McIver singled out the long slim key which must fit the safe. It was a single lock with a shutter to protect it from dust. He slid the key in and felt it fit like a finger in a glove. It turned with

71

scarcely a sound. He took the round flat handle below it and heard the weight of the three bolts drawn back. McIver knew enough about locks to know that a safe which is picked or opened with a duplicate key will reveal tell-tale scratches on the polished metal of the levers, when the lock is dismantled in the investigation of a robbery. But this time, there would be not the least mark. And that would leave Tarrant looking for the thief very close to home. It got better as it went on. McIver grinned to himself as he swung the heavy door open.

The three shelves of the safe were neatly stacked with bundles of documents and boxes. Several of the boxes were unlocked and contained leather jewel cases. Ma Tarrant's loot, perhaps. McIver had no intention of being lumbered with goods that could so easily be traced. There was a metal box, which occupied most of the lowest shelf. He drew it out and realized, as he should have done before, that the little key on the ring was not for the desk. It was surely for this box. He tried it and felt it fit. The lock seemed almost flimsy for what it guarded. McIver lifted the lid of the tin box and found himself looking at five-pound notes. There were four stacks of them, face-up, each containing five bundles of a hundred notes each. Ten thousand pounds. It was the best part of whatever swindle Tarrant and Foster had perpetrated on Customs and Excise over the bond whisky.

McIver took the notes and wadded them into his clothing. The sweater, tightened by the belt round his waist, held them easily. He locked the tin box and put it back on its shelf. He closed and locked the safe. There was no sound from the lower floor as he pulled the office door to, heard the Yale lock click, and then went up the narrower stairs to the projection box. There was no excitement now, just a bewildered sense of utter unreality at the extent of his success.

After the warmth of the projection box it was like a winter night on the iron escape platform outside. First came six feet on the little iron ledge above the drop to the coal yard. McIver did it almost without thinking. He gripped the iron ladder and went down it with the speed of exhilaration. There was no one in sight as he crossed the coal yard, heaved himself through the gap he had made in the wire and dropped down on the far side of the wall.

Billy Blake was still waiting in the car. He flicked on the torch and glanced at his watch. 'Twenty-five minutes,' he said.

'And ten thousand quid.'

'Ten thousand!'

'Well,' McIver said modestly, 'I haven't been through all the bundles to see if some of it's just paper. But this looks like the genuine article. I reckon it's the loot from whatever dodge Tom Foster had cooked up with Tarrant.'

Blake was beaming and flushed under his moustache. 'Ten thousand! Ten bloody thousand?'

'Come on,' McIver said, 'back to Pont Street. We haven't finished yet.'

3

But it was finished, McIver thought, surely. Only the very easiest part of it remained. He left Blake in the car, crossed the road, and cautiously entered the shaft of the Temple Court apartments where he had hung an hour and a half before. This time the service door was open for him. Tarrant's apartment door was open. He had locked the safe but the combination opened it again without a hitch. McIver returned the keys to their little cash-box. He took a final look at the little window and cleaned away a smear or two of putty.

The window was the weak point. Tarrant or one of his companions might look at it and see that a new piece of glass had been puttied in. But McIver's profession had taught him that such things are rarely noticed. Tarrant would see how the window appeared now but he would never have had reason to notice how it was in the past. With ordinary luck, it would appear as if one of his most trusted lieutenants had opened the door of the flat and the safe, using the keys to open the office safe at the Luxor. It would be a man – or a woman – who might be in the office during working hours without attracting suspicion. Certainly not Solitaire. She would seem to be in the clear.

It was neat, McIver thought as he dropped the catch on the door of the flat, neat as the ace of trumps. He moved down the length of the half-lit corridor and pushed open the heavy fire door of the service stairs. There was a sweetish smell of cement dust in the enclosed shaft. He dropped the latch on the door at the bottom and closed it behind him. It was just after three o'clock, the true dead of night in this part of London. No traffic, not a footstep. McIver moved silently towards the gap in the apartment building that led to the street. Billy Blake was parked in the identical spot by the railings of the public gardens. McIver moved along the last oblong of shadow by the basement skylights of the apartment backs.

Seventy or eighty feet ahead of him, the interior of the Chrysler Airflow went red.

McIver felt no alarm. Everything had fitted like clockwork. What scope was there for anything to go wrong? Even if Tarrant had walked into the building, Blake would now be flashing green like the devil to get clear. Billy Blake had pushed the top of the torch the wrong way. It was far the most likely reason.

Red again.

Annoyance, irritation, incomprehension, possessed McIver's thoughts. But neither panic nor fear. Still, Billy Blake could see the street. He, as yet, could not. There was nothing for it but to stand back in the shadows of the service yard and wait. The street could scarcely be swarming with policemen. Blake himself would either have been arrested or vanished. The thought of Tarrant returning was absurd at this time of night. Could there have been an alarm of some kind, either at the Temple Court or the Luxor, which he had set off without knowing it? But McIver had seen no trace of an alarm or its wiring. In any case, an alarm would have caught him long before this.

Red again.

It made no sense at all. Whatever the danger, it was not immediate enough to stop Blake from shining the torch.

Green . . . Green . . . Green . . .

McIver walked quickly to the gap. Instead of crossing directly to the car, he skirted along the near side of the street, away from the Chrysler, turned a corner and crossed, then came back down the other side. He opened the rear door on the pavement side and got in. Blake had started the engine and moved into gear before the door was closed.

'What the hell was all that about, Billy?'

Blake turned towards Belgrave Square and Grosvenor Place. 'Look!' he said. 'There! Man on his own in the parked Austin. Him! The copper that came up two days ago when we were stopped outside the Luxor. Talking to a uniformed policeman that told us to move on. It's him! He's been sitting there ever since we got back.'

'Can't be,' McIver said reasonably.

The Austin was parked facing them. As they approached, McIver screwed his eyes up, looked hard, and felt his stomach contract with a cold certainty.

'Christ, it is too,' he said, now looking back through the rear window. 'Watch your back, Billy, he's turning out to follow.'

They drove round two sides of Belgrave Square, the trees and shrubs of the central gardens, the pillared rows of embassies and consulates silent and dark in the street light.

'There was someone behind us when we were parked in Cadogan Square waiting for the girl,' Blake said. 'That's one. Then this face down the Luxor. That's two. And now him again. That's three. Something's cocked it up, Johnny.'

'Mightn't know who we are yet,' McIver said, twisting round for another view of the Austin. 'He's still there. Not even trying to be subtle about it.'

'He'll know who we are the minute someone at Scotland Yard phones vehicle registration. Unless he could be one of Tarrant's lot. In which case, they'll probably know who we are already.'

McIver braced himself for the bell on the other car to open up, signalling the pursuit. But the Austin kept its place, a dark silent shape through the rear window of the Airflow. They came to the junction with Grosvenor Place, the black angel of the winged victory outlined against the first daylight through a gap in dark clouds.

'Go left,' McIver said. 'Make for heavy traffic. Try to get in the outside lane at traffic lights with a lorry or something slow on the inside. When the cross-flow stops, go like the devil round the front of the lorry and down the left turn. By the time our friend tries it the lorry'll have moved far enough forward to block him. We shan't see him again.'

'Don't be a prat, Johnny! We could both be dead.'

'Right,' McIver said. 'When we stop for the lights, change places and I'll do it. It's not the first time.'

Blake circled Hyde Park Corner and came back down Grosvenor Place towards Victoria.

'Head south,' McIver said, 'Vauxhall Bridge. We might throw him there. There's plenty of traffic out of the goods yards and the depot.'

They passed Constitution Hill and the high dark wall round Buckingham Palace gardens.

'He's turned off!' McIver said incredulously. 'The bugger's just turned off. That's crazy.'

'It must be Tarrant's lot. I told you he wasn't law.'

'He didn't act like Tarrant's lot the other day. And he was a bit too friendly with that face in uniform.'

They were in Pimlico now, the first summer daylight making a fairyland of Victorian brick and baked stucco.

'He didn't show up in Pont Street by chance twenty minutes ago,' Blake said. 'He's been watching us all the time. He must have been. Why hasn't he done anything? Police don't just sit and watch a robbery and then drive away. And why was he on his own?'

They were coming up to the embankment; a light mist still gathered over the river and masked the arches of the bridges.

'Turn here,' McIver said. 'Next thing is to dump this crate. There's the Lex all-night parking at the back of the Regent Palace Hotel off Piccadilly Circus. We'll leave it there.'

Blake turned the car. 'So what's it all mean, Johnny? When Roddy Hallam borrowed that Rover, they chased him a good mile with bells ringing and rammed him when they couldn't overtake.'

'Search me,' McIver said. 'Unless, of course, we're dealing with a bent copper. It's not unknown, when the loot gets shared out, for there to be another place set at the table and a blue helmet hanging on the hatstand.'

'You think that?' Blake asked softly.

'Unless you've got a better idea,' McIver said.

4

McIver turned from Curzon Street into Shepherd Market. It was almost noon and the sun shone with a dust-laden glare on the buildings harshly outlined against a hot London sky. Banked yellow flowers on the stall by the new cinema gave off a scent that was thick as treacle in the heat. Shepherd Market was another world, its café tables on the little pavements in the French manner, shops that sold pre-war vintages and perfumed cigarettes from Egypt or Brazil. It was the cosmopolitan world of Johnny Zero and Solitaire, the little streets and exotic shops with hanging baskets of flowers that seemed more like Paris or Amsterdam than London.

76

He turned again into the narrower street. The pavement door of the house, between a tobacconist and an Italian grocer, was open. There was a bell for the first floor but McIver ignored it. Billy Blake would be there by now, in any case. He went up the stairs with their carpet worn to its threads and tapped the door on the first landing.

Blake opened it. 'It's all right,' he said. 'No one else is here and no one followed me.'

McIver went in. It was the waiting-room of Solitaire's other profession, basket chairs and cushions, an open door showing the bedroom with its pink-covered and canopied bed. That was what he had noticed about the furnishing and decoration of Tarrant's apartment. It had been chosen as if by a tart – or perhaps for a tart. The old woman, he guessed. Sofas that were for lying on or over. Padded stools that suggested kneeling rather than sitting. Heavy chairs that had been stuffed and shaped to support the human body in its contortions of pleasure.

Solitaire came through from the bedroom. She was wearing a long blue housecoat and, apparently, nothing under it. McIver thought it curious that she should appear so dowdy and domesticated in rooms that were dedicated entirely to desire and its fulfilment. Perhaps not. In his experience, prostitution was not usually a full-time profession. The girls of his acquaintance drifted in and out of it as necessary, by the day and even by the hour.

'What went wrong?' she asked.

McIver took her hand, sat her down, and placed himself in the next chair. 'Nothing went wrong that we know of. If it did, then it's nothing that involves you. The plan went like clockwork. Roddy Hallam was right first time about the number.'

'So were you,' she said. 'You picked the old woman's birthday as the most likely.'

'I'd got others to try,' he said modestly. 'And the money's OK. There's ten thousand quid, though we won't get that when it's changed.'

'So what's this about a policeman?' She looked from Blake to McIver.

'Christ knows,' McIver said. 'He was with a uniformed copper that came up while we were stopped outside the Luxor a few days ago. Causing an obstruction, he said. No sign of him after that until last night. I'd got the money and gone to put the keys back in the Temple Court safe. Then this face shows up outside and just watches from his car. Follows us when we move off. Then turns down Constitution Hill and vanishes.'

Solitaire looked at him and he could see, from the slight unfocused movements of her eyes, that she was deeply frightened while outwardly calm. 'It can't have been the same man.'

'It was,' McIver insisted. 'Two of us saw him both times. No mistake. No chance.'

'But he wouldn't just turn up at the Temple Court like that,' she said simply. 'If he appeared then, he must have been watching before. Why didn't he do something? He knew who you were before that. He wouldn't just watch you burgle Tarrant's apartment and the Luxor and then sit there while you went into the flats again. He can't be a policeman.'

'He could if he was bent. And that's better than him being Tarrant's lot.'

'Oh, God,' she said helplessly, 'what does it mean?'

McIver stroked the hand he held as if to emphasize the point of his explanation. 'It means that there are policemen who live off robberies. Not many and not for long. If this face had come up to us last night, he might wonder if we could be carrying a gun. After all, Tarrant's a big boy to go and see on your own. So what he'd do would be to watch and remember. He knows who we are. My fault. I should have done something about the car – that bloody number-plate. We could be hearing from him again.'

'What can he do?'

'Offer us five years inside – or a personal introduction to Sonny Tarrant – unless we cut him in.'

'So we cut him in?'

McIver shook his head. 'Can't say. What we do first is change the money. If that's done quick, we might not be around when this face comes calling.'

5

A red-funnelled steamer churned backwards through its paddle-wash, leaving the pier landing-stage on the afternoon return to Swanage. Shouts of children from the sands overlaid the beat of the engines and the wash of breakers from the finned wheels. Family groups were drifting home for tea through the camellias and rhododendrons of the central gardens. Sonny Tarrant got up as the phone rang on the mirror-glass table behind him.

'Mr Tarrant?'

'Speak up then,' he said. 'I can't hardly hear you. Who's that?'

'It's a friend, Mr Tarrant. I'll just say this once. You'd better come home, Mr Tarrant. You been well seen off.'

He glanced round to make sure the old woman was nowhere near. 'What the fuck's this? Who are you?'

'Just a friend, Mr Tarrant. I wouldn't be phoning you else. You lost something. Something what you been keeping for your pension down the Luxor Picture House. I think you'll find it's warming someone else's back-pocket now. I'm tipping it to you, as a friend. You been done up neat as a registered parcel, Mr Tarrant. If I was you, I'd be on the next train.'

'Hang on. . . .'

But he knew it was coming. The line clicked dead. Sonny Tarrant turned and stared out across the sparkling water of the afternoon tide. He was a man for whom people did not make trouble. That was his reputation. If there was to be trouble, after all these years, it might come from so many quarters that he was not sure which way to face. He looked at the holiday view beyond the balcony rail without seeing it or hearing the children's shouts. Then he went back to the phone and lifted the receiver.

'Hello? Operator? I want a London number. That's right. Streatham. Brandon's Garages. 4872. Yes. Quick as ever you can.'

5

HONEY-POT

1

The ancient bell on its metal spring jangled as McIver pushed open the door of the shop. There was no sign of Mr Champion. A young man of about twenty stood behind the corner counter in his shirtsleeves. His dark brilliantined hair was clipped short, the sides and back of his head shaved clean. His indifference was such that he looked at McIver without, apparently, noticing him. The wall behind the corner counter was faced with white peg-board. A number of new magazine issues had been clipped to it. *Lilliput*, *Men Only*, *La Vie Parisienne*. There were several productions of the underground trade, their covers crude and blurred by imperfectly registered colour plates.

'Mr Champion's expecting me,' McIver said.

'Is he?' The young man stood with hands gripping the edge of the counter at either end, as if to block the way to the back room more effectively.

'Tell him my name's Johnny McIver.'

'Is it?'

'I'm not the law,' McIver said patiently, 'I've got business with him. Tell him.'

'Right,' the lad said, 'I'll tell him when he gets back.'

'Gets back?' McIver said with a laugh. 'Come off it! He's here now.'

But the young man shook his head and stared past McIver, as if expecting to see someone beyond the shop window. In the hot afternoon of the Paddington streets, beer barrels were rumbling down a chute to the cellar of the public house opposite. Elsewhere, it was half-day closing and the street was empty. The young man turned his eyes on McIver.

'Not seen Mr Champion today. He's been poorly with his stomach. That's why I'm here.'

The door behind the counter opened and Mr Champion's head appeared. 'That's all right, Jimmy. I'm at home to Mr McIver.'

The young man shrugged. He opened the counter-flap and let McIver through. The back room was cooler and darker with its varnished table and chairs, its half-empty bookshelf, the photographs of the uniformed RFC pilot and the school rugger team.

'Sorry about that,' Mr Champion said. 'Just a natural precaution. I always look through the crack in the door first to make sure who it is. That's Jimmy, the wife's sister's son. Home on ten days' leave from the Royal Tank Regiment. Not much doing during the day for him, so he's happy to earn a few bob minding the counter. He's all right. Needs the money when the sun goes down. Don't we all?'

McIver took one of the two plain kitchen chairs. He shook his head. 'If the law ever comes here, Mr Champion, having someone on the counter won't help you. They'll put a man on the back door. You won't get out that way either.'

Mr Champion gave his long groaning cough and took a cigarette from McIver's open case. 'What I hear,' he said, 'they've not got the staff to send two at once. Since when did you start having monogrammed cigarettes from Bond Street?'

'They're the girl's,' McIver said.

Mr Champion had evidently not expected an answer and was already thinking of other business. He held up a cautionary finger. 'Your photographs of the damsel,' he said, savouring the description, 'sale of two sets only, I'm afraid. Not worth your while doing the work, m' boy. If you had it in mind to place any more, they'd definitely need to be stronger. Two young ladies simultaneously. Or domination and submission. Scout knots, perhaps. Definitely something more than straight up and down the wicket again. Savvy?'

McIver flicked the lighter-wheel and held its flame to his cigarette in profile, the way it was done by actors on the screen. 'I'm not here about photographs,' he said, 'I've got money.'

'Glad to hear it,' Mr Champion said.

'You remember we talked about money before? What might happen if I had a considerable bundle of it and if I brought it to you?'

Mr Champion looked down at an unwashed teacup. 'Can't say I do.'

McIver laughed. 'Come on! We talked a few weeks ago. About your friend the bookie. The one with race meetings all over the country and how he could get rid of banknotes provided he got a commission on them.'

Mr Champion tightened his mouth and shook his head slightly. 'Did I say that? Did I really?'

'You bloody well know you did,' McIver said sharply. 'See this?'

He reached into his pocket for his wallet and took a fold of banknotes from one of its compartments. He spread them out before Mr Champion, four large white five-pound notes with their old-fashioned engraving on thin crackling paper.

'Yes, I see,' the old man said.

'This is nothing,' McIver said eagerly. 'There's a couple of thousand like this. Genuine Bank of England notes. The real McCoy.'

But Mr Champion was unimpressed as he read the engraving. 'You must have gone to trouble,' he said sadly, 'a lot of trouble. Pity someone didn't tell you first that those notes are numbered and that the banks keep a note of people to whom they're issued. One-pound notes would have been the answer.'

'They're genuine.'

'Yes,' Mr Champion said. 'Might be better for you if they weren't. Fakes could be run off again by whoever lost these.'

'Banks aren't going to worry about this lot,' McIver said confidently.

Mr Champion sighed. 'It's not banks I'm thinking about. The numbers on those notes are consecutive.'

'So what?'

'So you might just as well take advertising space for yourself across Piccadilly Circus. By the way, they tell me Mr Tarrant had to come home from the seaside rather suddenly. Called back on urgent business.'

For the first time, Mr Champion's red-veined old eyes held McIver's in a steady stare. McIver laughed. 'Tarrant? He's a pensioner. He's nothing. Never would have been if people had the wits or the guts to stand up to him.'

There was a tap at the door and the young man put his head round it. 'Gentleman brought back a book and wants one of the new delivery. Mr Connolly. Said you'd know him.'

Mr Champion sighed and waved the youth to a large cardboard box which stood open on the floor. It was stacked with copies of a book in cyclostyled typescript and bound with insulating tape. *Sisters in Sin.* Its pen and ink cover was a drawing of two women, a blonde in a school uniform of some kind and a brunette with the sharp-eyed look of a female vampire.

'Two pounds,' Mr Champion said, 'if he's bringing one back. I never understand why they read another after the first. I suppose they always think the next yarn will be better.'

The door closed as the young man went out.

'Tarrant,' McIver said.

'Mr Tarrant.' There was no mistaking the pedantic courtesy in the old man's voice. 'I never had the pleasure of talking to him face to face.'

'He's nothing,' McIver said, 'unless you make him into something.'

Mr Champion twisted his mouth and nodded. 'You're a handsome lad, Johnny McIver. A clever lad, even. I like you. But don't start what you can't finish. As a friend, I wouldn't tell tales on you. Where's the purpose? But don't overestimate me. Mr Tarrant's got a workshop out the back of one of his garages. They reckon you can't hear a thing that goes on in there. If it happened to me like it did to poor old "Robber" Baron before the war, where Mr Tarrant and his friends put the gentleman's fingers and other valuables in the workbench vice and tightened up the handle, I'd be no good. I'd tell him anything he wanted to know long before the real damage was done. Mr Baron was too brave for too long. The mess he was in, they reckon they had to top him after he told them what they wanted to know. So the story goes. One thing sure, he was never seen again. I'm frightened of pain, Johnny McIver. Always have been and I'm not ashamed of that. I mean really frightened. There isn't anyone I wouldn't shop rather than have them start on me. Not family, not kids, if I had any. No one.'

He raised his veined eyes to McIver's again, as if seeking condemnation or understanding. McIver smiled. 'No one's asking you to put your hand in the fire, Mr Champion,' he said gently. 'Have a word with your bookie. If he doesn't want to know about it, we'll drop the whole business. That way, I'm not asking you to take a single chance.'

'You are,' the old man said mournfully, 'even asking questions is taking chances round here. But I'll go that far. Leave us a phone number where I can get you.'

McIver folded the banknotes. Mr Champion laid a hand on his.

'Don't put them away. If you've got all you say, then you won't mind leaving those for me to show him.'

They went out to the shop door together, out of the hearing of the young man at the counter. Mr Champion paused. 'One thing, Johnny McIver. A little bird said something to me a week or two ago that someone might be playing Mr Tarrant up deliberately. Capische? I hope that wouldn't be you.'

McIver smiled again. 'I told you, Mr Champion, he's another breed. I've got no interest in him now.'

The old soldier seemed relieved. 'Not even meddling with Sonny's young ladies, I hope. He's a devil, my boy, and I don't use the word lightly.'

McIver wrinkled his nose. 'I'll remember.'

Mr Champion paused, his hand on the door. 'Gus Pytchley,' he said gently. 'He was said to have crossed Mr Tarrant. Traded some stolen goods and made off with the proceeds.'

'Never met him.'

'No,' Mr Champion sighed, 'not likely you would now. He crossed Mr Tarrant. Consequently, it appears Mr Tarrant had him altered. Someone told me it was done under ether by a doctor that had been struck off and owed a favour for gambling debts. Worked on Pytchley's face. Gus used to be landlord of the Fox and Goose before the war. Doesn't go out by day much, not since what was done to his phiz. Works at night. Cleaning the muck up between railway tracks. You've got a nice new passport. Take you anywhere. I'll ask my friend, of course. Meantime, you think whether you wouldn't be better off gathering up all you've got, then going away as far as you can for as long as you can. At least until you hear that a certain gentleman has been gathered to his fathers.'

McIver laughed. 'Trouble with you, Mr Champion, you worry too much.'

2

The image on the screen was smaller than usual, the sound coming as if from the depths of a cardboard box.

'West London Coroner's Court this week saw the inquest on Latifa Noon, whose body was found in a burnt-out car in Surrey a fortnight ago. Miss Noon, a starlet of post-war films, had begun a promising career as a future comedienne in British cinema. The mystery deepened this week when the coroner's jury returned an open verdict. Scotland Yard, however, is determined that the investigation will not rest until the circumstances of Miss Noon's death have been fully explained and those who may have been responsible face justice . . .'

The clip ended with a reassuring library shot of the Whitehall Place archway, two stern-faced plain-clothes men striding purposefully through it.

'That's nice,' Rutter said, as the projector clicked off and its fan whined to a stop, 'I like being told I'm determined and resolute and so forth.'

The projectionist, an intruder at the meeting, worked the venetian blinds to their full height and left the room.

Rutter's predictions had been fulfilled. Superintendent Marriot now sat at the wide desk with the pale subterranean light filling the thick glass of the window behind him. He was a large dark-haired man with the look of an officer who owed his appointment to rugby football. His voice was that of a front-row forward leading the pack.

'Harold Gould would have been here,' he said cheerfully, 'but he had an appointment this morning that had to be kept.'

'How is he?'

'Fine, why shouldn't he be?' Marriot said in the monotonous tone of one who has said the same thing a dozen times before.

'That's good,' Rutter said. It would need only one more official voice to tell him that Gould was fine or perky before he believed that the poor old boy was dead.

'What matters most is to have this business of the young woman cleared up,' Marriot said. 'She's news, even if Royce and Foster aren't. Unfortunately I don't see how we can lay her to rest until we've done the same for them. I'm only standing in and I don't want to pull rank. But I think, Jack, that you'd better brace yourself for pressure.'

He checked the front page of Gould's brown folder and then looked up sharply, focusing on Rutter with a mixture of curiosity and reproof. Sunlight struck the dull brown surface of the scuffed linoleum with a prism-glaze like fuel splashes on water.

'The first reason I'm here is to make sure we all move in the same direction,' he said quietly. 'I'm not the expert in this case, you and the others are. But we're not having freebooters. All right?'

'Understood, sir,' said Rutter, respectful but non-committal.

Marriot left the brown folder open. 'The people on the top floor of this building have been through your memorandum, suggesting that the deaths of Royce and Foster were acts against Tarrant rather than by him. Anything you'd want to add to it now?'

Marriot's reading glasses were thick-lensed, making his blue eyes seem to swell a little as if with indignation. Rutter felt depressed.

'My point, sir, is that so far as motive and identity go, the cases hang together. Whether or not the killings were aimed against Tarrant, they certainly weren't carried out on his behalf. It's not Tarrant.'

Marriot reached a hand round under his jacket and scratched his back, as though this helped him to concentrate. 'That puts you on your own,' he said, 'perhaps with Sergeant Brodie's support. I can't have an officer in your position heading off in his own direction unless I'm given a better reason than any I've had to date. If you go down, Jack, you take everyone else with you. That's the problem. So, no brilliant mavericks, please. This has got to be a team game. We're certain of a basic fact. There's one major villain involved in this, by any calculation. Tarrant. No one else in this building is prepared to drop him out of it.'

Rutter took a deep breath. 'Then I'd like this on record, sir. These three people were certainly not killed by Tarrant. He was in Bournemouth when they died. Nor were they killed on Tarrant's orders, in my view. Contract murder in London, even among men like Tarrant, is virtually unknown. They know damn well that the clear-up rate for murder is high. The sentence is death. And anyone who committed three murders of this sort must know there wouldn't be a reprieve.'

'So what?' asked Marriot quietly. 'Murders still happen.'

'But not like that,' Rutter said. 'I could imagine two men killing to get their hands on Tarrant's empire. I can't imagine they'd love him well enough to do his murders for him. Suppose they got clear to begin with. How much money would you want to compensate you for living the rest of your life with the hangman two paces behind you? And would you throw in an extra corpse buckshee? The girl was killed simply because she happened to be there. That multiplied the risks they took. I'm not just saying that it doesn't have all the marks of a contract killing. It doesn't have any of them.'

Marriot shifted in his chair, his bulk almost obscuring the frosted pebble-glass panes of the basement window. 'Is that it?' he asked indifferently.

'No,' Rutter said, 'not quite. There's a rumour going round the clubs that Tarrant was robbed of a very large sum of cash last week, taken from his premises here while he was out of town. Apparently, it's the kind of cash that he can't report. It could be his loot from the swindle that Tom Foster masterminded. It could be from his Blue Chip Club tables off Carlos Place. There's evidence that he's got a share of the Blue Chip. Black Jack, roulette, faro. Three chemmy tables with nine players. Each player pays three pounds a shoe until three in the morning. From then until six, they pay six pounds a shoe. After six, it's ten pounds. You work out what Tarrant could be pulling in from that. Then comes this burglary. Now, a really cheeky robbery is not the sort of thing that happens to a man who can run a criminal empire and call up contract killers to help the odds. It happens to a man who's seen to be losing his grip. Even the people in this building must have some inkling that Tarrant's fighting for his life.'

'Does the rumour say who did this robbery?'

'No. We're watching Tarrant very carefully on the grounds that he may find the answer first. But we can't just go horning in. Officially, the robbery never happened until he says so. And he won't say it. He daren't.'

Marriot opened the folder and ran his finger down a freshly typed index-page. 'There's nothing here about a robbery.'

'There wouldn't be,' Rutter said, 'that's the point. Criminal intelligence won't process anything until they get it from us and we're not supposed to act on it until it comes back from them. It's a farce that goes back to policemen wearing tall hats and carrying bull's-eye lanterns. I don't suppose you've got the name Champion on that list either?'

Marriot looked surprised. 'No. Should I have?'

'Champion's a dirty-picture merchant in Paddington. He's not a target like the rest. On the other hand, he's had some very interesting visitors in the past few days.'

'I've got Pretty Boy McIver,' Marriot said, running his finger down the page. 'He seems to have connections of that sort.'

'Of all sorts,' Rutter said, 'including a girl who puts on acrobatic displays in Tarrant's apartment. Club dancer called Solitaire. When she's not dancing, she's posing naked for McIver's camera.'

Marriot shook his head. 'There's nothing here about that. Nothing.'

'No,' Rutter said, 'I don't suppose it tells you either that Tarrant's said never to have had a woman. Just a spectator at the ringside.'

'Never to . . .' Marriot paused. 'Is it relevant?'

'In this case, yes, sir. It establishes Tarrant's link with McIver and the girl's displays. We know that connection exists. Apparently, Tarrant doesn't know it yet. It's one place where we're ahead of him. I suppose it also identifies Tarrant as a man whose real lecheries are power and control. A born commander. I went to a lecture during the war. Army Bureau of Current Affairs. A psychologist who reckoned that some of the best military leaders had no taste for what he called procreation. Like monks.'

He stopped, aware that Marriot was staring at him hard and colouring a little at the explanation. With the confrontation over, Rutter made his way through the outer office. The blonde secretary was filling a newly installed set of shelves with box files.

'Still no Mr Gould, then?' he asked.

She looked back over her shoulder without letting go of the file. 'No, Mr Rutter. He was taken to hospital yesterday. They don't seem to think he'll be there long.'

Rutter made his way out to the street, his mood heavier at the prospect of Harold Gould's death. Frank Brodie was waiting behind the wheel of the car.

'What's the pitch then, Jack?'

Rutter sat gloomily in the passenger seat, the braided leather hot against his back from the sun. 'Same as before, Frankie. Sonny Tarrant decides to become an honest citizen. In order to cover his tracks he wipes out his two lieutenants plus his film star protégée Latifa Noon. Thereby printing tracks so clear that a blind man couldn't miss them. Our masters still think it's contract killers.'

Brodie snorted at the absurdity. 'Can't they see it's cock? Where'd you find contract killers in this city?'

'Search me, Frankie,' said Rutter helplessly, gesturing the sergeant to drive on. 'Trouble is, I can't find anyone in the hierarchy to talk to. Looks as if poor old Harold Gould has copped it. Taken to hospital. So we've got a stone-face stand-in. Marriot.'

'He was Vice Squad a couple of years back,' Brodie said. 'While you were away fighting for King and Country, Marriot was keeping London clean and decent for you to come back to.'

'That probably explains why he only just found out about old Champion selling dirty pictures in Paddington and never heard about young ladies who perform private theatricals for small audiences,' Rutter said sardonically.

They stopped at the Parliament Street traffic lights.

'So where does that leave us?' Brodie enquired.

Rutter watched an old man with his possessions in a perambulator, holding up the traffic as he made his laborious way to the far pavement. 'Where do you think?' he said grumpily.

3

McIver grinned at the two girls on the little stage of the Copacabana. They were dark-haired, like as twins, and dressed identically in silver-cloth shorts and monkey-jackets with matching boots. They smiled desperately from under the rims of silver top-hats and twirled their canes. McIver watched and listened. The pair looked as if they had escaped from small-town pantomime or a summer pierrot show. They would have died rather than perform Solitaire's fan dance.

> When my heart goes pitter-patter pitter-patter
> It pitter-pitter-pats for you . . .

The canes banged the floor together.

'I wouldn't,' Billy Blake said to McIver. 'Those tight costumes keep them in place. Without that, the one you're looking at might be on the generous side. Stout, even. Probably a bit older than she looks in that circus-girl costume. Not up to your class of popsy at all. Word to the wise, old son.'

> When my toes go clitter-clatter clitter-clatter,
> They clitter-clitter-clat for two . . .

One of the girls gave him a quick, awkward smile and he grinned back at her like an insolent schoolboy. Still watching her, he slid his hand round his glass and spoke to Billy Blake.

'A gun,' he said simply, 'that's all it takes. We need a gun. Just to fire it in the air would be enough for the sort of guttersnipes that Tarrant employs.'

Concern and incomprehension creased Blake's large, amply moustached face.

> You can make me hotter than a Hottentot
> You can make me blue . . .

'No,' Blake said, 'you don't want a gun. That's bloody well asking for trouble.'

McIver continued smiling at the girl who was slightly the plumper of the two. 'Not unless someone else asks first.'

> When I go swimming and my flipper goes a-flapper,
> My flapper only flips for you . . .

'Johnny!' Blake said. 'For God's sake, listen.'

'I'm listening to her, old bean. That's a young lady and a half. Louise.'

The girls were tap-dancing to the band now, the rhythm heavier in the wordless tune. The music dwindled to infrequent notes, leaving the rest to the girls' feet. McIver lifted his cocktail glass, drew a sip and watched the slight shimmer of powdered thighs below the tight hem of the silver pants in the energy and impact of the dance. The world, the universe had opened before him.

'Listen,' Blake said wearily, 'who're you going to use a gun on? Champion? His friend the bookie? Solitaire? Roddy Hallam? Me? Where's the bloody sense in it? Unless, of course, you were thinking of plugging Tarrant. Really bright move that'd be!'

McIver lifted his hands high to applaud the act. He met and held Louise's blue eyes, their saucer-wide mockery and innocence suggested by an edging of mascara.

'You know what they say, old boy. Better to have it and not need it than need it and not have it. I dare say if Royce and Foster and Latifa Noon had been carrying something of the sort, they might still be around.'

A dozen of the men and women at the tables were moving out to the centre of the dance floor again, the mirror facets of the central globe throwing prism lights and arabesques on the crimson velvet of the walls. McIver saw Solitaire coming towards them. He beckoned the waiter.

'Same again, old boy, if you wouldn't mind, and one for the lady.'

As the man turned away, Blake said: 'If you must have a gun, don't take chances looking around or trying to buy it. I've got one.'

McIver's eyes crinkled with amusement. 'You?' He sat back and grinned. 'How come?'

'My father had one from the first war. Kept it as a souvenir. It's a damn great thing. An Eley .455. Blow a hole in a wall. Still in working order, or at least it was when I tried it out a year or two back. Someone took the end of the barrel off with a hacksaw, years ago. Anything you fired from it might wobble about a bit. You'd just have to use it for show. But, then, that's about all you can do unless you want to make things worse. It's got no ammo now anyway.'

McIver screwed up his eyes, as if in thought. 'Ammo's not the problem, Billy. Size and weight might be. You can fire lots of bullets from a gun that size by filing the base of the cartridge. Tommy-gun bullets even. You can get those by the hundred. I dare say they'd wobble. No good for long range. Still, most quarrels take place very close up.'

They both stood up as Solitaire reached the table. McIver drew out a chair for her.

'How was your day at the Peek-a-Boo?' he asked, tugging his double-breasted jacket straight. 'Give the old raincoats a few sleepless nights, did you?'

She pulled a face. 'Bit of a wash-out,' she said, 'they're all puritans. The girls are worse than the punters. There was a poor old boy with a camera in the second row. Trying to hide it in a box of chocolates. One of the girls posing saw the lens. Asked the doorman to throw him out. I'd have been flattered, if I was her.'

'You forget,' Blake said, 'they're not all daughters of the middle class like you. Working-class girls are very narrow-minded. By the way, this idiot wants a gun.'

'Who's he going to shoot?'

'No one,' said McIver irritably, 'but so long as Tarrant's lot are equipped, I don't want them getting ideas. I need to know a lot more before I feel safe. That face outside the Luxor the other day and then following us from the flat that night was a bit too convenient. He'd got a warrant card for all I know. And to be where he was that night, when we did Tarrant's flat, he must have followed us from the Luxor. He could even have followed us down there. A village bobby would have seen what was going on, let alone CID. He even started after us when we left. And then he just turned off down Constitution Hill. If he'd gone home and told all the other little policemen, we'd have heard from them by now. Who did he tell? Did he keep it to himself? Until we know what we're up against, there's no harm being equipped.'

Solitaire shook her auburn hair into place along the line of her fine white shoulders. 'Perhaps it's Tarrant they're watching. If they went for you, he'd know it.'

'No,' Blake said, 'Johnny's right. We'd have heard something if that copper was on the level.'

'Not if they want Tarrant for three murders,' the girl said. 'Or what if this mystery man just saw his chance to take a cut of the money?'

McIver pulled a face. 'In that case, we'd have heard from him direct. He saw the car and the number. He wouldn't have left it this long. As for the gun, even if we've got it, we don't have to use it. If we have to use it, we'll be bloody glad to have it.'

'Tommy-gun bullets, he's going to load it with,' Blake said glumly.

McIver grinned. 'Last resort. You can fire tommy-gun bullets from a .45 if you file the base of the cartridges. No question.'

'You could blow your hand off too,' Solitaire said, 'no question of that. What did your chum Mr Champion have to say about the money?'

McIver watched the waiter loading his tray at the bar. 'We won't get face value, not with the notes being numbered in sequence. He thinks about three pounds for five but it could be more. It's a thousand each for us, however you look at it.' He raised his empty cocktail glass in tribute. 'No more bedroom displays in front of tired old men.'

Solitaire opened her handbag and spoke to its mirror. 'Why do I have to be the poor little girl who only does it because she's destitute and hates every minute?'

'You don't have to be,' McIver said, placating her.

'Good. Because in case it's escaped your notice, I'm an exhibitionist.'

Billy Blake was embarrassed behind the essential decency of his moustache. 'But not Tarrant, old girl! You wouldn't go back there.'

'Of course I would, if he asked,' she said, snapping shut her handbag and looking up. 'It would look bloody odd to refuse now. It might even be dangerous. In any case, the audience doesn't matter so long as there is one. You don't get people refusing to go on stage at the Old Vic or the Haymarket because they don't like the audience.'

McIver looked at her. 'Actressy' was still the only word to describe her. Solitaire's vanity was flawless. Performing with the Moke to warm Tarrant's libido entitled her to the prestige of a star part in the West End.

'What happened to the Moke, by the way?' he asked.

She smiled with the freshness of a schoolgirl. McIver noticed with approval that men who saw the smile from other tables were slow to turn away. 'I heard that a widow with some money happened to him,' she said. 'Not too old. He's hoping for full-time employment.'

'Drinks,' McIver said hastily, watching the waiter unload tulip-stemmed glasses from the tray. He laid a five-pound note on the round silver-plated tray. 'Change this for me, would you, old boy?'

The man bowed his head and walked away. Billy Blake looked back at McIver.

'That's not one of Tarrant's?'

'Of course it is.'

'For God's sake, Johnny!'

'We agreed to get rid of the loot carefully, here and there, apart from what Sam the bookie can do for us. A single fiver in a club is nothing. That's just the way to scatter it.'

'They could have a note of the numbers.'

McIver shook his head again and his eyes crinkled with school-boy mischief.

'Not unless Tarrant had gone to the law. Or unless this club was one of his operations. But it isn't. This is the kingdom of Solomon Grundy born on a Monday. OK?'

He watched the waiter hand the note to the barman. The barman said something and they both looked back towards the table. Then the waiter came across with the change laid out on the tray.

'Someone for you on the phone, Mr McIver. Will you take it here or in the booth?'

McIver smiled up at the man, helping himself to the change except for a half-crown. 'I'll use the booth, thanks, old man. No sense interrupting the party.'

The waiter stood back for him as he got up and went out

through the velvet curtains which led to washrooms and the rear of the stage. The door of the glass booth was open and the phone was lying on its ledge. He picked it up.

'This is John McIver. Who's that?'

The answer came in a lightly nasal pedantic voice, a delivery that McIver associated with pince-nez and counting-houses. 'Good evening, Mr McIver. I have been asked to speak to you on behalf of Mr Tarrant. I'm sure you know who I mean and to what I refer. Mr Tarrant has reason to believe that you have in your custody something belonging to him.'

'Does he?' McIver said humorously. He judged that there was no purpose in asking the name of the man at the other end of the conversation.

'He is quite sure of it, Mr McIver. Mr Tarrant knows that you will not find it easy to dispose of what you have. He is prepared to settle the matter on terms which I will put to you briefly and I shall only put them once. You will agree to restore his property by means which I shall outline. In exchange, Mr Tarrant will pay to your credit a banker's draft for fifteen hundred pounds.'

'And if I don't have his property?'

An old man's drawl that might almost have been amusement touched the voice at the other end. 'Oh, you still have it, Mr McIver. Mr Tarrant generally learns of such transactions very quickly, once they have taken place.'

McIver felt the nape of his neck getting cold, as if he was being watched.

'Who told you I was here this evening?'

The amusement in the thin voice grew broader. 'Really, Mr McIver, you are not a difficult man to find.'

'And suppose, whatever this property is, I've as much right to it by law as Tarrant and that's the end of it?'

'Well,' said the voice indifferently, 'I suppose you must take the consequences, Mr McIver. Mr Tarrant would regret that, I'm sure. Matters of this sort are best settled quietly.'

'Tell that to Sid Royce or Tom Foster, when you see them in Kingdom Come.'

'I'm sorry, Mr McIver,' the dry voice said, 'Mr Tarrant was quite specific. He is prepared to give you twenty-four hours to think over his offer. We shall be in touch again before that time expires.'

The line went dead. McIver stared at his reflection in the little mirror. He pressed the receiver-rest for a dialling tone and fed his coins into the box. As soon as he had dialled his number, a receiver was lifted and his coins dropped as he pushed the button in.

'Mr Champion? Johnny McIver. How soon can I meet your friend? The bookmaker. There's another possibility, that's all. Tomorrow's OK. As late as he likes, so long as he's prepared to agree the business then. He doesn't have to bring his own money yet. We could settle that the next day. What about tomorrow afternoon, then? All right. Two o'clock's fine. Just let me know if you have to change the time. I'll be there.'

This time, speed was his advantage. He smiled at himself in the mirror and put the receiver down. It would be over before Tarrant knew it had started.

Presently, Blake got up from the table and went after him. In the white glazed brickwork of the passage there was a perfume of body-paint and powder from the heat behind the little stage. McIver was now talking to one of the two tap-dancers who still wore her tight silver pants and coatee, waiting for her turn to come again. With the top-hat removed and her short dark hair slicked back, she looked suddenly younger. She was not, after all, stout in the way that Blake had suggested. What he saw now was more like the unshed puppy flesh of adolescence. McIver was trying hard with his smile and easy manner. But the girl, Louise, looked self-conscious and uncomfortable. Her natural command of the audience failed the moment she was caught alone like this.

'There's a lady waiting for you,' Blake said to McIver as he pushed open the washroom door. When he came back, McIver was turning away.

'See you again before you do your summer show.'

Louise was smiling now, perhaps with relief that the conversation was over, perhaps with pleasure.

'There's nothing there for you, Johnny,' Blake said irritably. 'For Heaven's sake, she's almost under-age.'

McIver chuckled. 'Not if she's working here, old son. And that's not really her sister, by the way. She's doing a summer show without her. Chorus line at the Boscombe Hippodrome. And I don't think she's shy of earning some extra cash in front of the old camera's eye.'

'It's not on, Johnny,' Blake said as they went out through the velvet curtain again. 'Stick to what you've got. Magazines aren't going to pay for photographs of that one.'

'Don't be a sanctimonious old bugger, Billy!' McIver said

cheerfully. 'If everything goes right, I shan't need the money. If it doesn't, then I don't care who's standing in front of the camera.'

'What's wrong with Solitaire?'

McIver paused as the velvet curtain swung to behind him. He gave his boyish grin at the table where Solitaire sat alone. 'She's got the conceit of the devil, old man,' he said quietly, 'worse than her leading man Roddy Tarrant. You'd think she was Betty Grable and Sybil Thorndike rolled into one. The truth is, she's skint – but for us. So skint that she'll share the bed of any of her friends that's got room in it for her. But she and this Moke of hers are artists, if you listen to her. Doesn't she see that whoever he is he's just one of Tarrant's lumberjacks from the blue films?'

'If it wasn't for Roddy,' Blake said fiercely, 'we wouldn't have twigged that business of the combination. And Solitaire's worth a hundred of that little tart back there. She's a good little scout, Johnny, and you know it.'

'All right, Billy,' McIver said amiably, 'I know it. But don't go sanctimonious on me. There's a good fellow.'

They walked back through the dancers and the swirling prism light to the table. McIver looked at Solitaire. Blake was right. She was magnificent by comparison with the young dancer.

'Seems we're in the money,' he said brightly. 'Come tomorrow and the deal's going to be done.'

Blake looked down at them. 'I'll let Roddy know,' he said. 'Best divide the spoils as soon as we can.'

6

WHITE LIGHTNING

The man whom Mr Champion called 'Mr Sammy' faced him across
the corner of the table in the back room of the little shop. To
McIver he seemed more like a bank manager than a bookie.
Perhaps a little of the schoolmaster as well. No wonder Champion
got on with him. Sammy had a large head, the sandy hair thin,
the hazel eyes mild. The broad face with its suggestion of a dewlap
was freckled and had a look of open and approachable decency.
It was the face of a reasonable man who would listen to any
argument. The voice was a pleasing baritone. It made McIver
think of velvet stout and dark syrup. Like Mr Champion's, it
suggested breeding and education misapplied. It was a confident
voice, lending force to its arguments. Though it was not a voice
to be trusted without testing, it was one that you instinctively
wanted on your side. All in all, 'Mr Sammy' was something other
than McIver had expected.

The three men were alone in the shop. Mr Champion had
bolted the street door, turned the cardboard sign to 'closed', and
announced half-day closing. They sat with their teacups before
them, the grey slops growing cold.

'In my experience,' Sammy was saying, 'the manner of carrying
out these agreements is every bit as important as the terms of
agreement themselves. Would you not agree, Mr McIver?'

'Yes,' McIver said, trying to sound as though he was not thinking of this for the first time. 'Absolutely.'

'You see the opportunities and dangers, then,' Sammy said
approvingly. 'It is seldom in acquiring money that the difficulty
arises. The element of surprise and the degree of planning are the

great advantages there. Disposing of the proceeds is the point at which these enterprises are apt to go awry.'

'Yes,' McIver said cautiously. The discussion was taking the wrong direction. Prepared to confront a check-suited bookie, he gazed at 'Mr Sammy' in his grey flannel suit and began to feel outmanoeuvred.

Sammy's mouth moved in a quiet smile. With a nod of his large sandy head, he indicated Mr Champion who sat at the far end of the table.

'Our friend tells me that you wish to negotiate an amount of currency. He assures me that it presents no difficulty in terms of legality. Perhaps I should say no criminal complications. I have, of course, to be sure that money of this kind is not the proceeds of a robbery involving serious charges to which I might be accessory. Had I been approached in the aftermath of an armed hold-up, for example, I would have nothing to do with it. There seems to be no question of such a connection here. So I will try to serve you as best I can. You smile at my caution, young man? Remember, please, that I must go to others in my turn. They will be quite as careful as I.'

Sammy's offer to serve him increased McIver's unease. It was not at all how he had imagined the negotiation with a racecourse villain.

'I'd like to have a price,' he said bluntly.

'Of course you would and so you shall, Mr McIver, in a little while. The amount in question is, I understand, ten thousand pounds. Five-pound notes numbered in sequence.'

'That's right.'

Mr Sammy smiled again, as if this pleased him. 'I did not expect that you would bring the money with you this afternoon, Mr McIver. In fact, I prefer that you should not. Mr Champion has shown me four of the notes and that is sufficient. The rest I shall see when we conclude our business. My suggestion is that if we can reach an agreement this afternoon, we should meet tomorrow at your bank, or mine, whichever you prefer. You will have the currency and I shall have a banker's draft made out in your favour. You shall see it paid into your account. Indeed, you may then draw it out in cash if you choose. Would that be acceptable to you?'

'In cash,' McIver said quietly, 'provided we agree. I'm not sure I'll be coming to the bank with you. I'll let you know.'

98

'Provided we agree,' Sammy said in his comfortable baritone. 'As to that, Mr McIver, I will do the best I can for you this afternoon. But let me be honest with you. As we sit here, I cannot tell you precisely the amount I shall get for the currency, in my turn. What I propose is that we should agree a price now. Whatever happens, that will be paid to you tomorrow morning. During the course of tomorrow, I shall begin to place the currency and shall soon have an idea of what it will fetch. You understand?'

'So far,' McIver said.

'We shall then meet here again tomorrow evening at ten, if our friend will permit us. If the disposal of the currency is more profitable than I allow for now, we shall share the difference between us. If, for example, the entire sum seems likely to be five hundred pounds more than I had expected, you shall be two hundred and fifty pounds richer for our meeting tomorrow night.'

'What if it's less than you thought?'

Sammy smiled and spread out his pale well-kept hands.

'Then I shall bear the loss. From your point of view, however, you shall have an agreed price now plus the extras tomorrow night. Is that fair?'

McIver's gaze rested on the bookshelf photograph of the RFC pilot. 'What's the price now? That's the main thing.'

'Of course it is.' As he sat with his elbows on the table and forearms in an arch, Sammy rubbed his finger along his nose. 'I won't conceal that the numbering in sequence of the notes makes it more difficult for me to assist you. That can't be helped. But any price you may be offered will include an estimate of all the risks.'

'How much?' McIver asked. The easy baritone voice was beginning to irritate him.

Sammy gave it some consideration. Then he looked up. 'Four,' he said firmly.

'Four thousand?' McIver dismissed it with an impatient laugh. 'Four thousand for ten thousand? That's ridiculous.'

Sammy sighed at the difficulty of what he now had to explain. 'My dear young friend, you make a common mistake of supposing that the face value of currency is what it will fetch. It will have to be widely dispersed. I must take it to someone else. He will offer me far less than its face value, knowing that the man who pays him must pass it on in turn.'

'Don't try kidding me,' McIver said,

Sammy shook his head. 'I had hoped that I might enlighten you. Tell me, how much did you expect?'

'Between six and eight for ten thousand,' McIver said. 'Probably somewhere about seven.'

Sammy gave him a sympathetic look and pulled himself up in his chair. 'In that case, Mr McIver, we had best bring this discussion to an end. By all means see if you can dispose of your currency to better advantage. I thought you were more fully informed. I remind you that I am here at your wish, not you at mine.'

McIver knew that he must keep the man at the table. 'Five at least,' he said. 'I've taken all the risks so far.'

'But not the risks that are yet to come,' Sammy said. 'I cannot believe you have tried elsewhere if you find four thousand absurd. There are places where you would be lucky to get two. Let me tell you what I will do. We will say four and a half. Then, tomorrow evening, we shall meet here again. If I have underestimated the enthusiasm of my associates, you shall have your share of the surplus. So, more now and more later, Mr McIver. Is that fair?'

In his mind, McIver heard the dry parsonical voice of the previous evening's phone call. *You will agree to restore his property by means which I shall outline. In exchange, Mr Tarrant will pay to your credit a banker's draft for fifteen hundred pounds . . .*

Sammy was looking at him.

'Four and a half?' McIver said.

Sammy waved his hand reassuringly. 'Plus whatever extras can be managed tomorrow night. We will see what can be done.'

'Four and a half,' McIver said, thinking about it. 'Suppose these so-called extras don't materialize?'

Sammy laughed. 'Then we shall just have a drink and shake hands. But, my dear young friend, you still won't lose anything. I may. That's another matter.'

McIver hesitated. Something that Champion had said had made him think he might get three or four pounds for each note. Even with the extras, Sammy was offering under three. The difficulty was to know the market price for ten thousand pounds in stolen banknotes. Tarrant had offered only fifteen hundred for their return the night before, hardly more than an insurance reward. Sammy's four and a half thousand, with or without 'extras', might be the best offer. Certainly it was the quickest.

Sammy gave that same tight little sigh of a man puzzling how to explain a difficult matter simply. 'I'll be as straight with you as I can, Mr McIver. All my life I've been a businessman, first and foremost. One thing I've learnt. It's the long term that matters. Now, you'll find rather stupid people in my line who think they get a bargain when they do someone down for a quick profit, leave him to go away and realize he's been screwed – if you'll pardon my directness. Now I don't work like that. To me, a bargain is when both parties go away feeling they've got something out of the deal. Prepared to meet and deal again. That's how business thrives. Am I right, Mr Champion?'

'Positively,' the old man said, his breath whistling in his teeth a little.

'And where's the result, Mr McIver? The smart alecs that rip you off and run, you know where they'll be tonight? They'll be bumming drinks off mug-punters down the saloon bar. I'll be sitting home in a nice house in Essex. Two motors in the drive. Two boys paid for at a school where they have blazers and keep their hair nice. A young lady that comes and keeps me company a bit. A girl that cleans. A lad that drives the motors for me when I'm tired and makes sure I don't get nudged off the pavement by some lout or other when I go walking. Right again, Mr C?'

Mr Champion's embarrassment at being appealed to once more showed as a lopsided grin. 'Indubitably,' he said.

'You get four and a half thousand, Mr McIver, and perhaps a bit more. I'll get a margin of two and perhaps a bit more. Further down the line there's a couple of dealers that'll want a thousand each. Now, my young friend, you may say why bother with them two? Well, I've got an older head on my shoulders than you. By the time these notes have been through two more sets of hands, no bother is ever going to come back to you. Isn't it better to have four and a half with no worries than six and a half with the law riding on your back?'

'I'm not worried about the law,' McIver said with a grin, but he knew Sammy had won the argument.

'Oh, dear,' Sammy said. 'Always worry about the law if you mean to keep clear of it. Take a leaf out of Mr Champion's book. For years he's run this business. Photographs, books, private movies, ladies and gentlemen, ladies and ladies, spankers, bondage. Never so much as seen the inside of a courtroom. A little worry at first can save a lot later on.'

'All right,' McIver said, 'but I'll need it in cash.' He did not particularly need it in cash but by making the point it seemed that his pride was soothed a little.

Sammy shrugged and stretched his hand across the table to shake on it. 'Any way you want it, Mr McIver. If we're at the bank, you can have cash as easy as a cheque.'

'I'll count it for myself,' McIver said. 'Not in a bank, either.'

Sammy gripped his hand firmly. It was a warm and dry pressure, as confident and reassuring as his voice. 'Where you please, my friend,' he said sincerely. 'May I take you to my club? National Sporting. Not difficult to find a quiet corner there first thing in the morning.'

'All right,' McIver said ungraciously. He liked being taken to clubs. On several occasions he had purloined headed stationery from their writing-rooms and put it to good use.

'Say half-past ten,' Sammy suggested. 'Then we'll all have something to celebrate.'

2

Something to celebrate. By the next afternoon, it seemed to have been a day for celebration, McIver thought. He and Sammy. He and Roddy Hallam and Billy Blake with Solitaire in Oddenino's at lunchtime for whisky and sandwiches, when each partner took eleven hundred pounds. He and Solitaire in Shepherd Market, where he went out for strawberries and a bottle of Sauterne. They ate, drank, made love and then drank more than McIver had intended. Three hours before he was due at Mr Champion's shop for the 'extras', he and the girl were back in Knightsbridge. McIver felt himself flushed but steady. There was nothing to negotiate with Sammy in any case. Either there would be a bonus at ten o'clock that evening or not. But the drink had gone to Solitaire's head, as it always did. It did not improve her mood.

'Beer and sandwiches,' he said with an air of command.

The first of the sunset was in the sky as they turned into the little mews that ran behind Sloane Street. Solitaire was coy and suggestive at first under the persuasion of drink. Later, she would grow morose. McIver had watched her progress on too many evenings to have any doubt. Their arms were about one another as they turned in under the mews archway. Her high heel slid sideways on the old paving slabs and she clung to him for support, laughing quietly in long nasal breaths.

'All right,' McIver said, 'just a little further. You can get all the beer you want down at the World's End. After that, as the doctor said to the newlyweds, we'll have you back in bed in no time at all.'

She paused, holding on to him. 'You are a bastard, Johnny McIver, you really are.'

'And you've seen enough of 'em to judge, darling,' he said softly.

She began to laugh again in the same quiet way. It was always possible, of course, that they might refuse to serve her unless she steadied up. The little pub was used by denizens of Sloane Street and Eaton Square. But Sally Brown, alias Solitaire, wouldn't be the first high-class tart brought there by a young city broker or an officer from St James's Palace guard.

'Buck up, old girl,' he said encouragingly, 'chin up and tummy in. We'll be there in a minute.'

They made their way more sedately towards the World's End, down the little mews with its artisan terrace now gentrified for the new rising class of Belgravia. Soon there would be lamplight in the quiet cobbled cul-de-sac, the flight of bat and moth against a dusk sky.

They sat in the front parlour of the mews house, the low-timbered opening of the bar little more than a buttery hatch. After beer and sandwiches, Solitaire's mood seemed unlightened.

'Tell you what, old girl,' McIver said, 'we'll go down to the Copacabana on the way back. Look in on Billy's celebration. Then I'm going to lock you in the hotel and go and fetch the rest of the loot. Tomorrow we'll make plans and buy tickets. Paris. Spain. Rio de Janeiro. Anywhere. Anything. There's nothing to stop us now. Go out to the Cape and fly our own plane. I've got a pilot's licence that's valid out there. Fantastic place. Where the real future is. You'd love it.'

She stared at her glass, silent and unenthusiastic. McIver blamed himself for letting her start to drink too early. 'All right,' he said, 'let's just go and pay a call on Billy.'

The Copacabana was crowded by half-past seven. Its modernistic entrance in Knightsbridge was like the foyer of a small cinema. In chromium frames on either side of the doorway, the performers smiled from their photographs. The picture of Louise in silver leotard and top hat had been removed at the end of her week's engagement. In the foyer, several couples were waiting for tables. McIver hailed the doorman.

'Flight Lieutenant Blake's party. He'll have a table busy in there already.'

They passed through the heavy swing doors into the din of the band and the revolving shimmer of light from the crystalier. Blake was talking to two men and a woman. McIver recognized one of the men from an evening at the bar of the Falstaff in Fleet Street. A reporter on one of the Sunday papers.

'What're we having?' Blake called to them.

'Nothing too much,' McIver said with a grin, 'we began celebrating too early. I rather think we're going home for a little orgy to round off the day. And there might be more good news, Billy, to add to what you've already received today. No promises, but you can never tell.'

He winked at Blake who shrugged and spread out his hands with amiable incomprehension. Conversation with the journalist and Blake's two friends rumbled on. It crossed McIver's mind that Billy might have hinted something to them. But then he smiled at his friend and knew that Billy was far too sensible for that. A very careful type. They drank a glass of the house champagne to Blake's health and then McIver glanced at his watch. It was ten past eight.

'Must be pushing on,' he said amiably. 'See you all in here tomorrow, I expect.'

At first he thought that Solitaire was going to stay. Then she pushed back her chair and got awkwardly to her feet. When McIver went to help her, she fell against him and he had to hold her upright. Then she began to move with his arm round her, though her head drooped. Guiding and steadying her, he tried to make it look like an embrace.

'Cab, if you don't mind, Larry,' McIver said to the doorman, and waited close by her while Larry hailed a taxi that was coming down from Hyde Park Corner. He helped her inside and gave the name of the hotel. It was not far, scarcely more than a quarter of an hour, but there was no other way of getting the young woman there. The last thing McIver wanted just then was an encounter with the law. Having paid off the cab, he found his key and guided her into the lobby of the hotel. During three weeks as a guest, he had cultivated the desk clerk with their shared tales of military service, McIver's always being self-mockingly the more heroic. This amiability had always paid off when living on credit and cheques that were likely to be returned. In the end there would have to be a reckoning, but a pleasant manner always bought him time.

The desk clerk looked up from the evening paper on the counter with a smile and a nod. 'Anything else for you tonight, Mr McIver?'

'No thanks, Freddie. Early night tonight. Do not disturb until quite late tomorrow. You might ask them to bring my bill up to date, though. I'll settle it in the morning. We'll have to think about moving on soon.'

'Right you are, Mr McIver.'

They went up in the lift. McIver looked at his watch again and saw that it was half-past eight. He had intended to leave her at the hotel entrance to make her own way up to the room but that was too risky. While he was out, he wanted Solitaire safely under lock and key. As the old-fashioned lift creaked slowly up to the second floor, she leant back against the polished mahogany of the panels and stared up at the frosted glass of the light.

'I feel awful,' she said breathlessly, 'bloody awful. That bloody club was the last straw. Those bloody people . . .'

Sliding back the steel lattice of the lift, he led her across the passageway and unlocked the door. There was time to sit her on the bed and then take a look through the curtains at the street outside. A man was standing in the doorway of the florist's shop on the opposite pavement. He was reading a paper. To McIver, it looked as if he had been standing there for some time and would be there for as long as was necessary. McIver had expected something of the kind. He knew what to do.

Turning back to the bed, he took Solitaire's hands between his own. 'Listen, my sweet. I'm going out now. I'll be about an hour. Stay put here, keep the door locked. If anyone asks, you don't know where I am but I'll be back any minute.'

She nodded. He put his hand under her chin, raised her face to kiss her, and grinned. He stood in the doorway and winked at her.

'With a bit of luck, old girl, we'll be a few hundred quid richer when I get back than we are now.'

McIver had said nothing to Blake or Hallam about the 'extras'. Solitaire was too drunk to comprehend. He promised himself it was pride, not trickery. They must all have their share. But in case there should be nothing to share, he decided not to mention it in the first place. Nothing had happened that he couldn't take care of on his own, including getting in and out of the hotel unseen by the man on the opposite pavement. The desk clerk seemed a decent type but it was best that he should not see McIver coming and going now. Just in case there was a connection between the two. Perhaps the man in the entrance to the florist's shop was merely waiting for a girl, or a bus. McIver wondered who the watchers might be this time. The law? Tarrant? Even Tarrant's rivals? He walked down to the end of the bedroom corridor.

The hotel, like the Temple Court, had its service stairs which doubled as a fire exit by regulation. At this hour, they would be deserted. He went down and saw the empty kitchen through an interior window. The door to the little street running alongside the hotel would close automatically behind him, unless he prevented it. McIver took an empty cigarette packet from his coat, wadded the card tightly, and jammed it into the recess of the lock.

There was no one outside, no one watching in the narrow chasm of the alley beside the hotel. McIver turned away from the street and came out by the arcade of shops. The man in the entrance of the florist's was still there. And the best of luck, chum. McIver turned under the midnight-blue glass legend of the underground station. A ticket to Paddington. The smell of dust and tobacco smoke in the tunnels, warm pneumatic air and the thunder-smell of electric traction. The whine and whoop of the trains bursting like brilliant serpents from their dark burrows. For McIver the underground had always been a stairway to theatreland and neon magic, bars, pubs, cafés, and the excitement of his dream city at night.

At Paddington, he got out and went up to the street, a warm breeze blowing paper scraps about the heads of the pedestrians. A corner pub off Praed Street had the last of the bare sawdust floors and a swirl of Irish music. Voices rose with the roaring breath of a furnace at the open door. Coloured bottles and men in shirtsleeves. A woman's scream of laughter. Then the dark of the little streets beyond it.

McIver turned a corner and faced Mr Champion's shop. Champion and his friend would be careful, of course. Using the back room again. The view through the street door showed no glimmer of light, only the thin illumination of street lamps falling on rows of cellophane-wrapped magazines behind the glass panel. The dark windows of the upper floor were uncurtained and the rooms appeared unoccupied. McIver looked for a bell-push and found none. Three raps on the glass. Nothing. His watch-hands stood at ten precisely. Three more raps, louder this time. Still nothing. Perhaps there was no more money to share. Why, no message, then? Why nothing, after Sammy's homily on the importance of trust and satisfaction in a bargain?

McIver stepped back and looked at the building. A lane behind it would show him whether there was a light in the rear window or if the curtains were closed. He walked round the corner and turned into a narrow lane. It was like a dream, after all. The buildings had vanished, invisible from the rear. Nothing but a blank wall about eight feet high ran along the lane. McIver went back for the longest possible run, sprinted, and leapt, catching the coping stone that topped the wall. He looked into blackness. It might have been the centre of the earth. It had never occurred to him that the underground railway ran behind the buildings of the little street, though the metal track was open to the sky at this point. A wall of blank cement rendering lined either side of the chasm in which the trains ran. The rear door of Mr Champion's shop opened into a tiny communal yard between the buildings and the blank wall on that side.

No wonder the old dodger had never been caught. There was no obvious means of putting a policeman at the back door, no sign from any point of view that there was separate access to it. And then McIver saw the iron ladder stapled down the far wall at the end. The way down for engineers to inspect the track. A bunk up on to the wall and even Mr Champion might be down that ladder while the policeman was still at the shop counter. McIver grinned at the thought of the old fellow weaving his way after an electric train to appear among the crowds fifty yards away on the platform at Paddington.

One more heave. Astride the wall, McIver pulled his feet up, crouched, then stood at full height above the abyss. A train clattered past twenty or thirty feet below him, carriage lights flashing along the opposite wall, a shower of sparks rising from the conductor rail like a disintegrating cigarette butt in the night. But now he saw the rear window of Mr Champion's premises. The curtains had been left open and the room was dark.

McIver dropped down into the alley again. At the worst they had shafted him over the 'extras' of which Sammy boasted. But four and a half thousand pounds was safely delivered, drawn from the bank and guaranteed genuine beyond any question. The money had been divided with Blake, Hallam, and Solitaire. At the worst, McIver knew that he and the girl together had two and a quarter thousand pounds. It was enough to take them far enough and long enough away. He walked round to the shop door again, banged hard, and then rattled it in its frame. There was no response and no more to be done.

As McIver turned away, one of the cars which had been parked down the little street drew out from the kerb. It passed him and stopped at the road junction. He felt again the chill at the back of his neck. In the light of the lamp, he saw plainly and without the least doubt the face of the same policeman who had been outside the Luxor and then at the Temple Court apartments. The face was not to be mistaken. It had a hard-set jaw but the eyes looked almost gentle in their indifference. The mouth was pressed rather tight as if with perpetual exasperation. There was a square look to the head and the fair hair was clipped unusually close. Something else which McIver now knew he had seen before but without noting it was the tension in the face. It looked as though the jaw was always about to bite hard on something, though never quite doing it. The man turned and looked straight at McIver without apparently recognizing him. Their eyes met for a second or two as the stranger let in the clutch and moved off.

But this time McIver was the hunter. They had nothing against him now. Nothing they could prove. Let them damn well try. He also knew that the traffic lights at the Praed Street junction might be against the car. He sprinted after it and saw that the lights were red. There was time. There was plenty of time to cover the fifty yards. McIver drew level with the driver's window. It was open. The man turned and looked at him.

'Who the hell are you and what the hell do you want?' McIver shouted.

In reply, the man wound up his window. McIver snatched at the door handle and found it locked. He rapped the window as he had done the door of Mr Champion's shop. From the corner of his eye he saw the red light turn amber. The car began to move. McIver tried to put his arm across the windscreen, blocking the driver's vision. Instead of braking, the driver swerved clear of McIver and shot across the road junction, almost on the wrong side of the road. An elderly man riding a bicycle on the far side steered for the kerb and shouted as the car went past him, dangerously close.

'I've got your number, mate. And I'll bloody well report you for driving like that!'

McIver looked round. No one seemed to have noticed him in the noise of the street and the bustle of the brightly lit cafés by the station. He turned away and went back down the steps to the underground station. At least he'd given the bastard a shock, for what good that might do.

3

It was almost eleven o'clock when he reached Knightsbridge again. The lamplit street outside the hotel was quieter. The man who had been in the florist's entrance had gone but there was another figure in a suit and trilby hat waiting by Timothy Whites the Chemists. McIver looked up at the heavy Victorian façade of the hotel, smoke-darkened red brick with pale stone banding. The edge of the bedroom curtains showed him that the lights in the room were still on. Either she had not gone to bed yet or had fallen asleep fully clothed. He turned away and went round the back of the building to the door of the service entrance in the little side-street. The folded card of the cigarette packet had kept the lock open. There was no one in sight as he pushed the door ajar, went through, and locked it after him. He moved silently up the stairs to the bedroom corridor of the second floor.

McIver slid the key into the lock and opened the door. The lights were still on in the frosted-glass pendant lamps at the centre of the ceiling and the two opal shaded lamps by the twin beds. On several nights they had managed with one of the twin beds. There was no sign of Solitaire, nor of her clothes. It was inconceivable that she would have gone out in her present state. The bathroom. McIver listened but heard nothing beyond the drip of a tap. He waited for a moment and then called out. There was no response.

About to pick up the phone and call the desk clerk to see if she had gone downstairs, McIver paused. He went across and opened the bathroom door. It was in darkness. He pressed the switch. The strip light came on with a series of flashes and then an abrupt and steady glare. He had found Solitaire.

She was at the far end of the peach marble bathroom, half kneeling and half lying on the tiles with most of her clothes scattered on the floor around her. She was still wearing the pants and stockings but, at a distance, it seemed that she must have collapsed while trying to undress. Her right arm was stretched up at full length against one of the vertical pipes, as if she had clutched it for support. Then McIver saw something thin and silver-coloured round that wrist.

He walked across, knowing and dreading what awaited him. Solitaire was dead, of that there was no question. Now it seemed that he had known all the time, subsconsciously, that it would end in this way. Death was the price of wealth in this Sunday School morality. Her head lay to one side, the auburn hair falling aslant. A folded linen hand-towel was half in and half out of her mouth. A pillow from her bed had been left on the little bathroom chair. A blue chill showed round her lips. Her face was not otherwise disfigured but the eyes were half open, squinting grotesquely at something beyond the door. She had not fallen straight to the floor because the steel cuff holding her wrist to the pipe was not wide enough to pass over a junction in the pipe several feet higher.

McIver tried to lift her but the dead weight of her body hung awkwardly. He was possessed by the thought that if only he could pull her free and lay her on the bed, it might look like an accident. But the steel cuff was locked and there was no key. Whoever had done this did not intend that the scene should have an innocent explanation. McIver stopped and realized with a shock that by wanting to move her, he had admitted his part as the only suspect in her death.

It was like a dream, in which his normal processes of thought were absurdly paralysed. Was it possible that she might not be quite dead? Was there not something still in her eyes? He drew the linen towel cautiously away from her mouth. Life and death were so finely divided, the line between so imprecise, that men and women certified as dead had still revived. He let the body down gently and went into the bedroom for the dressing-table mirror. He held it to her mouth and whispered, 'Come on, old girl! Come on!'

He began to cry, not much and only briefly because McIver knew that he was crying for his own stupidity, the howl of the fox in the trap. They had caught him so easily, in the end. There was no cloud on the mirror glass. Worse still, as he let her go, he noticed for the first time two marks on her back, close to the shoulders. It seemed that the colour of the imprints had deepened while he was with her. It was as if she had been struck by a stick or rod, or perhaps had fallen back against a rail of some kind. It no longer mattered what.

He felt the first true desperation of a man in a labyrinth. Apart from the real or bogus policeman, there was not a single witness to suggest that he had been absent at the time of Solitaire's death. Tarrant, or whoever had taken this revenge on them both, had arranged matters with precision. Tarrant, he supposed, must have discovered the part that Solitaire was playing.

If the police believed him, McIver knew that he might still be safe. But who would believe him now? He could prove nothing. The choice was between staying and facing the music or running for his life. He went back into the bedroom and sat down on the first bed. In that case, the choice was surely between staying and being hanged or making a run for it. Solitaire had the appearance of a victim shackled to the pipe and choked by the linen towel.

There were two marks on her shoulders which might suggest that she had been beaten when she resisted. McIver could hear himself explaining to the police that another man had done it. Which other man? Tarrant? Tarrant would have an alibi. 'Mr Sammy'? What had it got to do with him?

He sat on the bed and knew that every line of accusation would lead to him. The man in the entrance of the florist's shop and his successor outside Timothy Whites the Chemists. If they were watching him, they would confirm that he had gone into the hotel with the girl and only reappeared after she was dead. The desk clerk would say the same. McIver's story of having been to Paddington for an hour and a half would sound like the worst defence of all.

What else? There was the passport which Champion had got for him. There was the money. Two shares for him now that Solitaire had no use for hers. They had bought two large-format second-hand novels from a barrow near St Giles's Circus, hollowed out the pages, and folded the banknotes inside. McIver went to the drawer of the dressing-table and saw that the books were still there. But even before he opened them and saw that the money had gone, he imagined what had happened. Solitaire manacled to the pipe. The killer – or killers – asking her where the banknotes were. Getting no answer, someone hit her across the shoulders the first time. Whatever she told him then was not enough. He hit her a second time. There would be no prevarication then. McIver guessed that she had never been hurt like that before. Solitaire was the pretty little girl and the beautiful young woman, admired and treasured, even by those who exploited her. Manacled there and knowing that the pain would continue and get worse, she would have told them anything. Mr Champion had explained all about fear and pain at their last meeting. The warning had proved a prediction. The interrogators of Solitaire need only turn the bath taps on full for the thunder of water to cover the small shrill sounds of the questioning. And then, with the towel in her mouth, they had smothered her with a pillow over her face. McIver shuddered and guessed that was it.

Hastily, he unzipped a cushion in one of the two Parker-Knoll armchairs, slid his hand inside, and touched the hard edge of the passport. Since it was still there, Tarrant could not have known about that. So long as the passport was safe, 'John Guy Walker' had a way out. A passport, a cheque-book, and a little more than thirty pounds in cash. Enough to survive on for the next week or two. Solitaire's purse. The black patent-leather handbag was on the other chair. He clicked it open, found the purse, and looked. Three single notes. Enough to be worth taking. Almost a pound in coins. That too. And, to his surprise, a first-class railway ticket, return from Waterloo to Bournemouth, stamped with the previous day's date and valid for three months. Who the hell had bought that for her and why? McIver guessed the reason for her mood that night. She had been about to ditch him after all.

His last compunction about what he intended was removed. Christ knows what she had told other people about him. Did they know she was about to walk out on him? If the police heard that, her death was going to look like McIver's revenge. A lover's anger. Worse still, a pimp's vengeance. In two days they'd discover how Solitaire earned most of her money and how much of it went to him. Run like hell, McIver thought. And do it quick.

Sitting on the bed, he thought that perhaps if he disappeared, if John Patrick McIver died to the world, the investigation would turn up clues to Tarrant or the true killers. If he stayed, the law would look no further. Surely the room must be marked by traces of the men who had been there. He thought that it would have taken more than one man to overpower the young woman and manacle her to the pipes. Give it time and the police would find the clues. Apart from that, his instinct was to run rather than stay. He and Solitaire had been going away anyhow. Why not stick to that plan, even alone? As a schoolboy, McIver knew that the best course was to run away from trouble. Let the indignation subside. Eventually it would be forgotten.

So that was it. Only a fool would stay and tell the police the best story that could be offered them. Far better to take the passport and vanish. He would be looked for, certainly suspected. But the passport was his answer. The photograph showed him in uniform. Wing Commander John 'Johnny' Walker. He could keep his first name. And he was not just any Wing Commander Walker but the officer who had been an equerry to the young Edward, Prince of Wales, in 1935. No red-faced village bobby would come pedalling forward to arrest a former royal equerry. Given half a chance, he would tell stories about this past, stories good enough to charm the birds out of the trees.

It was possible, of course, that he might encounter someone who had heard of Walker being killed when a flying-boat was shot down on the Lisbon run. But they would suppose it was a mistake, merely a rumour, or another Walker.

As he thought of this, McIver began to pack his suit and shirts into a suitcase. There were two cases and between them they would hold everything. Park them in the left luggage at Victoria or Waterloo. Then think what to do. The all-night News Theatre would give him a chance. In any case, get the hell out of these rooms while he still had a chance. He was locking the first case when his heart leapt to his throat with such force that he almost vomited. The phone bell rang. Leave it. No, if he left it they might wonder why and come up. He lifted it to his ear.

'Mr McIver?' the desk clerk said. 'Call for you, sir.'

Who the hell could it be? Who knew where he was? Then his heart sank.

'Mr McIver?' It was the same dry parsonical voice as the night before, the pursed-lip pedantry of an ancient lawyer or loss adjuster. 'My client is most disappointed in you. He had hoped that you might have listened to our advice.'

'You've done this!' McIver shouted. 'You and Tarrant. If they string me up, I'll make bloody sure they do the same to you! I've got enough to prove it! Don't you know what being an accessory means?'

There was a pause. It lasted so long he thought the connection was broken. Then the voice replied. There was an uncertainty, even worry, in its tone, suggesting that this was something for which no script had been prepared.

'I have not the slightest idea what you mean, Mr McIver. You and your two associates in Paddington will be called to account. That is all.'

McIver felt the chill again. But he was stronger than the man at the other end and he knew it. 'I'm talking about the dead body of a young woman, manacled to the pipes of a bathroom. You can tell Tarrant that his name's tied to her. And as soon as they get to him, you'll be an accessory.'

The phone clicked dead. If they knew where he was, they had only to phone the law now and catch him before he could leave the hotel. McIver needed a strap to hold the second case. He found one, buckled it and looked around him. The camera, the silver and black pre-war Leica. Leave the rest of the equipment. The bathroom door was slightly ajar, the light now turned off.

McIver had a last brief qualm that he was doing the wrong thing. No. He had thought it all out while sitting on the bed. They wouldn't believe him. His sole witness to the alibi was a bent or bogus policeman. Never worth the risk.

He opened the door and barged the two bulky suitcases awkwardly through the space. The door shut behind him. The lock clicked. He listened and heard no movement ahead. The service stairs were in darkness now and he dared not turn on the light. McIver slid and bumped his luggage a little, hauling it down flight by flight. But sound carried very little from here. He came to the last door and pushed it open, punting his two cases into the dark side-street. He picked them up again, the bulky cases bumping awkwardly against his legs.

There was a way through narrow streets which came out beyond Belgrave Square and then into Grosvenor Place. The immediate danger was past. Even with two cases in the small hours of the morning, he would not be stopped by a policeman. He was near the station now, just another traveller struggling on foot to a train at Victoria after the buses had stopped running. There was a cloakroom open overnight for the channel ferry train. McIver left the two cases there. The neon-banded News Theatre, which was open through the night for servicemen in transit, gave him warmth and shelter. He bought a ticket and went up the stairs with their chrome-railed and white-enamelled balustrade to the quietness of the circle seats. There was room to stretch out and relax. Despite the hunt that would soon gather behind him, McIver felt safer now that he was away from the hotel. In a way, life was simpler than it had been for months past. Now he would get away or he would not. He felt only a wry regret for what he was leaving. There had been good times and good types, Billy Blake especially. He would tell Billy what had happened. Put him on his guard. McIver turned his attention briefly to the screen of the little cinema where the Silly Symphony cartoon was ending. Then an abrupt orchestral vibration led into the weekly magazine feature. Settling back in the plush seat, while images of post-war reconstruction flickered on the screen, McIver went to sleep.

4

As the first office workers who came in on Saturday morning were stepping off the early trains, McIver went down into the station barber's shop for a shave. One chair had been uncovered for the early trade. His reflection, as he saw it in the electric-lit mirror, was pale and sober. His mind was still in the mood of unreality which follows a death. He expected to grieve for Solitaire and was surprised that as yet he did not. He wanted, in some way, to feel more frightened of his pursuers. But the unreal world of loss and shock enveloped and comforted him. They would find her body, of course. Yet he had an uncanny feeling that he might never hear any more about it. Once or twice at school, until the point when he was expelled, he had expected to be sacked after the perpetration of various offences. Lesser things were brought against him. Of the greater crimes, nothing was said. It was as if they were too appalling to be spoken of.

McIver watched the spare consumptive reflection of the elderly barber, beating up fragrant lather in a bowl, and relaxed in the remote warm dream of the tiled washroom below the trains and travellers. Waking in the cheap plush seat of the News Theatre, he had watched the monochrome images of world events and wondered how many of the previous night's memories were accurate.

If he walked back to the hotel now, Solitaire would be sitting up in bed with her green silk jacket on and the breakfast tray across her knees. But as the barber brushed the lather over his cheeks and chin, McIver watched his Father Christmas reflection in the glass and felt in his pocket the hard pasteboard edge of the first-class return ticket to Bournemouth and the flimsy claim slip for his cases in the cloakroom. Solitaire was dead. John Patrick McIver was dead. Only Wing Commander 'Johnny' Walker remained.

The barber stropped his razor and then cut the rasping whiskers through the layer of soap. McIver made conversation in reply to the elderly man's prompting.

'Been ferrying an Auster trainer to France, actually, old boy. Hurn Airport to the flying club at Le Bourget. Came back on the boat train. Lovely little plane. No effort. Flies like a bird. Anyone could do it. Bit different to hauling away at a bloody great Lancaster bomber with a ton of TNT under the seat.'

The white-coated barber listened, nodded, and smiled at him in the mirror. He liked McIver on first acquaintance. Men and women usually did. The gaunt grey-haired man finished and handed him a linen towel. McIver took it, stood up and felt a sudden pang of nausea. He steadied himself with a hand on the leather arm of the barber's chair. A similar linen towel in her mouth had choked her. But he pulled himself together quickly and handed the barber back a shilling from the change. The man touched McIver's arm.

'You take a tip from me, sir. A good breakfast. That's what you need to see you right.'

McIver walked up into the thin diffused sunlight that filtered through the soot-dimmed glass of the station canopy. The back of each concrete step was inset with a coloured advertisement for cigarettes. Players Please . . . Capstan Cigarettes . . . Craven A . . . Du Maurier Filter Tipped . . . He stood in the stale sooty air by the bookstall. When would they find her? Not yet. Not for a few hours. He turned into the station buffet. Two urns were spitting steam and a woman was cleaning the tiled floor with a mop. He went to the counter and ordered breakfast.

Money. That was the next thing. Billy Blake would help him. Billy would help anyone. He could always ask Billy, wherever he was, and Billy would send him money. McIver looked at his watch and saw that it was after eight o'clock. Probably safe until midday. But not at Billy's place. If by some chance they had found her, Billy would be one of the first names on their visiting list.

Still, there was Mr Champion. The old dodger had something to answer for! There was a story McIver could tell the law about him, if ever he was caught. Faked passports and changing stolen money. Photographs of girls with men and girls with one another. Men with boys. And that wouldn't be the worst of it for the old man. What the law did to Mr Champion would be kindness itself compared with the vengeance of those who were betrayed in their turn. So it would be in Mr Champion's interest to pay something of what was owing.

For the last time another temptation nagged at McIver's mind, echoing a schoolboy code of honour. Do the decent thing. Own up and take what was coming. What was it they used to say? Always get off lighter if you own up and tell the truth. But how little they knew! Go to the police now and tell the whole story? No. They'd want to know why he hadn't called them at once. According to their simple inflexible rules, he was the last person to be seen alive with her by the clerk. They always got you on that one. All the evidence would point to him being there when it happened. There had even been that bloody phone call just before he left, put through by the helpful desk clerk. Worse still, McIver now had an image of himself trying to move her, touching the metal cuff that held her to the pipe. He felt sure that he must have touched the metal itself. They'd have his fingerprints on that, perhaps only his. He wished now that he had wiped it over. Still, it would have been pointless to try wiping his prints from everywhere in the room – it would only have made it look worse, in fact.

He sat at the table with its yellow laminated top and knew what he must do. He could always go to the police and tell his story, if it seemed the best thing to do. There was no advantage in going now. If he was known to have run off anyhow, the length of the run mattered little. But Mr Champion was another matter. Mr Champion might be in this up to his scrawny neck.

McIver came out of the station buffet and saw that it was almost nine by the big four-faced clock that stood above the platforms. The warm morning air smelt of fruit. Railway stations have their individual smells. Victoria always smelt to him of fruit. Citrus and strawberry. He stepped out into the brightness and the boom of traffic, crossing to the bus for Paddington. The little shop opened at ten. McIver had never understood why anyone would want to buy Mr Champion's merchandise first thing in the morning. But the old man seemed to know better about the vagaries of human desire.

117

The bus stopped by St Mary's Hospital and McIver got off. It was a few minutes before ten by his watch. He walked down the little street and saw that the shop door was open slightly, as though someone had just gone in. There was a young man behind the corner counter, one of the hirelings. McIver pushed the door wider and went in. The young man turned. He was stoutly built and soft faced, the untidy hair and beard giving him the look of a sun-god emblem. He was perspiring already.

'Mr Champion?' McIver said. 'Is he in yet?'

The young man put down a box behind the counter. He looked up. 'No Mr Champion here.'

'When's he in?'

The young man rolled his shirtsleeves down. 'I think you got the wrong shop, mate. There's no Mr Champion here. Never heard of him.'

'I talked to him here the day before yesterday,' McIver said softly, 'in the back room. There are two chairs and a table in there, bookshelves and two framed photographs. One officer in RFC uniform. One rugby football team. I'm not the police, if that's what worries you.'

The young man shook his head as if to clear it. 'Hang on,' he said, 'there's never been anyone of that name here.'

He took a black Bakelite telephone receiver from under the counter and dialled a number.

'Del? It's me. There's a bloke here in the shop asking about a Mr Champion. We know anything about that, do we?'

He listened and then put the phone down. 'Seems no one don't know Mr Champion. But you're to hang on and the guv'nor will have a word with you.'

There was no point in arguing. McIver waited with his blood beating faster, scanning the covers of the magazines on the wall without taking in anything that he saw. Five or six minutes passed very slowly. A car drew up by the far pavement and, as he turned at the sound of it, two men got out. They were solidly built and similarly dressed in dark suits with trilby hats. They looked either way for traffic before beginning to cross the road to the shop.

McIver spun towards the young man. 'You miserable little shit!' he shouted.

Though bigger than McIver, the young man looked helpless. McIver raised the flap of the counter, pushed him aside and threw open the door of the back room. There was no one in sight and the room was almost bare. The chairs and table had gone, also

118

the photographs, though the little set of bookshelves remained on the wall. They had sprung the trap all right, not knowing that he had seen the way out of it.

The back door was open. It would be, McIver thought. He braced himself for a sprint, ran, jumped, and caught the top of the blank wall above the underground railway. The men were in the shop, he could hear their voices raised. He was on the wall, walking along the top to the point where the iron inspection ladder ran down to the track. They were in the back room now. But as they came out through the door, he was going down the ladder, hand over hand, faster than they would ever do.

He had no idea who they might be. It was possible her body had been found by now but surely they would not have had time to prepare such a trap as this. These men were Tarrant's or, perhaps, the genial Sammy's. He jumped and his feet slipped on the gravel. No sign of a train. But as he stood there, he heard the rumble and whine of an electric motor approaching on the opposite track. It ground its way along the rails from the underground platform at Paddington, came out briefly into dusty sunlight with a jolt and a trail of sparks, then moaned into the darkness of the next tunnel beneath the houses.

The two men were on the wall above him. But they were making heavy weather of it, McIver thought, as he picked his way across the tracks. One of them was on the ladder now but pausing. McIver ran leisurely along by the far wall, level with the track, the platforms of the station clearly lit a hundred yards ahead. In the wall of the short stretch of tunnel, there was a door. He tried it and was surprised to find that it was open. Inside there was a long dimly lit storeroom of some kind, probably used by the night cleaners. He opened the door at the far end of this and stepped out into one of the tiled corridors of the station complex. A wooden escalator creaked upwards at the far end, its shaft lined with identical framed advertisements for Alan Ladd in *The Great Gatsby*, a Gaumont Release.

To one side, the passageway crossed the line and went down steps to the platform. McIver ran, went down, and found himself in the middle of a morning crowd. At one end, he saw the light of the approaching train. Packed securely in the middle of the moving crowd, he boarded the train and was carried towards Kensington. At Victoria, he went up with the crowd and paused at the ticket barrier, handing a shilling to the collector.

'Paddington, thanks, chum,' he said cheerily and walked on.

The events of the last half hour left him with no option, as he saw it. He crossed the busy concourse to the cloakroom and retrieved his two cases. Pushing through the crowds, he made his way to the taxi rank. The office workers who came in on Saturday mornings were at their desks, the shopgirls behind their counters. The crowds that filled the concourse now were pressing patiently and hopefully towards the trains with head-numbers for Brighton, Eastbourne, and the holiday coasts.

'Waterloo station, please,' he said to the driver of the cab.

They turned down Victoria Street to Westminster Bridge and the Southern Railway terminus. In his pocket, McIver felt the little oblong of pasteboard which would carry him to Bournemouth and back by first-class rail. The concourse at Waterloo was crowded with men in slacks and open-necked shirts, women in print frocks with children clutching their hands. Few of them were travelling first-class. Twenty minutes later, his luggage stowed aboard by the steward, McIver relaxed at a table with pink-shaded lamps, in the brown and cream Pullman car of the Bournemouth Belle. The white cloth had been laid for lunch. As the train moved slowly from the platform, there was a brief shiver of trembling glass and a tiny percussion of silverware. He smiled at the steward and ordered bottled beer.

7

SQUAD CALL

1

Saturday afternoon of the holiday weekend was quiet as a Sunday in the long streets of commercial offices, banks, and insurance companies. Even Trafalgar Square was a sunlit desert of stone as the car turned into Cockspur Street. Frank Brodie stared at the scale models of grey-hulled cruise liners in the display windows of the shipping companies.

'Rogers reckons the trippers were sleeping on the beach at Brighton last night, thousands of 'em,' he said quietly. 'Hotels overflowing.'

Rutter nodded and tried to ease the binding anticipation in his chest. 'Did Rowley say how they found her exactly?'

The car was level with the Duke of York's steps and the United Service Club, tall darkened portraits of Crimean generals in red tunics glimpsed through Regency windows.

'No ring for breakfast,' Brodie said. 'They usually rang about ten. The chambermaid went to do the room about twelve. Knocked the door and got no reply. McIver and the girl sometimes came in from a night-club about dawn and slept until lunch. The bedsprings used to get regular exercise before they got up. Anyway, when the maid got no answer, she decided she'd go and do the top floor, then come back. No one had handed in the room key, so she assumed they must still be in there. After that, she still got no reply to her knock. Getting on for one o'clock by then. So she went down and told Mrs Rees, the manageress. First thing Mrs Rees thought, naturally, was that they might have done a flit during the night to save paying the bill.'

They passed the old weathered brick of St James's Palace, turning up towards Piccadilly.

'How long'd they been there?' Rutter asked.

'Three weeks, I think she said. For the last ten days or so, McIver spun some yarn about waiting for money. Reckoned his living-out allowance from the RAF was overdue. Phoned the Flying Crew Accounts section at the Air Ministry every day, he said. The RAF hasn't known anything about him for a twelve-month. Anyway, according to DC Soper from Chelsea CID, when there was no reply at one o'clock, Mrs Rees went up with a pass-key. Knocked the door and opened it. Curtains still drawn, so she turned on the light. No sign of them. Beds not slept in. She was sure they'd done a bunk. Didn't smell too sweet in there, so the first thing Mrs Rees does is pull the curtains back and open the windows. I told Soper to leave them that way. Then Mrs Rees thinks that perhaps something in the bathroom needs attention. Goes in and finds the girl on the floor with one wrist cuffed to a pipe. She didn't let the maid see anything. Pushed her out, locked the room, went straight down, and dialled three nines. That put her through to Chelsea CID.'

'How's she taken it?'

'Better than Chelsea CID, by the sound of it. Especially Soper. Seems it's his first dead body.'

The driver picked up speed along Piccadilly, the road before them almost empty to Hyde Park Corner.

'Soper will learn,' Rutter said. 'We've all got to start somewhere.'

'Still,' Brodie said with a chuckle, 'I reckon that's one young shaver that's going to be off his white meat for a bit.'

'One thing about you, Frankie,' Rutter said quietly. 'Sense of taste and timing. I don't know how you do it.'

Brodie shrugged and fell silent. The Georgian elegance of Apsley House and the lush bowers of the park shrubs beyond the Serpentine swept past as if a movie camera had panned steadily across them.

As the car drew up outside the hotel, half a dozen uniformed men were keeping back a handful of reporters and about twenty sightseers.

'By the way,' Rutter asked suddenly, 'did Mrs Rees tell Soper what names they were registered under? Or hadn't Soper enquired yet?'

'Nothing but the best,' Brodie said, 'Squadron Leader and Mrs John McIver. Everyone liked him.'

122

'Everyone always does like him,' Rutter said bleakly, 'until they cash a cheque for him.'

In the hotel lobby a small grey-haired woman was talking rapidly to two uniformed men, a constable taking her statement while a sergeant tried to slow her down. Henshaw, a burly man with an incongruously ornamental quiff of hair, walked up to Rutter.

'Hello, Jack. This one's not yours, is it?'

Rutter shook his head. 'Too grand for me, Max. It's Mr Marriot's case.'

'Where's he, then?'

'Half an hour ago, Mr Marriot was on the fourteenth green at Moor Park Golf Club with the Deputy Commissioner. Now he's in a car, being driven this way very fast with the bell ringing, just like on the flicks. I was sitting down to giblet stew in the Whitehall canteen. Of all days, it has to happen on a Saturday.'

'You want to go up?'

'Can't say I want to, Max, but I'd better. Mr Marriot's going to need detailed briefing when he gets here. What's the score so far?'

'Dr Clarke's doing his stuff. Fingerprints and photography got here about twenty minutes ago. We need both lots finished as soon as possible so that we can do an inch-by-inch up there. She's been dead since yesterday, they reckon, so we'll move her soon as poss. Dr Clarke wants her taken to Fulham mortuary for an autopsy this afternoon. There's an undertaker's hearse on standby a few minutes away. DI Fisher out of Chelsea is scene of crime officer. Thing is, Jack, this caught us short-handed in the middle of Saturday.'

Rutter looked at the hotel entrance. 'What's happening about the press?'

'We reckon that's down to Mr Marriot,' Henshaw said. 'The vultures know there's a woman's body found. So naturally they're waiting on a sex murder. Could well be right. One way or another, we might need all their co-operation if this bloke McIver has to be found. He's not been seen since last night, just after nine o'clock, and the thinking seems to be she was dead soon after. But he was still in the room when the desk clerk put through a call about eleven. McIver answered.'

'Right,' Rutter said, 'I'll go up. You'll probably see Mr Marriot in a little while.'

With Brodie beside him, he went up the stairs to the second-floor bedroom, his gut tightening a little with apprehension at what awaited him. A uniformed constable was posted outside the suite. The door handle had been encased by a cellophane bag and the door itself stood open. When Rutter went in, Giles the photographer was already packing away part of his equipment into two large black cases. Four fingerprint men with brushes and powder were working painstakingly over the window-frames, chairs, and tables, moving with speed and precision, like stage jugglers demonstrating the impossible. Giles had left a smaller camera to one side.

'Just the snaps of the dabs to do now, sir,' he said to Rutter with quiet professional satisfaction.

Rutter nodded, took a deep breath, and moved to the bathroom doorway. A low screen of dark green canvas closed off the far end of the tiled room at waist height. Rutter, thankful for this, saw only a woman's arm raised above it and the thin metal which held the wrist to the pipe. The skin had a bloodless and slightly wrinkled look, as though it had been too long immersed in water. Clarke, who had been stooping behind the screen, straightened up, his beard and moustache concealed behind a white surgical mask.

'Afternoon, Jack,' he said breezily, 'Mr Marriot with you?'

'He's on his way,' Rutter said.

'Had to wait for a printed invitation, did he? We're almost through here.'

Rutter heard a voice behind him and saw Jeff Fisher, Chelsea Division's scene of crime officer. 'Mr Marriot's going to need briefing fast, Jeff,' Rutter said. 'What've we got so far?'

Fisher, a tall balding intellectual with ginger hair, pulled a face. 'Not much. Probably enough, though. The woman's name was Sally Brown, known professionally as Solitaire. Professional model, club dancer, and everything that goes with it.'

'Rooms in Shepherd Market,' Rutter said. 'She's been in business there a couple of months.'

'That we didn't know,' Fisher conceded. 'Thanks. She and McIver came in last night and spoke to the desk clerk about nine o'clock. They came straight up here. McIver wasn't seen again. He answered a phone call from the desk about eleven. The girl wasn't seen until her body was found just about one o'clock this afternoon. Body temperature, according to Jim Clarke, suggests she was dead by midnight. Suffocation, unless he finds something cleverer at the post-mortem. No sign of a break-in. No sign of the room being entered except by the guests' key. They'll take the lock apart and see if there's scratches on the mechanism from a duplicate key or a pick-lock. I reckon they're wasting their time.'

'Sounds a bit open and shut,' Rutter said mildly. 'Any of the other guests nearby hear anything between nine and midnight?'

A look of ironic satisfaction touched Fisher's face. 'It's Saturday, Jack. Three lots moved out this morning. One couple is now somewhere between here and New York. Another, known as Mr and Mrs Smith, probably a bogus address anyway. They left early. But the couple immediately above heard nothing. Nor did the ones in the suite that adjoins the bathroom.'

'What's the lay-out of the rooms?' Rutter asked.

'Bathroom above the bathroom, bathroom next to the bathroom,' Fisher said. 'See what I mean? And water gushing in a bath and rumbling in the pipes would cover a certain amount of yelling. The American couple on the other side were the most likely to hear what went on.'

Rutter sighed. 'If she screamed, someone heard her, water running or not. If she didn't scream or struggle, I want to know why.'

'Mr and Mrs Abrahams were the nearest,' Fisher said. 'They left on the 8.30 boat train for Southampton this morning. The *Queen Mary* sailed at noon. Almost three hours ago.'

'She'll call at Cherbourg about five,' Rutter said firmly. 'They always do. Frank! I want someone back at the office to contact Cunard's agent at the Gare Maritime in Cherbourg. Put the call through the Ocean Terminal at Southampton, if that's quicker. The *Queen Mary*'s probably due to dock in France about five. She's not likely to sail again for New York before seven or eight. Mr and Mrs Abrahams, passengers for New York, get the rest of their details downstairs from Mrs Rees. I want them questioned about last night. Where they were and what they heard. Times, details. Take 'em off the ship, if necessary.'

'Can you do that, Jack?' Fisher asked nervously. 'In France?'

'They're witnesses in a murder enquiry, Jeff. They'll want to clear themselves. If not, they could be suspects.'

Giles was packing up the last of his photographic equipment.

'John Patrick McIver is what we want,' Fisher said. 'We've got

Criminal Records Office on to his name. His belongings have gone, most of them. Just a few photographic accessories. Presumably he made a run for it during the night. Even took the key with him.'

Rutter gave a derisive snort of laughter. 'I can tell you about McIver. Including things that CRO doesn't know about yet.'

Fisher looked at him uneasily. 'Anything like this?'

Rutter shook his head. 'Nothing like this, if this is what it seems like. McIver's a nice simple type. Officer and gentleman gone bad. Chucked out twice for embezzlement. Army and RAF. Otherwise known as thief, con-artist, expert in defrauding women of love and money, dirty picture merchant. Not known to be violent. Unless, perhaps, in the line of sexual duty. Shot down a Jap Zero at Imphal. If he hadn't had such a rotten record, he might have got a mention in despatches for that.'

'So what's Mr Marriot's interest?'

'Bigger fish,' Rutter said. 'Some of whom had reason to gobble McIver up.'

Fisher shrugged. 'Looks like your party, then.'

Dr Clarke came out of the bathroom, untying his surgical mask. 'Mr Marriot still doing his best to reach us, is he?'

'You never stop, do you, Jim?' Rutter said philosophically. 'And what does medical science tell us about all this?'

Clarke dropped the mask into a plastic bag, rippled off his gloves and dropped them too. 'She died between nine and midnight or a very little after. I can't believe that the cause of death was other than suffocation. She was handcuffed to that pipe by her right wrist before she died. There's also a post-mortem flush on the left wrist. Made by a ligature of some sort, probably a twisted towel or linen of some kind, pulled tight to tie her by that wrist as well. The clothes that were taken off were taken off after that. I haven't examined the blouse but you can see that it's been cut. There's a linen towel that seems to have been in her mouth. Perhaps it choked her accidentally. Perhaps she was suffocated deliberately by someone who hoped it would be hard to detect. They could have pressed a pillow or a cushion to her face. Strung up like that she wouldn't be able to do much. There is slight bruising on the face which may indicate something held there. Perhaps they just kept her nose closed. However it happened, I don't think we'll get much closer without a witness.'

Fisher looked at him quickly. 'You think it was sexually motivated?'

126

Clarke shook his head. 'Motivated, maybe. But I don't think there was any attack of that sort. There was some kind of assault. Two marks across the upper back and shoulders. Made by something thin and rigid. Not a great degree of violence, though. Done to frighten rather than injure, probably.'

Rutter heard voices raised in the street below. He went to the window and pulled the curtain aside. The uniformed men were holding back the press from a Rover saloon car.

'Mr Marriot,' he said.

'Good,' Clarke said. 'Nice timing.' He turned away to make arrangements for the unvarnished mortuary coffin.

'What's eating him?' Fisher said softly. 'Needle, needle, all the time.'

Rutter pulled a face. 'He's all right. Got a wife that's a complete neurotic. Fit as a flea but keeps bashing his ear about all the illnesses she's got. If you're a doctor, I suppose that must be the last straw.'

Marriot, tall and broad-shouldered, appeared in the doorway. 'Jack!'

Rutter turned; the details of the investigation were pigeon-holed in his mind as he stood aside with the superintendent and rehearsed the story. While Marriot listened, Rutter watched the entry and departure of the plain coffin with Clarke in attendance. Giles took his last photograph of the fingerprints revealed by white dust. One by one they left until Rutter and Marriot were accompanied only by Fisher and two uniformed constables.

'Right,' Marriot said presently, 'we'll press on to Whitehall. Forensic ready to do their inch-by-inch, are they? Good. Let's see what we can start doing about this bird McIver.'

2

This time it was Whitehall, deserted and empty as if a death-ray had cleared the streets. The pale obelisk of the Cenotaph rose in the centre of the long vista, its flags furled at the base. They went down the stone stairs and the bright summer day was reduced to an underwater gloom through the basement pebble-glass of the window behind Marriot's desk. Rutter had no need to be told that surveillance of Tarrant and the black market was in other hands until McIver had been brought in for the death of Sally Brown.

'After all,' Marriot said, 'we can't run a murder hunt as well. Not set up for it. Catching a killer takes priority. Whoever did this might do it again. The way she was strung up was premeditated. Nothing impulsive. Nothing accidental. We've got a real one this time, Jack. I'd say this is going to be one for the textbooks.'

'And we're hunting no one but McIver?' Rutter asked.

The question caused a shadow of impatience on Marriot's broad big-boned face. 'With that evidence, Jack? What else would you suggest? We'd get nailed to the mast if we didn't stop McIver now. You're not suggesting Tarrant or one of her other gentlemen friends had a hand in it?'

Rutter stood at the window. 'No, sir,' he said quietly, 'I'm sure you'll find Tarrant was a long way off, especially if he had anything to do with her death. McIver was there last night with the girl. McIver could have done it. The only thing in his favour is that it's not his style. Dishonest, unscrupulous, even callous on occasion. But not violent. Not that I know of, anyway.'

'He's a degenerate, at the very least,' Marriot said glumly, 'and don't tell me about style. Facts are what matter. Either he killed her or he didn't. Fact. And if he killed her like this, then it's his style.'

Rutter bowed to Marriot's logic with an inclination of the head. But he still believed in style. 'Photographs certainly,' he said, 'living on her immoral earnings, I dare say. But Clarke thinks it wasn't a sexual assault.'

Marriot turned in his chair. 'Leave out Tarrant and the fancy stuff, Jack. Stick to what the evidence says. McIver. He went up to the room with her at about nine. He still has the key of the room, so far as we know. Within about three hours of their going into the room together, she was dead. McIver had not been seen to leave during that time nor, apparently, had anyone else been seen to arrive. McIver was still there to answer the phone at eleven. At some later point, he managed to leave unseen. But ask yourself, Jack. Why would McIver want to sneak out unseen, if everything was all right with the girl? And if it wasn't all right with her, then he's got the rope round his neck already. There's no sign of a break-in or any kind of forced entry. Whoever was with her entered that room in the normal way, either using the key or being admitted.'

Marriot picked up the telephone on his desk and asked for a

number. He gave his name and listened. Then he put the phone down and turned again to Rutter. 'Cherrill's boys found what you'd expect, Jack. Not many sets of recent fingerprints, seeing that McIver and the girl had the place to themselves for three weeks. The girl's prints are everywhere. So are McIver's. We matched his from his Criminal Records set. Mrs Rees and the chambermaid we've found and eliminated. And, in case we need more, McIver's prints are on the metal handcuffs that were on her wrist. They were toys, by the way, not too difficult to open, so long as you were free to do it and knew how.'

'I still wish it was McIver's style,' Rutter said quietly.

'So do I,' said Marriot coldly. 'Which is why I put out an enquiry on the way from Moor Park. From what we can gather, Tarrant was a hundred miles away last night. With his mother, at the seaside. Probably he had half a dozen witnesses with him. Now, the fingerprints again. Two sets probably belong to Blake and Hallam, suspected as accomplices of McIver in theft and fraud. We'll check Hallam from the prints taken at the time of a dangerous driving charge. He was acquitted of the theft when the owner changed her mind. All the same, we got him for dangerous driving. Patrol car had to ram him to stop the bugger killing someone. Blake doesn't have a record. Still, he'll be keen to co-operate.'

Rutter heard a lone taxi rumble down Whitehall.

'Anyone suggest where McIver might have gone?'

Marriot shook his head. 'Robert Locke is organizing eyes and ears in the usual pubs and clubs. Also the places McIver used to frequent in Soho. Clubs where you could do anything or anyone for a price. And Blake and Hallam can expect to have us to lunch every day until their friend is caught. And so can anyone else who was close to McIver.'

'Waste of time,' Rutter said, 'he'll have done a complete bunk by now.'

Marriot sighed. 'But if he hasn't and if we didn't watch the clubs and pubs, Jack, we'd get crucified. Given McIver's record, he'll run as far as he can. We're having a display for the cover of the *Police Gazette* issued tomorrow. McIver's photo from his file. It's going to every police force in the country, especially ports and airports. I had this done by Locke while we were on our way from Knightsbridge.'

Rutter took the sheet of paper with its typed message as Marriot handed it to him. The wording had all Marriot's ponderous efficiency.

It is desired to trace the after-described for interview respecting the death of Sally Brown, a night-club dancer and model known professionally as 'Solitaire', on the night of 20th–21st inst. John Patrick McIver, alias Cunningham, Trumpington, Mitford, etc., born Wimbledon 29 May 1916. Criminal Record Office File 19356–35. Sergeant Pilot RAF 1943–45. Convicted at Bow Street Magistrates' Court, December 1945, for wearing uniform and medals without authorization. May be in possession of trainee civilian pilot's 'A' licence. Thought likely to attempt passage to South Africa or other English-speaking dominions. May stay at hotels accompanied by women.

As Rutter handed the paper back, the phone rang on Marriot's desk. The superintendent listened, then handed it to Rutter. 'Frank Brodie for you, Jack.'

Rutter took the receiver. 'Jack? We found Blake all right. Sitting in his flat minding his own business. He was getting drunk with half a dozen people at the Copacabana last night from nine until after two in the morning. Seems to let him out. McIver and the girl were in the club between eight and nine. They went off saying something about having an orgy back at their hotel.'

'An orgy?' Rutter said glumly. 'That's nice. Anything else on Blake?'

'We've got Blake's fingerprints. Took them off him down at Chelsea. But there's one bit of bad news.'

'What's that, then?'

'Blake had a service revolver. First World War, Eley .455. McIver's got it now. He reckons he can fire all sorts of ammo from it, including tommy-gun bullets if he files the base of the cartridge to fit.'

'Thanks a lot, Frankie,' Rutter said, 'that's cheered me up no end. Anything else?'

'Yes,' said Brodie firmly, 'we've got the girl's address in Shepherd Market. That'll need to be searched today. You going to be there?'

'I don't think so,' Rutter said wearily, 'I'm sure you'll do it very well.'

'That's nice.' Brodie sounded uncharacteristically depressed. 'That's really nice, that is.'

'See you later,' Rutter said, and put the phone down. He turned to Marriot. 'You'll have to add a line to that appeal, sir. It seems that McIver's got a gun. He's going to try firing mismatched cartridges from an Eley .455. They'd roll quite a lot but he could easily hit someone at close range. Even at medium range, he's only got to fire for long enough before he hits somebody or something.'

Marriot made a note on the paper. 'We can't send armed officers to every police force in the country, Jack. Still, we can warn them and let them make up their own minds as to what they do.'

'And Frank Brodie says they've Blake's prints, sir. I imagine they'll pay a visit to Hallam, just to check on him.'

Marriot nodded, thinking of something else. 'One thing, Jack. We need an officer down at Fulham. Someone as our man at the autopsy this evening.'

'I'd go,' Rutter said hastily, 'only I've promised Brodie to take charge of the search of the girl's room in Shepherd Market. Best to send someone who's almost on the spot at Fulham. DI Fisher out of Chelsea. He gets on well with Dr Clarke.'

Marriot drew a long breath. 'All right, Jack. I'll see. But we all have to take our turn with things like that.'

'Yes, sir,' said Rutter sincerely, 'I was at Clarke's PM on that taxi driver in Lambeth. You'd think a scalpel cuts through flesh like a knife through butter. It doesn't. Skin is tough. It makes a noise like someone tearing canvas. Sounded like Clarke was having a go at the big top of Bertram Mills Circus.'

'Yes,' said Marriot flatly, 'well, that's just a fact of life. So you're going to Shepherd Market now?'

'I'll make a start,' Rutter said, 'no harm in being there first.'

'Take a man with you,' Marriot said sharply. 'You don't want to be alone in private premises without a witness.'

Rutter went through the outer office and up the stone stairs. He came up into the warm summer afternoon. Beyond the windows, a cloud moved and river wavelets chopped and glittered by County Hall on the far bank. As the Sally Brown murder enquiry began, he felt sealed off from the real world of summer, as though he might be part of someone else's winter dream.

3

The low-ceilinged room at the top of the little house was silent as a country cottage in the weekend calm. In the late afternoon, it had the smell of warm wood and dusty cushions, which came from having been closed up during the day. There was very little to suggest the profession that the young woman had carried on there. The bed-sitting room itself, with its pink covers and the pale satin-finished wood of the dressing-table, took up most of the space. To one side there was an alcove curtained off and furnished by a single armchair. Comfort was provided by a portable radio on a shelf, a low cupboard built into the corner with a gas-ring on top. Its shelves were filled with enough food for breakfast and a few pieces of crockery.

He went back to the main room. A golliwog pyjama-case lay on the bed and three imitation-porcelain shepherdesses stood on the narrow mantelshelf. A copy of Upton Sinclair's *Dragon's Teeth* with a stamp from Boots' Library had been left on the dressing-table. Apart from this room and its alcove, there was only a closet-sized compartment with a toilet and hand-basin. It was not a flat in which anyone lived, Rutter thought, or at least it was not a place where meals were cooked or baths taken. The great advantage was that it could be fingerprinted and searched in no time at all.

He went back downstairs to the little street, where Giles and one of Cherrill's men were waiting.

'Nothing much to it,' Rutter said, 'but I'd like it as quick as you can.'

He went back to the car to call Marriot. As he finished, a second car drew up at the Curzon Street entrance to the market and Frank Brodie appeared.

'Didn't expect to see you here, Jack.'

'No,' said Rutter philosophically, 'well, I didn't expect to be here, to tell you the truth. But then it was either this or an evening down the morgue while Jim Clarke exercised his talents. This shouldn't take long. Giles and his friend are doing their stuff now. I'd expect to find McIver's prints again, possibly Blake's and Hallam's. There'll be some from anonymous clients. There's just a chance we might find dabs from someone who appears elsewhere. Meantime, Mr Marriot's sending McIver's photograph and description to every force in the country. Did you get much out of Blake, apart from the news of the gun?'

Brodie shook his head. 'Mr Blake's out of his depth. Whatever they were up to, I reckon it's his first taste of major crime. He's scared as hell at being mixed up in all this, so scared that we're not going to get much more out of him. He says he doesn't know where McIver is. I think that's true. But he's not saying any more without his solicitor present.'

'Nothing else at the hotel room?'

'We went through her handbag but there's not much there, except something odd written on the back of a shop receipt for a pair of stockings. *Mrs T's birthday?* That's got to be Ma Tarrant's birthday, I'd say. As if the girl was reminding herself to ask about it.'

'Meaning?'

Brodie shrugged.

'You tell me. I showed it to Blake. He didn't respond much. He looked scared but then he's been looking scared all the time. Perhaps we'll have to ask Tarrant about his mother's birthday.'

'What about Hallam?'

'Nasty little wart,' Brodie said, 'repertory actor before the war. Bit of thieving nowadays, I should think. The girl was with him when we rammed the car he'd taken away. We could have another word with the lady who owned the vehicle. She got suddenly confused about whether she'd given him permission or not. He got off that charge but he was done for dangerous driving. Seems he introduced the lovely Solitaire to McIver several months ago.'

'Alibi'd, is he?'

'Looks like it,' Brodie said philosophically. 'He's had a bed-sit in Maida Vale for the past fortnight. Says he had a bath about nine last night, someone saw him on the way to the communal bathroom. He was either coming from the bathroom or going to it. You don't usually have a witness while you're in the bath. Anyway, he didn't. He says he was definitely in the Copacabana by half-past ten. It's not impossible that he could have gone like hell for Knightsbridge, killed her, and still got to the club. On the other hand, there's no evidence for that. His fingerprints in that room weren't new, according to Cherrill's experts. Anyway, McIver was there from nine until eleven, wasn't he? So he's still top of the list.'

The evening sun was slanting lower at the bedroom window when Rutter and Brodie began their search.

'Only what you'd expect to find in a home-made knocking-shop,' Brodie said, 'and not very much of that.'

133

Rutter opened the first drawer of the dressing-table. Brodie was right. He stared at the tricks of the trade that were about as erotic in themselves as the contents of the kitchen cupboard. There was little to suggest that the young woman's clients wanted anything but the most orthodox pleasures. Then Rutter pulled open a lower drawer and stared at the open metal loops of a pair of cuffs. They looked identical to those which he had seen in the hotel bathroom several hours earlier.

'Come over here and tell me if we've struck gold, Frankie,' he said softly. 'Look at this but don't touch it.'

Brodie looked over his shoulder. 'You reckon that's the same make?'

'I'd say so. And whatever prints there may be, I want them.'

'Where's the key to them? That might have prints.'

'I don't think these have keys, Frankie. They're toys. Children's toys, rather than bedroom toys, I'd say. You just press that button. Easily done, unless you happen to be wearing them. Unless you happen to be strung up by them. Even then, you might do it, if you knew how.'

'Well,' Brodie said, 'seems like she didn't know.'

The bedroom was full of warm late sunlight. Rutter stared into the drawer.

'Oh, I think she knew how they worked, Frankie, but she wasn't allowed to open them. If she used these on her clients for fun and games, she must have known how they worked. I don't reckon that stockbrokers, members of parliament, and high court judges came hurrying out of here looking for a locksmith. She wasn't allowed to open them, that's the point.'

'Strung up like that,' Brodie said, 'she probably couldn't press the button against anything.'

Rutter sighed. 'All right. Then what about McIver? Suppose you were him, Frankie. If she died accidentally during some extravaganza, even if he did it deliberately, would you leave her the way she was? Surely he could have pressed that button if he used the things? Why leave her as we found her? Cold-blooded murder. The kind juries don't have doubts about and the kind that never gets a reprieve. He might as well put the rope round his neck now. Why not take her down and put her on the bed? Wouldn't you, at least, try and make it look like manslaughter? Sorry, officer, but we were having a brisk bit of mattress-exercise. She turned over and we were so carried away. I must have leant on her too hard and pushed her face into the pillow. Not good, but better than nothing.'

'With something like this on her wrists?' Brodie asked sceptically.

'And another thing, officer,' Rutter intoned, 'she did like wearing funny bracelets. You look in her flat and you'll see for yourself. Come on, Frankie! Why didn't he try to make it better for himself somehow? He could still have done a bunk but he'd have had a better prospect to come back to.'

Brodie turned and looked out into the street. A waiter was arranging small tables on the pavement under the awning of the Brasserie Parisienne as the dinner trade began.

'I don't know how McIver's mind works, Jack. You don't think like that in a real panic.'

'I reckon McIver does,' Rutter said firmly, 'I think that's exactly how a petty crook like McIver would think.'

'Well, he obviously didn't this time, did he?'

'I don't know, Frankie,' Rutter said thoughtfully, 'I just wonder if he couldn't open the cuffs because he didn't know how – he'd never seen them before. I'm wondering if she'd ever seen them before either.'

Brodie frowned at him. 'But there's a pair of 'em here, Jack.'

'I know that, Frankie. And I'm still wondering who put them there.'

'She did,' Brodie said.

'If you say so, my son,' Rutter said, his interest now elsewhere.

There was a Kodak envelope of photographic plates under the metal cuffs. Rutter drew it out by its edges. He shook the prints out on to the dressing-table, moving them aside one by one without touching their surfaces.

'Nothing in those,' Brodie said, 'she must have been in dozens of sets of under-the-counter snapshots. Ask the dirty squad. They'll tell you. She never made it to the magazines but sealed packets of photographs were definitely in her line.'

Rutter lifted them carefully and set them aside. There was Solitaire naked and in profile. Solitaire in a practised sprawl of animal abandon across the silk covers of an anonymous bed. Solitaire looking back over her shoulder with disdain and then with timidity. Her poses and expressions were the small change of the trade in such packaged photographs. He lifted another.

'Hang on,' Brodie said softly, 'that's more like it.'

Rutter would not have thought it an obscene photograph, scarcely indecent by the standards of the law, but it was powerfully suggestive to him at that moment. The naked model was seen from the rear but only from just below her shoulders to the upper swell of her hips. The edge of her hair was just in view where it ended across her back. Her arms were pulled behind her, wrists crossed in the small of her back, hands turned so that her palms faced the camera, fingers lightly clenched to show the crimson-painted mannequin gloss of long elegant nails. Round the wrist that lay on top of the other were three circuits of cord drawn tight. To one side, the frayed ends of the cord had been securely knotted.

'Could be her,' Rutter said, 'except that it's not the sort of thing she went in for, according to information received.'

'It wouldn't be in her collection of self-portraits if it wasn't her,' Brodie said sceptically.

'In any case,' Rutter said, 'you can't see the wrist that's underneath. That rope's just round the top wrist for effect, I should think. She's just wearing it, like a watch-strap. Still does the trick for the punters.'

He lifted the print by its edges and looked at the next photograph. This was what he had feared. The entire menu. Wrists showing the bright metal of the cuffs. It was the bedroom of the hotel, Solitaire face-down on the bed at the centre of the composition.

'Heavy stuff for the private trade,' Brodie said. 'What d'you think, Jack? You reckon McIver and she tried some experiments like this until it all went wrong? Not hard to choke someone or suffocate them if you fool around with these things. Trouble is the fans see it on the movie screen and they think it's all jolly fun and no harm done.'

Rutter shook his head and put down the print. 'I don't think it makes a damn bit of difference, Frankie. And McIver did a bunk because he reckons it doesn't make any difference either. He's got to answer for the half-naked body of a young woman, hanging from the bathroom pipes in a hotel suite. That suite was booked in his name. He'd lived there with her for three weeks. He'd got the key to it. He went up there alone with her just before she died. No one else was seen going there and he wasn't seen leaving. The metal cuffs have got his prints on. He's taken photographs of her for the picture market and among them we get stuff like this. Assumption is, McIver could have an obsession about tying up his lady friends. But it doesn't matter much whether he has or not. You think he's got a defence?'

'Accident?' Brodie suggested.

Rutter shook his head again. 'It might be true but it wouldn't save him. Most murders are an accident, in the sense that the murderers usually wish afterwards that they hadn't done it. No, my son. What happens if McIver goes along to court and says it's all a terrible accident? He admits that he strung her up and shoved a towel in her mouth and left a couple of marks across her shoulders. She died in the course of festivities. So far as the law is concerned, that's not accident. Can you imagine how the judge is going to sum up for the jury? McIver wouldn't last five minutes with a case like that. The girl was alive and then, after what he did to her, she was dead. End of story. He knows he killed her, the judge knows it, and the jury knows it. He had to do a bunk.'

'So he reckons that he'll be topped whatever happens?'

Rutter shrugged and took a cigarette from a packet. He offered the packet to the sergeant. 'Unless he can get clean away. Mind you, there's a fair chance McIver might top himself. That's the form for a chancer like him when his luck runs dry. He could have done it already.'

The discovery of the photographs and the metal cuffs prolonged Rutter's working day into the night that followed. He was still at his desk when the first traffic of Sunday morning began to stir in the quiet Whitehall streets. Marriot had gone home, promising to be back at lunchtime. Rutter took his towel and razor from the top drawer of his desk and shaved in the communal washroom. He returned and tipped the overflowing ashtray into the wastepaper basket. At nine o'clock, he went out and bought a paper. There was an ABC near Trafalgar Square that stayed open on Sundays. Rutter sat down at one of the little tables, ordered breakfast and opened his paper. The front page of the *News of the World* had pictures of the holiday weekend crowds at Brighton that made him glad to be in London. He turned through the pages of news-print. Three inches of a column on a centre page were devoted to the story, under the headline WOMAN'S BODY FOUND IN KNIGHTS-BRIDGE HOTEL. Marriot's name was mentioned as leader of the investigation. As usual, it was misspelt with an additional 't'.

After breakfast, there was McIver's earlier file from the Crimi-nal Records Office. Petty theft and financial trickery. Frauds perpetrated on his friends. Two of their houses robbed. But that was a long time ago, in a sunlit summer before the war came to save him. The exploits of 'Flight Sergeant Johnny Zero' had set him on his feet again. Rutter stared blankly at the colourless light beyond the office window.

'You stupid bugger!' he said helplessly to the absent McIver. Then he returned to the file.

There were two schools of thought. One insisted that the petty thief and embezzler of today, devoid of all moral sense and conscience, would mature into the murderer of tomorrow. The other held that the young thief and trickster merely became the middle-aged and elderly thief and trickster, never learning and never progressing. Nothing in McIver's files helped to resolve the question.

When Marriot arrived, Rutter was still thinking about this. There was little to do but think. None of the police forces who had received McIver's details had so far reported any sightings. Marriot was impatient.

'See what happens in the next twelve hours, Jack. If there's nothing, we'll have to give the full story to the press. Get them to join the hunt. I don't want to spoil our chances of a conviction in court by naming him in the press at this stage. But we need this investigation tidied away before McIver kills himself or someone else. That means we may have to identify him and take our chance on what that does to a prosecution case.'

'I'll get the press office going first thing tomorrow, sir. Unless someone spots McIver today.'

'Good,' said Marriot, looking up with enthusiasm. 'And I should get off home to bed now, Jack, if I were you. You look absolutely terrible.'

4

Jack Rutter was back in the Army again, with an extra pip as acting captain. He tried to protest, to explain that he had an important job at Scotland Yard. The regimental adjutant brushed his complaint aside . . . Somewhere an alarm bell went off, putting the battalion on alert for an imminent attack. Rutter awoke from his dream and heard with gratitude the familiar sound of the telephone by his bed in his own bedroom. It was broad daylight, almost six o'clock on Monday morning. The dream of being back in the Army was less frequent now than at first. It was one that most conscripts shared in the months after their release.

'Jack?' Brodie's tone conveyed excitement and astonishment. 'You there?'

'Yes,' Rutter said irritably, 'where did you think I'd be? It's not six o'clock yet.'

'Letter in the early post,' Brodie said, 'mail room sent it straight up. It's from McIver.'

'McIver?'

'He's written us a letter,' Brodie said patiently.

'Has he, by God! When?'

'Posted Saturday, right on our doorstep. London SW1.'

'Cheeky sod! What's he say?'

'Rather a lot,' Brodie said. 'It's his version of what happened in that hotel bedroom the night before last. I think you'd better get down here and read it for yourself.'

5

In half an hour Rutter was standing in Marriot's office with the superintendent and Brodie. Marriot handed him the sheet of paper without comment.

Chief Commissioner of Police,
Scotland Yard,
London SW1.

Sir,

I feel it is my duty to place before you certain details respecting the death of Miss Sally Brown. I had been staying with Miss Brown at the Paris Hotel for several weeks. On Friday evening, I went back there with her at about nine o'clock. I then left to keep an appointment in Paddington at ten. I did not go out of the main entrance of the hotel because I feared that I might be followed. I went down the service stairs and returned by the same way.

On my return, about an hour and a half later, I found Miss Brown in the condition of which you are aware. I realized that I would probably not be able to establish an alibi for the time of her death and also I might have to face the music on other charges.

Two people who I was to meet in Paddington did not appear. However, I was seen by a man I believe to be a CID officer. I had seen him a few days before outside the Luxor cinema in Croydon and also recently one night in Pont Street, when he followed the car in which I was travelling. He is clean shaven with fair hair cut short and a large build. He was driving a dark saloon car that was either black or dark blue. It was at the junction of Praed Street and Eastbourne Terrace that I spoke to him, when he stopped for the lights. I tried to detain him but he swerved across the road when the lights changed. I do not know his name but he spoke to a uniformed officer outside the Luxor.

On finding Miss Brown in the condition described, I hesitated what to do. But knowing that it was bound to look bad for me whatever happened, I packed my bags and left by the service stairs. It was after half-past eleven. In the past few hours, I have been uncertain whether to come forward or not. At present, I am reluctant to do so. If you find evidence that might exonerate me in respect of Miss Brown, then I would be prepared to surrender myself. If you wish to contact me over this, an announcement in the personal column of *The Times* will find me.

J. P. McIver.

Rutter handed the paper back.

'Mad,' Marriot said, 'completely mad. Does he suppose that we would be likely to advertise in the personal column – or that he could trust us if we did?'

'Not insane, though,' Rutter said thoughtfully.

Marriot jumped on it. 'Definitely not insane! Devious and deranged but not insane. When we catch this ray of sunshine, I want the bugger strung up, not eating his head off for the next forty years in a lunatic asylum at the public expense! This is the sort of case that the public wants settled in the good old-fashioned manner. I suggest we all put our talents to that forthwith. See what you can get out of this letter, Jack, for a start. What was he doing in Paddington, supposing the story is true? And who's this so-called CID officer? Phone round the divisions, if necessary.

See who was in Paddington on Friday night. And check this car. See who owns it.'

<h1 style="text-align:center">6</h1>

Alone in his office as the morning came to an end, Rutter read through the contents of the letter again. There was nothing more to be gained from it. Wherever McIver might have been on Saturday, there was no sign of him this Monday morning. Brodie knocked and entered.

'I've done a search, Jack. There's no unmarked car that was on patrol two nights ago where McIver described it in his letter.'

Rutter frowned. 'No one from Paddington saw him?'

'No duty CID officer in the Paddington area saw McIver nor anyone like him on Friday night. He's on their books over the trade in photographs around there, so they'd probably keep a note if he showed up. Anyway, if one of our chaps was there and also down near Croydon, he'd be part of this outfit, not division. There's no one here owning up to that. He's not one of ours, Jack, unless you reckon there's something very fishy going on.'

'All right, Frank,' Rutter said, 'let it ride for the moment. Anything else?'

Brodie had the air of a messenger who has kept the best till last. He sat down uninvited in the chair across the desk from Rutter.

'We've had a man on Blake. Nothing on Hallam. But first thing this morning Blake was out down the Strand at Somerset House. Registry of Births, Deaths, and Marriages. He was there waiting, almost fell through the door when they opened up. If our man was right, this was a very important errand that Mr Blake was running.'

'You think he could be fiddling a passport application somehow for himself or McIver?'

Brodie shook his head. 'Our man watched him round the corner of the stacks. Not hard to do. Blake was taking down volumes of birth registrations.'

'That could be a passport. Applying in the name of someone safely dead.'

'Jack! These were volumes for the 1880s! He's not more than half that age. Nor is McIver.'

'So he's tracing his family history.'

Brodie grinned. 'He took down the same volume for each year from the same bit of the alphabet. *Taplin* to *Taylor*. Nothing else. Just the names covered by that.'

'Tarrant?'

'It's got to be,' Brodie said enthusiastically.

'Too far back for Tarrant himself. Tarrant's father, perhaps, supposing that matters to anyone. If it was Mrs Tarrant he was checking, he'd need to look under her maiden name.'

Brodie smiled again. 'He would, if she was really Mrs Tarrant. I daresay Sonny's friends might cut you up small for mentioning it, but she's actually Miss Tarrant. No one's called her that for the past thirty or forty years. Sunshine was born on the wrong side of the blanket. I've just checked that with his CRO files. I reckon Blake was looking up the old woman's birth. The man we had watching him didn't want to get too close but he's positive it was Tarrant. And when Blake got to the volume with the old woman's entry, he stopped looking and left the building.'

'What in hell does he want? However Tarrant or his mother was born, why should it suddenly matter to Blake?'

'Same reason as the girl had that scrawl in her handbag. Reminding herself to find out about Mrs T's birthday.'

'But who the hell cares when the old trout's birthday was?'

Brodie shrugged. 'Someone cared all right, Jack. Maybe someone cared enough to do murder for it,' he said reasonably.

8

GOLDEN SANDS

I

McIver stepped on to the café terrace of the Regent Cinema, its tall windows rising over the tables with their sun umbrellas. He walked across and rested his arms on the smooth brass rail. A gull rose in a tiny feather of spray, far out beyond the pier and the miles of crowded sands, where the emerald sea darkened to a black horizon band. On the warm lunchtime air the bird's wings rose easily shoreward, light and rigid as a paper glider.

He knew that his best protection would be to have a woman on his arm. Give it time. The beach was strewn with girls in flower-pattern swimming costumes and young women in the tight elastic skins of their Martin White water-suits. Sun-suits and straw hats filled the Central Gardens, white flowers perfuming the hot shade. Rows of elderly men in panamas and their wives in wide-brimmed summer hats occupied the deck-chairs below the band-stand. Geraniums and the tall flowers of red-hot pokers framed a vista of blue water across the pier approach.

Death had no place in McIver's thoughts, as he gazed at this sunlit world of public gardens with their pampas grass and camellias, palm trees and Monterey cypress. On high ground, the Pavilion and the rock garden shimmered with heat above the glittering waters of the Channel. He had not as yet bothered to look at the morning papers for an account of the police investigation. The passport and cheque-book in his pocket were his security. Johnny McIver was dead, as surely as Solitaire. Give it a few more weeks and the law would assume that his body was lying undiscovered wherever it had fallen. For Wing Commander John 'Johnny' Walker, DFC, the fresh paint sparkled on the fretwork of the pier and the fish-scale silver of its roofs. The waves to the west were a glare of burnished silver as the sun slanted fiercely in the sky above Sandbanks.

The man who shadowed him was still there, of course, but McIver knew that the bulky figure in the light suit was no policeman. Better still, a man who had impersonated a plain-clothes officer was in no position to go running to the law. He was Tarrant's man or perhaps even 'Mr Sammy's'. It mattered very little which one. McIver looked down at him, seeing the same powerful moon face and flat blond hair. There was the same air of indifference on that face, not caring whether he was seen as he watched his prey. It was the steady gaze of impersonal contempt that McIver had first encountered outside the Luxor at Croydon. It was also the impassive look of the driver who had followed Blake and McIver from Temple Court to Constitution Hill. It was the casual hostility of the man who had wound up his car window and driven off, when McIver confronted him under the Paddington street lights. The life or death of the person looked at would be equally insignificant in those steady eyes. Not a policeman, then. A bent copper, above all others, would have let well alone after Solitaire's death. So long as he was just one of Tarrant's guide-dogs, there were easy ways of dealing with him.

McIver adjusted the blue and red silk of his Royal Air Force cravat, the tight smart fit of the dark blue blazer just outlining the silver cigarette case in his breast pocket. One or two of the women at the tables glanced up at him. Tall and personable, his breezy manner and casual charm matched the firm jaw, blue eyes, the fair hair in a matinée idol's wave across his skull.

The large man waited, as if on sentry-go, where the asphalt paths meandered among flowerbeds whose colours looked neat as embroidery from this height. He stood by a varnished board that had been pasted with theatre bills for the summer season. Lettered in blue and red, they announced Evelyn Laye with Frank Lawton in *Elusive Lady* or last week's appearance by Billy Cotton's Stage-Band at the Boscombe Hippodrome. From time to time, the man looked up at the café terrace of the Regent, as if to make sure that his quarry was still there.

McIver turned and leant his back against the rail. He had never believed in fate or any other power of its kind beyond thinking that if your number was up there was nothing to be done. Yet all roads had led him to this warm Bournemouth summer. So many threads were drawn together now. Tarrant's holiday apartment was in one of the new blocks that rose among Victorian lodges and villas on the West Cliff. The ticket which McIver found in Solitaire's handbag had been for Bournemouth. First class. Where would she have got the money to travel first class? Who but Tarrant would have bought it for her? He turned again and looked down into the gardens. The sunlit trap. But when such a trap failed, it might destroy the man who had set it.

Presently McIver walked back across the terrace and into the Regent lounge, through the warm draught of cooked meat and a faint perfume of Virginia tobacco-smoke. He ran down the main stairway and out into Westover Road. The crowds were moving towards the tile-hung department stores and the streets beyond the clock-tower as the lunch hour began. A good time to talk to Billy Blake. He made his way to the phone box by the pier turnstiles. Counting out a handful of coins, he lifted the black Bakelite receiver that was sticky from use by so many hands and waited for a voice.

'London, please,' he said to the operator, 'Kensington 9418.'

He listened, fed the coins in as instructed, heard the ringing answered and pressed Button A. In the background, he heard the murmur of lunchtime at the Copacabana Club.

'Wing Commander Walker,' he said smoothly, 'Flight Lieutenant Blake there, is he? . . . No? . . . Later, perhaps . . . Just a message . . . Would you tell him that I'll ring him at his hotel . . . Better have a time . . . This evening at six . . . Or any evening this week at six . . . I'll try until I catch him in . . . Thanks awfully, old boy . . . Cheerio . . .'

He stepped out into the warm tobacco-scented sunlight between the pier pavilions. Let them make what they could of that. Billy Blake had no hotel. But among the 'standing orders' of the group was an arrangement for making contact in an emergency, using the public telephone in the foyer of the Strand Palace Hotel. The furthest in the row of phone-booths was less frequently in use and both men had memorized its number. If the message to the club was delivered, Billy would be at the Strand Palace this evening, either in the booth or standing close by it. If he was not, then McIver had lost his ally.

He turned from the pier entrance and began to walk along the lower promenade of the West Undercliff. There was no sign of the large pale-faced man. He was there somewhere, of course, probably following at the upper level. On the warm sands, the squawking puppet-battle of a Punch and Judy show was surrounded by children. Further on a white-haired and black-coated man stood on a soap-box with a Biblical text unrolled on a stand beside him. He was flanked by several companions. The curious watched him from a distance.

'I call each of you!' the old man cried. 'You, poor sinner, hell-bound in Satan's captivity, lost in the meshes of sin and grief! Receive the gifts of joy, strength, gladness, holiness! Receive your risen and ascended Lord! . . .'

McIver stood among the little crowd, watching from the promenade. Looking round him, he still saw no sign of his shadow. He glanced up at the higher promenade of the Overcliff. Nothing. Nothing in either direction at the level of the sands.

'Oh – believe me!' cried the elderly evangelist. 'I could tell you such stories of what God's power has wrought in this very place. To each of you I promise it. Dear sinner, hear the Voice that sounds in your heart. In Me is strength, says that Voice. You are dissatisfied and restless. My people shall be satisfied with my goodness, says your Lord . . .'

McIver felt awkward and irritated by the old man's cry. He drew back towards the cliff, where the slope and the foliage would conceal him from above. He took a cigarette from his case, lit it and waited. The cigarette was half smoked when the pale blue car of the cliff railway rumbled gently downwards, passing its twin at the mid-point of the rust-coloured scar in the yellow gorse and scrub. The large pale man was there, sheltering at the centre of a dozen people who had stepped out on to the promenade. Then he turned and walked quickly away from where McIver was standing.

Got him! No policeman, no one but a beginner would have given himself away that easily, McIver thought, by making a panic move when his target was no longer in sight. He was Tarrant's man, surely, a sad relic of old-fashioned villainy that had died ten years before. It was time to finish the job. Time to give the poor mutt a surprise. Time to see him on his way. McIver smiled at the yellowing haze of the afternoon tide below him. A light breeze shivered the silver glare of the sea as he turned towards the black silhouette of the pier and the nutshell shapes of the distant rowing-boats. He whistled quietly to himself and walked away.

At the landing stage of the pier, the red-funnelled steamer

heaved slightly against the wooden timbers of the structure, its deck filling with passengers for the crossing to Swanage. McIver knew exactly what to do. His shadow had orders not to let him go and would obey to the letter. With a look of purpose, he walked quickly along the promenade to the pier gates, snapping his cigarette into the gutter. He passed through the turnstiles and on to the echoing planks. No need to glance round and see that the pale man was following – and probably sweating over the problem of how to join the steamer without being seen by his quarry.

But at the end of the pier McIver turned away from the landing-stage and began to walk back down the other side of the glass windbreak towards the turnstiles again. He grinned and thought that the large pale man's troubles were only just beginning. Lengthening his stride, he reached the turnstiles well ahead of his pursuer. In the warm enclosure of the pier entrance a board with yesterday's photographs pinned on it stood to one side. The little man with his camera waited to snap each face and press a ticket into the hand. McIver reached him first.

'Not me, old boy. But do us a favour. My friend coming down there. Tall chap with fair hair. I'd like one as a surprise for him. Four prints. I'll pick them up tomorrow.'

He pressed a pound note into the little man's palm and turned aside, into the doorway of the sweet stall. The large man was hurrying now. The turnstiles clattered as he pushed through. The photographer looked down into the viewfinder of his square box-camera and pressed the shutter-lever. At the same time, the large blond man turned and raised his crooked arm for concealment. The photographer aimed again, with difficulty because the range was close now and the big man was moving fast. But McIver saw that the shutter-lever was pressed.

The large man moved in, barging like a rugger player, to knock the photographer to the ground and try to tear the film from the camera. In that moment, a group of men and women pressed round the photographer. An assistant came out from a little room in the pier buildings to pin another row of damp prints on the board. There was a uniformed policeman by the phone box and a dozen witnesses. The trivial coincidences of the summer day turned the big man's aggression to panic. Perhaps he had already been photographed by one of the bystanders. In that case it was already too late to do anything about it. He glanced round once and began to walk quickly towards the laurel paths and rhododendrons of the central gardens.

McIver had expected to unnerve him but not as easily as this. In a moment, the hunter became the prey. The large man shoved through the crowds in the gardens. A voice shouted after him, 'I'll give you in charge, if I see you do that again!'

He began to run. McIver moved quickly. By sprinting along the upper garden level of the pavilion, he kept him in sight without following close. Who the hell was he? Why had the danger of being photographed driven him off like this? As a boy of sixteen, McIver had set a school record for the hundred yards which, he understood, had still not been broken. He could outrun the large man any day. He continued his cautious pursuit on the crowded pavements by the modernistic department stores and through the glass vault of the arcade with its window displays of jewellery and fashion on either side. The fugitive was winded by the time they came up past Bobby's. McIver drew back under the awning of an ice-cream parlour, its polished mirrors reflecting a cool marble interior. From this concealment, he watched as the man stumbled, rather than ran. But at that moment, the bulky figure in the light suit turned aside and sprang for the platform of a custard-yellow bus which was pulling out on the hill to the Lansdowne intersections.

McIver made a guess at the destination of the bus. He ran more leisurely after it, across the Lansdowne and into the shabby commercial length of Holdenhurst Road. Ahead of him was the Victorian red brick of the railway station. McIver followed more slowly. There was no sign of the large pale face among those at the booking-office. From the bridge above the platforms, it was simple to watch the steps on the London side. But the man was not there. McIver, at least, could not see him. The Waterloo express with its sleek green flanks steamed out twenty minutes later. Perhaps the bus had not taken him to the station after all. All the same, McIver thought, the large man could hardly run back to Tarrant and explain his blunder.

But why should the hunter now be so scared? Who was likely to see his photograph on the board? Who would care that he was in Bournemouth?

Before he left the station, McIver bought an *Evening Standard* and a *Bournemouth Evening Echo*. He unfolded the Bournemouth paper first and read it as he walked back towards the Lansdowne and along Bath Road to the promenade. There was a headline on a centre page: HOTEL MURDER: POLICE SEEK MAN WITH MILITARY GAIT. McIver smiled as he read. Military gait? It was absurd and merely showed how far they were from having anything on him. No name was given and it seemed to him that he was reading about some other man and some other death. The *Standard*'s headline was on the front page but far down in a corner. WOMAN DANCER MURDER HUNT. They seemed to suggest it was not of great importance. A cab-driver in the Strand had phoned Scotland Yard and reported a suspicious passenger. The man had been questioned and released. The truth was, McIver thought, that they weren't looking very hard. The way the papers reported it, the police were waiting for the answer to fall into their laps. By next week, the story would have been buried by other news and bigger crimes.

He paused in a shop doorway to light a cigarette, the petrol-scented flame of the smooth lighter sheltered from the mild breeze that carried across the sands. With a sense of euphoria, he opened the Bournemouth paper to see what it had to offer him. Boscombe Hippodrome. He thought of the dancing twins, Louise and the other girl, whose act had followed Solitaire's at the Copacabana. If he needed a partner on his arm and a model for his camera, she was two for the price of one. Better than a popsy who would cost a packet to take round the town and show nothing in return. There was no reason why Wing Commander 'Johnny' Walker should not try his snapshots on a glamour mag. If Louise danced in the same costume, she was half-way to taking her clothes off already.

2

With time on his hands before he could phone Billy Blake, McIver surveyed the talent at the Pavilion tea-dance. There was nothing doing. To the tango rhythm of Albeniz, young men steered their girls across the narrow polished boards of the dance floor, surrounded by individual tea-tables. The silver-plated instruments of the band on its dais, the square glass-lined pillars, and high stucco ceiling reflected the marine brilliance of the sky. Here and there, pairs of girls danced together. McIver smiled and watched cautiously. It would be too risky. He needed a girl with no attachments, certainly not a second girl without a companion. Louise was the best bet. Louise, with her show opening at any minute, would be too busy to pay much attention to the news. But these were girls with time to read the papers. To the girls on the sunlit dance floor, he was a stranger, a man from anywhere. To Louise, he was the good-natured acquaintance from the Copacabana. That was the other thing, McIver thought. None of the newspaper reports had said anything about Solitaire's appearance at the Copacabana. There was no reason for Louise to make any connection. With her on his arm, he would surely be safe.

He went back early to the Adelaide Hotel, the room with its gas fire and a view from the west cliffs across the sparkling tide to the Isle of Wight. It was a decent medium-sized hotel with a few single guests and married couples.

McIver was aware that he had made something of a hit as Wing Commander Walker, easy-going and approachable, a man still young to hold so high a rank. He had decided to emphasize his modern outlook, rather as the Prince of Wales did before the war. It would look good when someone discovered that he had the name of the prince's equerry.

At the dressing-table he caught himself whistling, 'Every little breeze seems to whisper "Louise" . . .' and grinned at his reflection. On the pretext of having sent his suit to the cleaners, he would wear his mess gear for dinner. Three rings on each cuff for a wingco. The grey-blue tunic was also stitched with two Far East campaign ribbons and the diagonal striping of the Distinguished Flying Cross. It would do no harm to show them before the bills came in and he had to duck out.

At six o'clock he cantered easily downstairs, turning a handful of coins in his trouser pocket. The empty lounge was large enough to make an intimate dance floor when the carpet was rolled back. A large walnut-cabinet radiogram was pumping out the music of Harry Davidson and his orchestra. McIver turned aside to the telephone booth, closed its door, and picked up the black Bakelite receiver.

'London, please,' he said when the operator replied, 'Strand 4821.'

He heard the bell sounding in another world, where the evening traffic rumbled and fumed between Charing Cross and Fleet Street. He thought of the smart modern lobby of the Strand Palace in its caramel-coloured marble, the elegance of the Savoy across the busy street, the crisp new suits and blazers on the dummies in the Savoy Tailors' Guild . . . The phone rang a dozen times before Billy answered.

'Hello, old boy,' McIver said cheerfully. 'How's the weather your end?'

'Not good,' Blake said quietly. 'I'd no idea what the hell happened to you. I've had visitors. They're not with me just now, of course, as far as I can see. Listen, Johnny. It wasn't you, was it?'

'Don't be a prat, Billy! Of course it wasn't me! I was out, supposed to be meeting Champion and his money-changer in Paddington. They never showed up. When I got back, she was dead and both our shares of the money had gone. I can't prove a bloody thing.'

'Then there's something you'd better know,' Blake said. 'We've been screwed. Both of us. I warned you about Hallam.'

'Sorry, Bills. Don't get you.'

'You remember a number that was the same as an old lady's birthday?'

'Sure.'

'Who told you it was the same?'

'Roddy told . . .' McIver checked himself. 'Roddy told a certain young lady of our acquaintance. She told me.'

'I was asked by a visitor yesterday why she should have written a note reminding herself to check on the date of a certain old lady's birthday,' Blake said. 'My visitors had found it written on a piece of paper in her handbag. Mrs T's birthday, it said. With a question-mark.'

'She never said anything about it to me. You sure?'

'The face who asked me about it was certain sure. Anyhow, there was such a smell about the whole thing that I went to check the registers of births at Somerset House. The number you were given isn't her birthday. It's three years out, Johnny. And the wrong month as well. Hallam reckoned he got the date for us from those records. He can't have done. Someone told him the right number for the combination and he made up the bit about the birthday. Where does that put him? In Tarrant's pocket!'

McIver listened with the feeling he used to have at school when he roused himself from a reverie during class to discover that he was being asked a question to which he had missed the answer. Blake's voice was back again.

'Who do you reckon told Hallam, Johnny? Must be Tarrant. If

151

that little shit Hallam knew the right number, it was only because Tarrant or someone told him. He simply can't have got it from anywhere else. He certainly didn't get it from those records of the old woman's date of birth. And if he was told a number so that you could use it, that means he was working for the other side all the time. So we're both screwed, Johnny.'

'Wait a minute,' McIver said. His face in the little mirror of the booth looked blankly back at him. 'There's no sense in it.' Nothing made any sense.

'Johnny?' Blake said. 'Do you get what I'm saying? If it was all set up, you were meant to open that lock. The stuff you took to Champion could have been duds for all we know. Don't you see? And whoever our young lady let into that hotel room of yours must have been someone she knew. Someone who even knew where the money was likely to be. Tarrant's got that money back, Johnny. All that you and she had. And he's probably got whatever Hallam had. For all you know, Mr Champion's money-changer could be his man as well. Christ, Johnny! He's been on to us from the beginning, thanks to Hallam. He's screwed us both and left you to face the music over the girl. Don't you see?'

McIver drew a breath. 'Listen, Billy. I need time to think.'

'Johnny! There isn't time! Tarrant reckoned we were the opposition and he's screwed us! You worst of all! Perhaps the man you met at Champion's screwed us. Perhaps they both did it. Are they friends or enemies with each other, after all? I don't know. All it's cost them is the money I've still got. Cheap at the price. If word gets round, no one's going to try touching Tarrant again. No one's ever going to squeal on him either.'

'Any news about Champion? The shop reckoned he'd never existed.'

'He's gone, old son. Vanished.'

'We'll talk tomorrow, Billy. Same time, same place. And there's one bit of news from Tarrant's holiday town. That face we saw outside the Luxor that afternoon has been following me here. He's definitely not law. I even saw him in Paddington that night we've been talking about. He could have been tailing me there to give someone else the OK about the girl being on her own. There was a bloke hanging about opposite the hotel when I left earlier on. All it needed was the big man to make a call to him in a public box. The one that was hanging about could have been up the service stairs of the hotel and done it before I was half-way back. For that matter, the big bloke in the car could have driven back and helped him, easily. I saw him off today. He took to his heels and ran. I'm going to find out why he was so scared of being photographed. I reckon it's because someone knows him. Knows him well. He ran like he could be arrested for murder or something. There's too many questions in this, old boy. I'm going to find some answers.'

'Hallam,' Blake said bitterly. 'That's answer number one. He's got to be.'

The telephonic pips sounded. 'Hang up, Billy,' McIver said. 'Give me until tomorrow or the day after.'

He pushed open the door of the booth and went into the carpeted lounge. The walnut radiogram was still pumping out Harry Davidson. At the little bar with its string of coloured bulbs, Phyllis Barnes sat on a stool, staring at the coloured glass. She was wearing a dark blue dress with a pleated skirt and belted waist. He put her at about thirty-three and thought that it showed a little. Perhaps it was just that the pancake make-up formed one or two tiny cracks. The cloud of fluffy dark curls with team-captain features suggested Worrals of the WAAFS or some other heroine of wartime fiction. Someone had mentioned that she had been an Army driver. Yet, as he walked across, McIver was surprised by the thought that she was two or three years his elder.

'Evening, Mrs B,' McIver said cheerily. 'What's your poison?'

She looked up ruefully but he could see that she was taking in the pressed air-force blue of the uniform, the young wing commander's cuff-rings, the three medal ribbons on the breast.

'That's very good of you,' she said lazily, 'I'll have a sherry if I may. Not too dry. Dry ones taste like lighter fuel to me. Something special this evening?'

'No,' McIver laughed self-consciously, 'civvy suit at the cleaners. I'm dining in tonight. Thought I might try to catch a show afterwards. Second house at the Boscombe Hippodrome, perhaps. I've got a chum who's in it.'

'In the show?' As she spoke he heard the tell-tale hesitation in her voice. Mrs Barnes was prepared to be impressed.

'Yes. She's a dancer. Only a small part but she's definitely on the way up.'

He turned to the boy behind the bar and took the glasses.

'Thanks, old man. Put them on my crime sheet, would you? I'll catch the bank tomorrow and settle up.'

He saw the boy's eyes also taking in the medal ribbons and knew there would be no argument. Then McIver carried the glasses across to a table in the bay-window, overlooking the evening sea, and waited for Phyllis Barnes to sit down.

'I say,' he said suddenly, 'I've got two tickets – couple of comps from my chum, actually. I don't suppose you'd care to have the other?'

Phyllis Barnes looked at him closely but she was smiling at his nerve. 'You mean alone? Go with you alone?'

McIver spread out his hands. 'It's only the Boscombe Hippodrome, old girl. Not exactly Port Said after dark.'

'And there's my husband . . .'

'He's not here, is he?'

'Not until the weekend. I'm just wondering what he'd say.'

McIver wrinkled his nose at her like a mischievous but decent schoolboy. 'Tell you what,' he said, 'I won't tell him if you don't.'

She lifted her head back and laughed at him. That was a good sign. Almost always. 'All right,' she said, 'but no funny business. I've seen some fast workers but you'd leave them all behind.'

McIver raised his fingers in a Boy Scout's pledge. 'Promise,' he said. 'Honest. I wouldn't know how.'

The encounter was everything he had hoped. If ever the police questioned Phyllis Barnes, she would name every other man of her acquaintance as a possible murderer before she thought of Wing Commander 'Johnny' Walker. Not that she could be more than a companion, a 'pal' as they said. With a husband in the background, anything more serious would be asking for trouble. While she was getting ready, he phoned the Boscombe Hippodrome and arranged to collect the tickets on arrival. That would look good, as if they were complimentary tickets always held for him. Despite the news from Billy Blake, he felt that something had been accomplished by the time that he ordered a taxi.

No two ways, Phyllis Barnes blossomed with the pleasure of being seen on the arm of a young wing commander with his DFC ribbon. They sat in the front row of the stalls. Louise appeared in a dance number, where half the young women were little Dutch boys and the rest were little Dutch girls, white hats and pinafore bands with either short blue skirts or short blue pants.

> Down by the old canal,
> The old folk used to say,

154

> There was a moonbeam path
> To light the lovers' way . . .

The energy of the young voices was a little harsh and they were
not quite synchronized, like dancing-school girls in a pantomime.
But as the ensemble clicked and clacked about the stage, the
childish lyric was accompanied by bare thighs, pants that were
skin-smooth and short skirts that flew tantalizingly. He guessed
Louise would see him through the footlight's glare. As she looked
in his direction, McIver raised his hand in a half-salute. She
seemed puzzled at first and then, recognizing him despite the
uniform, she smiled before looking away again. Phyllis Barnes
noticed and looked aside at him, as if surprised that he had not
spun her a yarn after all.

It went like a charm. After the show, he took her round and
introduced her to Louise. The girl was reassured by seeing him
with Phyllis Barnes and the woman was impressed by his famili-
arity with the young dancer. If those who hunted him imagined
that his companions had the least cause for suspicion, they were
making one of their habitual mistakes.

In the taxi that took them back from Boscombe to the West
Overcliff, he was on his best behaviour. The women of his experience were, on the whole, more inclined to respond than to have
a row in the presence of the taxi driver. But this time McIver
knew better. Put a foot wrong and it wouldn't just be a slapped
face and a slammed door. More likely his wrists strapped behind
his back and rough weave of a rope round the sensitive skin of
his neck. Not that it need come to rope, he thought. You could
do it yourself with a silk tie before they got to you. Chaps certainly
did. The fellow at Imphal who got the jitters about flying
again . . . He turned and grinned at Phyllis Barnes in the faint
reflection of the lamps along the East Overcliff. Across the water,
a coppery moon glittered on the dark movement of the waves
from its ascent beyond the Needles and the faint outline of the
Isle of Wight.

'That was a bit of all right,' he said bravely. 'We ought to do
it again somewhen.'

She smiled at him and he knew that she would try it again,
almost anywhen during her husband's weekday absences.

Alone in his room, McIver got out the pre-war Leica, a silver-
bodied camera with black facings. Its f1.5 Xenon lens might be

good enough to take photographs by natural light in the room on a sunny day. Or it might even be cheap enough to hire a studio from a commercial photographer with a couple of photo-flood lamps for the afternoon thrown in. McIver tried various angles through the viewfinder. In his mind he rehearsed the names of the more reputable magazines who would pay for images of Louise. How could she object, when dressed in her Dutch costume of pants and blouse? Nudity would be useful but not essential. As McIver knew better than most of her admirers, even in her dancing costume, the right posture and the right look in her eyes would blow the brains of Mr Champion's customers clean out of their skulls.

Better still, there might be another girl from the show who would partner her. A little Dutch girl and a little Dutch boy who also happened to be a girl. He grinned and thought that Mr Champion's readers would see the point. So would the more respectable market for *Lilliput* and *Men Only*. When that happened, Wing Commander 'Johnny' Walker had only to become plain Johnny Walker, photographer. If there was a living in it, the police might go on looking for John Patrick McIver until they got tired and gave up. And they certainly would tire of it. Despite the public image of stern-faced men implacably hunting down their prey, regardless of time and cost, McIver knew the truth. In six months there would be more urgent matters than the death of Solitaire. The inquiry would be scaled down. After twelve months, he would be unlucky if a single policeman was still looking for him full time. Keep his nose clean for a year or two and that would be the end of the matter.

This view of the future left Tarrant and possibly Roddy Hallam to be considered, if Billy Blake was right. But McIver had learnt a little jungle training at Imphal and he knew that worrying about Hallam was a waste of time. Never tangle with a snake. Cut the head off. That meant Tarrant.

He took down a suitcase from the bedroom wardrobe. It was finished in polished calf with silver-coloured locks. McIver had even had the initials 'J. W.' stamped on it in black. Cost a little but meant a lot. He unlocked the case and took out a dressing-table casket whose shape might have graced a pharaoh's tomb. This one was made of dark brown Bakelite with a deep green knob on its lid, a handkerchief box that had been a birthday present. He took the lid off. Under two folded handkerchiefs lay the heavy metal stub of the sawn-off Eley revolver. In the angle of its barrel and stock was a rolled handkerchief with eight rounds of ammunition, the cartridge bases filed to fit the .455. There were enough bullets for Tarrant and Hallam. Enough to have a couple spare. McIver smiled at the melodrama of the gunman's one-way ticket. Still it was an option, if things got too hot.

The oil from the old revolver had marked the handkerchiefs and stained the bottom of the box. He wiped it off and put two clean handkerchiefs on top, before returning it to the locked suitcase and going to bed.

9

GLAMOUR PUSS

1

McIver wrinkled his eyes at the girl and moved his lips slightly with the cigarette held between them. It was the smile he had grown up with, the one that girls were supposed to like.

'That's smashing,' he said, looking through the viewfinder again, 'that's an absolute cracker.'

Louise looked back over her shoulder, the dark-lashed saucer eyes and impudently pretty face ready for anything. To one side, at shoulder height, she held a beach-ball whose segments in blue, red and yellow made it look like a multi-coloured pumpkin. Her body, in the tight blue pants and sweater of thin wool, was twisted round a little to emphasize the lines of her figure. With one foot cocked up behind her, she was caught running away into a cyclorama sky of Saharan blue. The studio sand on which she posed was almost white in the glare of the photo-flood bulbs.

McIver felt the perspiration gathering in the heat of the hired studio, at the back of the commercial shabbiness of Holdenhurst Road. The sharp fit of his dark blue blazer was immaculate, except where the contour of the thin silver cigarette case was outlined as usual in his breast pocket.

'Super,' he said, 'hold that once more and then we're done.'

Louise tensed herself as the shutter-button clicked. McIver knew it was good, this time, and his enthusiasm was not just the photographer's fanning of his model. The girl with her cropped dark hair and impish prettiness appeared to be running, almost airborne. He had caught the energy of the bare thighs, the silhouette of the breasts as she half turned, and an agile contortion of the hips. This was a cut above Mr Champion's trade, better

158

than anything in *Lilliput* for the last twelvemonth. It was superbly sexy, McIver thought, but with nothing in it that the law could complain about. Louise was wearing no less than on the stage of the Boscombe Hippodrome. The pose was everything.

'Finished?' she asked with mock weariness, lowering her foot to the ground and turning round.

'Yep,' McIver said, giving her a non-committal hug, 'that's it. Absolutely great. And you own half of the action, remember. Take this, if you want it. Any lawyer can tell you it's as good as a legal contract. Like writing your will on a cigarette packet. Still valid.'

From his side pocket, he drew the letter he had shown her before they began. It was written on the notepaper of the National Sporting Club, which McIver had purloined during his meeting there with Champion's money-changer. It was addressed to Wing Commander J. G. Walker at his Bournemouth hotel, the envelope torn open so that it made illegible the round post-mark which would otherwise have shown that it was posted in Bournemouth. In the letter, Major 'Dicky' Doyle wrote affably to his friend, 'Johnny' Walker, explaining that he had just landed a cushy number as picture editor of *Lilliput*. He commissioned McIver, as a pre-war freelance photographer, to produce a set of six pin-up photographs for the next issue. The fee of £300 would be paid in equal parts to the photographer and model. McIver doubted whether Louise had made £150 in the last twelvemonth.

'I can't take your letter,' Louise said, laughing at the absurdity of it.

McIver smiled his favourite smile again.

'Fair enough, old thing. Just so long as you remember that a bargain's a bargain.'

The next letter would be the one in which 'Dicky' Doyle was bowled over by the photographs. There might even be a small payment on account. In this second letter, Doyle would wonder if the model might consider being paid more for something a little bolder. It might not work but, with Louise, McIver guessed there was a good chance. Even now, she left the door of the little cubicle half-open as she went to change into her dress.

'Johnny? Would your friend Dicky use more than one set of pictures in his magazine?'

McIver smiled, to himself this time.

'That's the thing, old girl. He might very well, if they were a bit different. In any case, he's got a lot of other contacts. Paris and New York, as well as London. He started as a photographer with *La Vie Parisienne* before the war. If that's what you want, he's the one to put you on the map.'

Louise came out in a polka-dot blue and white dress.

'Well,' she said uncertainly, 'at that rate it beats hoofing round the stage twice a night.'

Among the props in the hired studio was a basket-chair with a fan-shaped peacock-tail back. It stood with this back to the camera. Beyond it was a dark-veneered walnut dressing-table with square drawer-handles in dark green glass and a modernistic triple mirror. The model who occupied the basket chair would be seen from every angle.

McIver guided Louise. She knelt on a cushion which filled the seat of the chair, her hips raised, embracing the back of the chair and her head turned aside on the basket-weave.

'Like this?' she asked.

'Like that,' he said softly, 'that's absolutely perfect.'

Louise waited for him to walk back to the camera on its tripod. Then she knelt upright, pulled the dress up, raised her arms and tugged it off over her head. Holding it to one side, she let it fall to the floor. Behind the lattice of the chair-back, she made several quick movements with a comb. There was no protest and no hesitation. Louse had made up her mind to do what must be done. She knelt forward again with her arms about the chair-back and her head resting on it in profile.

McIver switched on the photo-flood lamps in their blinding umbrellas of silver foil. They shone on the girl from either side behind her, so that her profile was half in silhouette. Their brilliance fell full on the sleek-fleshed pallor of her body as it was reflected in the triple mirror. He adjusted the focus of the camera-lens for a softer image of the profile and sharp reflection in the mirrors. This was art, he thought, something too good for old Champion. It was enough to knock dead any reader of *Lilliput* or *Men Only*.

'That's it,' he murmured to the girl, 'that's absolutely it. Keep it like that.'

The shutter fell with a metallic click. She was so relaxed in this improbable position that she might have chosen it for rest.

'One more,' he said softly, 'and one more again for luck.'

Before the hour was up, he had captured images of Louise

sitting nude on the chair with her hands demurely folded in her lap as she gazed into the mirrors. Then she appeared with the coloured beach-ball, always holding it to cover whatever the censor might object to.

Afterwards she picked the summer frock up from the floor and went into the cubicle to dress. She was a little subdued but as much part of the conspiracy as he.

'What happens to the photographs after they've been in the magazine?'

'They're yours, old girl. They can't be used by anyone but you, anywhere, or any time.'

'Why not? What's to stop them?'

McIver laughed. 'The law's to stop them. They're your property. In any case, once we've done the prints for the magazine, I'm going to give you the negatives.'

'And the ones kneeling on the chair . . . ?'

'They're terrific,' he said reassuringly, 'wait till you see them. Of course, we won't use them if you don't like them. You're the boss. But, in any case, no one could identify you through the basketwork. All I could see was that it was a pretty girl's face. Apart from that, it could have been anyone.'

He switched off the photo-flood lamps, breathing the hot-metal air of their reflector shades. It was as if Louise had shared his thought of her images captured in the camera, her youth and reputation in the possession of a man she scarcely knew. But she was over that now, he guessed. Of the girls who had been his models, only Solitaire had shown no reservations. Still, all of them had been happy in the end.

'Tell you what,' he called, 'we'll celebrate on Sunday evening. Dinner and drinks. I know somewhere we can go dancing, if you like. OK?'

She appeared in the doorway of the cubicle, ready to leave.

'Sunday?'

'Not otherwise engaged, I hope.'

'No,' she said hastily, 'of course not. We work through the next week's numbers on Monday morning. They leave us free on Sunday.'

'Right-o. I'll book dinner at my hotel. I'm living there until I can find the place I want to buy. It's pricey but they look after you pretty decently.'

McIver opened the door. He had paid the studio hire in

advance. 'Best lock up the old home,' he said, 'I paid a packet for the equipment in here.'

Louise watched him close the door. 'You must have done well to afford all this.'

'I do all right,' he said, and winked at her. 'Let's go down the cocktail bar of the Royal Bath, if you've got the time.'

They walked up to the Lansdowne junction and turned to the promenade.

'Just a jiffy,' McIver said presently, 'a spot of business while I remember it.'

He left her standing by the pavilion steps and walked across to the pier entrance. Three photographs of the large fair-haired man were on the board. In two of them the camera had been aiming at someone else and the man was merely there in the background. They had been taken as he went on to the pier and before he noticed the photographer. In one of them he had moved so quickly that his face was like a monochrome flash of flame. Another showed him only from the side and at a distance. But the third had been taken in the moment that he moved into focus. It was perfect. No mistaking him in that. McIver walked across to the little booth and saw the photographer through its open window.

'Thanks a million, old man,' he said.

'You still want those photos? Two of them were a dead loss.'

'Okey-doke. I'll take the other.'

The little man in his trilby hat and shiny suit came out and unpinned the print from the board. 'I can't say I care for your friends,' he said. 'As well he never damaged the camera or you'd have heard more about it. Him barging about like that.'

The photographer handed him the prints in a brown trade-envelope. McIver guessed that it was his generous payment in advance which had saved him trouble over the big man's aggression.

'Not much of an advertisement,' the photographer said, nodding at the prints. 'I suppose this is funny business, is it?'

McIver smiled at him. 'Funny business?'

'Yes,' the little man said, 'I know it when I see it. I've had one or two people wanted to use pictures of mine for divorce cases. That sort of thing. I don't do that. Never did. Never won't.'

McIver laughed, handing the man a banknote as though paying him for the first time. 'Not this one,' he said. 'He's never been married, let alone divorced. Come to that, I don't think his parents were ever married either. Sort of family tradition.'

He walked back to Louise and took her arm. They went up the steps, into the warmth and lunchtime chatter of the Royal Bath Hotel's lounge bar. McIver drew his arm away and hugged Louise gently.

'What's your poison?' he asked.

2

Children's voices, harsh and high as gull-cries, rose among the rush and swirl of waves on firm sand. A sunlit water-pattern played on the high ceiling of the hotel room. McIver stubbed his cigarette out and pulled himself off the bed. One thing sure, he was going to have to be careful about money. The thirty pounds he'd had in London were less than twenty now. When the photographs of Louise were ready, he really would try them on the glamour mags. But that would take time. He could take copies to several of the offices. Offer them for sale on the spot. Ready cash. But that meant going back to London. With a cheque-book and a passport in Walker's name, he could pay his hotel bill. But once the cheque bounced, the police would know. Walker would be finished. But, of course, they wouldn't know who Walker was.

He paced up and down by the window, unaware of the sunlit beaches and glittering tide as he tried to put his plan in sequence. It was too late for honesty, too late to tell the truth about Solitaire. No one would believe that. It was asking to be strung up by old man Pierrepoint or whoever did the hangman's job now. What then? Go back to London. Cash a cheque at every bank he could, using the passport to prove he was Walker. Take the money and go Union Castle to Cape Town. Find a job. Work the glamour trade from there. Either that or turn on the gas fire, lie down on the rug, and get it over with.

Louise was no good for money, having none herself. In any case, if he tried something there, it would give the game away, the game of being a successful freelance photographer. There was Phyllis Barnes. That was more likely. She was older than he. Old enough to be flattered by his attentions. She had a husband, absent on business except at the weekends. There was money there, somewhere, McIver felt sure of it.

And there was Tarrant, of course. Tarrant, by some freak of geography, was not a mile from him now in the new Albeira apartment block on the West Cliff. Tarrant had something to answer for, something to pay. If Tarrant's man was so scared of being photographed at the pier, that meant Tarrant had reason to be a little scared as well. Perhaps the photograph was worth money to Tarrant. McIver decided to try that before having any more thoughts about taking the gas pipe. In any case, he must move soon, before Tarrant went back to London. Hit him while he was still on holiday and off his guard. And then there was Billy Blake. Good old Billy, the one person in London he could trust. The one man who might see him right. Talk to Billy first. McIver glanced at his watch and saw that it was just after half-past five.

Standing before the mirror, he combed his hair sleekly into place and pulled his jacket straight. The bar downstairs was empty but someone had left the evening paper on a high stool. He sat by the window and opened it. Nothing on the front page. The story was dying fast. At the foot of the third page there was a report that filled three inches of a narrow column. The police investigation into the death of Sally Brown, known professionally as 'Solitaire', was still continuing. Several of her male friends had been interviewed. The police were anxious to trace John Patrick McIver for questioning. It was a shock to see his name in print. Still, it was bound to happen sooner or later. Best to get it over and out of the public mind. Thank God they hadn't used a picture of him. Not that the mug-shot after the medals and uniform charge last year looked much like him. The final bit of the report was not so good. Mr McIver had shared a hotel room with the dead woman. That was as close as they dared go to saying that he'd done it. What were the rules of the game? They weren't allowed to say you'd done it before they arrested you. Couldn't have a fair trial in that case. Something of that sort.

Would they be watching the London railway stations? Probably. If he was going to bounce cheques off a string of banks in one day, it might be best to travel up as far as the first underground station. Wimbledon or Richmond. Then mingle with the crowds on the tube. Billy Blake would tell him what the best thing was. Billy would see him right.

He waited impatiently for six o'clock, counting out change from one hand to another. He watched the hands of the little clock above the bar touch the hour. There was movement behind the shutter and a clink of glasses. Bar-room clocks were always kept fast. Give it five more minutes to make sure that Billy was in place. Then he went into the telephone booth and closed the door.

'London, please,' he said as the operator's voice replied, 'Strand 4821.'

He listened, fed the coins into the machine as she instructed him and waited to press the silver button on the black coin-box. He heard the sharp ringing of the bell far off in the Strand Palace Hotel. It rang half a dozen times, and in his mind he saw Billy Blake turning from the marble lobby towards the line of glass-fronted booths. About now. The phone rang and rang. But it would be all right. Billy was not the sort to let him down. Anyway, if he was caught, Billy would be in the clag as well. Billy knew it. Come on, Billy. Come on, old son. The phone rang again. It was bound to be all right. They had nothing on Billy. Nothing.

'I'm sorry, caller. There is no reply from that number.'

'Could you try again? No . . . Hang on. Get me Kensington 9418.'

Another phone began to ring, its tone identical with the first. There was a click as it was lifted and a faint tidal sound of voices in the background of the Copacabana Club.

'Wing Commander John Walker. Flight Lieutenant Blake there, is he? Billy Blake? Well, has he been in today? Right. I see. If he should come in, tell him I rang, there's a good scout. I'll try his hotel at six tomorrow evening.'

McIver put the phone down and counted his change. Enough for one more go anyway.

'Operator? Try Strand 4821 for me again, would you?'

The coins dropped on to the metallic heap of change. At the far end, the phone rang twice. 'Hello, Billy?'

'I'm sorry, sir. This is a public call-box in a hotel lobby.'

'I know that. This is urgent. Family matter. Can you see a chap standing anywhere in the lobby? Well-built, about thirty, RAF moustache?'

'Sorry, sir. There's no gentleman of any description standing in the lobby at the moment.'

For the first time, McIver felt a chill certainty that something had gone wrong with Billy Blake. The lifeline had broken.

'Operator? Can you get me London again? Bayswater 9090. I've got about enough change for three minutes.'

For half a minute the phone rang in Billy Blake's digs. McIver could see it in his mind, the black receiver on a shelf at the front of the communal stairs. Billy's two rooms on the next floor of the tall Victorian house in the long terrace opposite Kensington Gardens. A woman's voice answered. McIver spoke quickly.

165

'Hello. Can I speak to Billy Blake, please? When will he be back? . . . When did he move? . . . Yesterday? Who collected his things? . . . Yes but which man? . . . Isn't there someone there who could tell me who the man was that collected Mr Blake's things after he left? . . . Well, did this person look like a policeman or someone official when you saw him? . . . All right, then was he a large man? Very large with fair hair? No. A small chap with dark hair? Might have been called Roddy? All right. Thanks, anyway.'

He put the phone down. That was that. If ever he was on his own, it was now. If Tarrant had paid a visit, Billy could be dead. If not, he could be answering questions to the law. Or else he might just be so scared that he'd taken cover. With more than a thousand pounds as his share of the loot, Billy could be on the other side of the world in a few days.

Billy wasn't the sort to let him down. Unless. Unless, of course, they had made the poor mutt believe that his friend Johnny really had killed his friend Solitaire. Evidence. Newspaper stories. God knows how Billy had been got at. Perhaps, in the end, he just ran for it. Perhaps Billy was the one destined for sunshine and flowers in the Cape. Or perhaps he was lying dead where no one would find him. McIver felt no resentment nor grief. What the hell did it matter? One way or the other, he thought, the lifeline to London was gone.

He went out and sat at the table again. The evening paper was still there. When a body was found, they reported it. There was nothing. Not a word about Billy Blake. No news of an arrest. In any case, they wouldn't hold Billy for two days and move his things out of his digs as well.

He went up to his room and took down the suitcase from the top of the wardrobe. Unlocking it, he opened the dressing-table casket. The Eley .455 lay stubby and polished in its old silk scarf. If he was going to swing for Solitaire, he'd swing for Tarrant too. For the moment, he put the gun back in its hiding-place.

10

DANCING IN THE DARK

1

The crooner's voice from the radiogram in the bar carried across the tables of the hotel dining-room.

> If I should ever make you cry.
> I'll say 'sorry' bye and bye . . .

McIver and Louise sat with their coffee-cups, the only couple still there.

> If you'll let me promise you,
> All the sweet things that we'll do . . .

He put his hand on hers.

'All I'm saying is that this could open the way to bigger things. How much do they pay you for a week at the Boscombe Hippodrome?'

'Seven pounds.'

'And when the season's over?'

She shrugged but made no answer.

'Exactly!' McIver's hand tightened a little on hers. 'Where's the fun in being on your uppers? Just hoping to find something in the pantomime season.'

'I shan't starve,' she said indignantly. 'The other girls get work in shops or hotels between shows.'

'And some do worse than that,' he said significantly, 'only they're not likely to tell you. What I'm talking about is regular work in a dance company. Posing at the back of a Windmill dance is nothing different to what you're doing now. It's all in the mind. Nothing to be ashamed about. The dance routines there are only what you're doing already. Thing is, once you're part of a regular company, you're made for life. No more touting for work when the summer ends. Being a model in a decent magazine could be your big break.'

She blushed a little at this. The wide blue eyes showed indignation as she looked up at him.

'I'm not ashamed. That's not the point. It's just that I'd no idea that people buy these magazines everywhere. That's all. Every railway station and bookshop.'

The corners of his eyes crinkled in their practised smile.

'But that's what you want, old thing. Once you're that popular, you can name your price. And if you're afraid your local vicar might see you, he won't see anything unless he reads the magazine anyway. So where does that put him? You're not drinking your cherry brandy.'

She drew her hand away. 'I don't think I want any more. You drink it, if you like. I'm not talking about a local vicar. I've got a family too. I don't want to upset them.'

He smiled at her again and took the unwilling hand. 'But it was all right yesterday morning, wasn't it? It'll be all right tomorrow morning. You'll see. Sleep on it. Give it that long.'

Louise looked away slightly but said nothing. Presently they got up and went into the bar, so that the waitress could clear their table. The walnut radiogram was playing the 'Anniversary Waltz'. Someone had rolled back the carpet and half a dozen couples were moving like clockwork models round the polished parquet. McIver squeezed the girl's hand. 'We'll put some life into this.'

He stood by the radiogram, smiling as he waited for the number to finish. When the record ended, he replaced it with a foxtrot rendering of 'Doin' What Comes Naturally'. Steering Louise to the centre of the floor, he saw the other dancers draw back and watch as the girl's feet flew to the rhythm and McIver kept pace.

McIver was good at it, aware of the looks of admiration from those who were now spectators. It was only half for the speed of his feet in the dance. The rest was for a young-looking wing commander with the Distinguished Flying Cross who had been briefly equerry to the Prince of Wales but who had no side to him whatever. McIver guessed that he could have had his pick of any woman in the room just then. He felt on top of the world.

168

Her sudden unease over the photographs nagged him as he grinned at her as they danced at one another, the cigarette still clipped in his mouth. Poor girl probably needed cheering up. Nothing more than that. There was a burst of applause from the other guests at the end. Louise looked brighter already. At the centre of the group round the bar, McIver said modestly, 'My boss could knock spots off me at that. We had a party when the *Renown* was docked at Halifax on the American trip. HRH did a number like that and his feet never went outside the space of a table-top. He could have been Fred Astaire.'

As always when he tried it, someone asked him about the prince and his opinions. McIver was ready for it. He gave a quick smile of utter decency.

'You know what they say, old boy. Never talk politics in the mess. Besides, you might get me sacked.'

They believed him. They believed him without further question.

Just after nine o'clock, he saw Louise talking to the barman.

'Anything up, old girl?'

'They're going to get me a taxi,' she said, 'I'll have to go back presently. We start early with rehearsal on Monday morning.'

McIver put his arm round her gently. 'I'll see you back.' He turned to the barman. 'Scrub the order for the taxi, would you, old man? I'll see the lady home.'

Louise seemed too overwhelmed to protest. McIver fetched her coat and they went out through the hotel lobby. Louise led the way, down the hill fifty yards to the bus stop above the Square and the central gardens.

'I can get a bus from here,' she said with a determination greater than he had expected of her. 'It passes the end of my road.'

'If that's what you want,' McIver said patiently.

'Yes,' she said, 'it is. The other thing – I'm sorry – I don't want those photographs published.'

'You're the boss,' he said gently. 'But it's crazy. There's no harm in them.'

Those photographs were going to be published whether she liked it or not. Perhaps she need never know.

'Another girl lost her place in the company last year,' Louise said, 'because of photographs like that in a magazine.'

'But you'll have left them by then.'

'Other people won't give you work. I've been told that.'

McIver felt warm with anger. She could not know it, but Louise might have been helping to put a rope round his neck by her reluctance.

'Don't be such a little fool,' he said sharply, 'you could have the chance of a lifetime.'

'I don't want it!' she said with the first touch of anger, 'I don't want to be seen like that. I'm sorry. I'll pay you whatever it cost to take the photographs. You said I could have them, if I wanted them.'

'All right,' he said quickly, 'but don't make a scene about it. I can't give them to you this minute. The film has gone to Dicky Doyle in the post. He'll develop and print it. He's got a professional service for that. I'll get them back for you.'

The custard-yellow bus stopped with an abrupt shriek of its brakes. To McIver's dismay, Louise seemed suddenly on the verge of tears.

'How could you?' she cried. 'How could you give them to someone else just like that?'

'Because you wanted me to,' he said irritably, 'you wanted them to go to the magazine. Next time, tell me what you want done – and stick to it.'

'Next time . . .' Louise left the retort unfinished. McIver must think as he chose.

She turned from him and stepped on to the platform at the rear of the bus. A bell tinged and the custard-yellow hulk lumbered down the hill towards the department stores on the Square and the central gardens by the pier. McIver clenched his fists in his trouser pockets. A row like that in full view of the hotel entrance was the last thing he needed. As for the photographs, that was Louise's bad luck. He would damn well use them any way that he chose. But, uncharacteristically, he felt badly shaken by her outburst.

2

Across the Channel from the distant Normandy coast, the same moon-path tapered like rippled copper on warm languorous waves. McIver stared at it. He was angry but also frightened for the first time since Solitaire's death. Odd though it seemed, he was more frightened now than on the night when he had found her body. Billy Blake had gone. Roddy Hallam had betrayed him, one way or another. He had probably seen the last of Louise. For the first time, he was utterly alone.

Christ! he thought. Roddy Hallam had something to answer for. And what of Tarrant? McIver had no illusions about his own fate. He knew that he had been caught in order that he should be destroyed. Was it Tarrant who had made robbery easy in order to teach other contenders a lesson? Or had one of Tarrant's enemies given Hallam the number of the safe? What of the other deaths? Had Sid Royce and Tom Foster died because Tarrant thought they knew too much? Or had they died because a rival wanted Tarrant's support wiped out? In his mind, McIver saw the bookmaker, Sammy, sitting across the table from him behind Mr Champion's shop. Where the hell was Sammy now?

He felt himself struggling in a web of circumstance and deceit, the veined translucence of the wings torn and the shuddering body exhausted. He was about to die from lack of ambition. He had been content to rob in a world where the game was murder. Someone – Tarrant or 'Mr Sammy' or a man unknown – had ordered the death of Sid Royce or Solitaire, Tom Foster or Billy Blake, and then had gone home to dinner. McIver himself might have been punished for his challenge by a broken nose or a fractured limb. But they meant to make an example of him to others. That was why Solitaire had been killed. To get McIver hanged. It was more effective than any bullet in a dark street. The great pageant of an Old Bailey trial. The three-week nightmare of the death cell. All the newspaper headlines. A public example to anyone else who crossed Tarrant and his kind.

He thought about it calmly, staring at the moon-beam across the water. It was a weekend. So Tarrant was probably sitting in the old woman's clifftop apartment not more than a mile away. McIver felt the threads of circumstance tighten round him again. How was it that so many of those threads were drawn together in this seaside town? He could ask Tarrant. Suppose Tarrant had involved him in murder. Suppose that he could now involve Tarrant. At least Tarrant might pay money to save his own neck.

The more he thought about it, as he stared from the Overcliff at the tranquil moonlit sea, the more plainly McIver saw what he must do. Confront Tarrant. Call his bluff. Now. Tonight. If it was all up, if there was no hope, then he had nothing to lose by taking Tarrant with him. Tarrant might be alone at this hour. There might be a single bodyguard, not more. The Eley revolver would be a match for that.

Turning from his view of the sea, he saw the backs of the hotels along the cliff. How to do it? To shin up the iron fire-ladder to his room would be child's play. They would think he was still out with the girl, if it suited him to say so. Take the gun. Return the same way. No one would see him coming in later. If it suited better, he need only say that he had come straight in from the bus stop when no one was around to see him.

McIver walked down a side path to the back yard of the hotel. The iron ladder was a piece of cake and the window of his room was not even closed. He slipped half a dozen cartridges into the chambers of the heavy revolver and pushed it into his pocket. He also tucked into his cigarette case the photograph that the pier photographer had taken of the large fair-skinned man. Presently, he came out of the side pathway and walked along the cliff-top road.

The substantial villas stood well back behind tall and deep rhododendron hedges. In the darkness, only the mauve flowers remained luminous and velvet against the wreath-green leaves. Here and there among the red roofs was the green tiling of a modernistic house whose white walls and shutters added a hint of the Mediterranean among the heavy baronial style of an earlier age.

McIver's researches into Tarrant's habits had given him the name of the apartment block. It stood on a newly developed stretch of the cliff-top road, a balconied building in black marble facing with the look of a cabinet whose drawers were all pulled slightly open. It was much like the Temple Court apartments in its layout. The immaculate shape of a new Humber Snipe in aluminium-grey stood sleek and streamlined in the gravel drive. He recognized it as Tarrant's car. One way or another, matters would be settled tonight.

McIver stood in the darkness and looked in at the lighted lobby. There was a night porter on duty behind the desk. No more. Along the wall on one side were metal mail-boxes with the names and numbers of the apartments. Even from where he was standing he could see the bold black print. '36 Tarrant.'

It needed a little nerve. Nothing more. He waited for something to distract the porter. McIver thought to himself that it would happen, sooner or later. He had all night to spare, if necessary.

Standing by the Humber Snipe, like a chauffeur smoking a cigarette, he watched his chance. Being a chauffeur would be his story, if confronted. A bell rang. The porter came out from behind his desk and went through the double doors.

After all the fuss, it was that easy. But, of course, whatever security Tarrant had must be in the apartment itself, not at the porter's desk. McIver pushed cautiously through the double doors beyond the lobby and went up the softly carpeted stairway with its wide brass rail. The black glass and white tiling of the walls had been copied from the Odeon cinema modernism of the pre-war years. Beyond other heavy double doors with their spring action he heard muffled music from one of the apartments, the thumping rhythm of a band.

With his hand in his pocket, McIver rang the bell on the apartment door. It was opened by a slightly built man with dark hair and a thin pale face. McIver held the squat stub of the revolver steadily.

'Turn round,' he said quietly, 'walk back in and keep your mouth shut.'

He followed the thin man closely into a wide lounge whose balcony windows looked out into the night and towards the sea. It was a room of quiet brooding lamps and Spanish rugs in red and black. Bookcases sunk into the walls displayed shelves set out with alabaster and ivory, porcelain and jade. By the low glass-topped tables were deep cream-coloured chairs and a sofa. Tarrant sat in one of the chairs, his grey-blond pompadour hair carefully combed, a cigarette between his fingers and a tumbler on the glass-topped table. In the chair beside him sat the old woman, a fading ghost.

'I'm sorry, Mr Tarrant,' the thin man said, 'I thought he was service or something.'

'That's all right, son,' Tarrant said, looking past him at McIver. 'Well, my friend, you goin' to shoot us all with that thing, are you?'

'It's you I want,' McIver said. 'You're the one that's in the shit.'

'You don't use language like that in my home, in front of my mother.' Tarrant made it sound like a polite request. 'Not if you want me to do anythin' for you.'

The old ghost beside him smirked with pride in her son.

'Sit down,' Tarrant said to the thin man. 'Just sit down there on the sofa and we can all be comfy. I suppose you want to stand up, whoever you are.'

'I'm McIver,' McIver said. 'That's who.'

'Are you?' Tarrant said, unimpressed. 'The one that killed a young lady and that the law is lookin' for? And now you've come here to shoot us, have you?'

McIver hesitated.

'Well?' Tarrant demanded. 'Have you or haven't you? If you have, you'd better do it and get caught. If you haven't, then you might as well put that gun away.'

McIver glanced down at the ugly metal shape in his hand but he kept his aim on Tarrant. 'I've come to give you a chance of not being charged with murder.'

'And you're goin' to save my life by pointin' a loaded gun at me, are you?'

'Sally Brown,' McIver said. 'Otherwise known as Solitaire. I want the truth. The same as someone wants the truth about Sid Royce. And Tom Foster. And Latifa Noon because she had the bad luck to be there with Foster.'

'And you'd know all about that, would you?' Tarrant said bitterly. 'Royce and Foster were my friends.'

'They knew too much about you.'

'Yes,' Tarrant said, 'and if I had them killed, you just think how much someone else would know about me now. You think you got a story? You go to the law with that load of cock any time you want, my friend.'

'Sally Brown . . .'

'A young lady that deserved better than what happened to her. If they catch the dog that done it to her, I'll pray they hang him long and slow. And that goes for you too.'

McIver looked at the three of them, the old woman's eyes moist and unblinking, her face wrinkled like lizard skin. 'Hallam worked for you,' he said. 'Don't deny it.'

Tarrant turned to the thin man. 'You know anythin' about any Hallam, do you, Foxy?' The thin man shook his head and Tarrant turned to McIver again.

'You got any idea how many people I got on my pay-roll? No. Nor have I. You think I'm in attendance every time they take on a new grease-monkey down one of the garages? I got men to do that for me. So I never heard of your friend.'

McIver's jaw tightened. 'He worked for you. Close enough to

174

get the number of the safe in your flat, so that the girl could give it to me. That's how I opened it, took the keys to the Luxor safe, and took the money from that. Champion arranged the rest and a bookmaker called Sammy changed the money. Someone killed that girl and took the money from the hotel room. I'd lay odds Hallam was mixed up in it. He always treated her like dirt.'

Tarrant sighed. 'If you say so, my friend. After all, you're the one holdin' the gun. I never heard these names personally. Still, you believe what you like. I was down here the night that poor young lady died. With a dozen witnesses. And why would I want her dead?'

'Because she helped to rob you of ten thousand pounds.'

Tarrant shrugged. 'As I say, you're the one holdin' a gun, so I won't argue. Only I'm not complainin' of bein' robbed. No cause to. As for the rest, why tell me when you could easy tell the law?'

The old woman sniggered again at her son's cleverness. Tarrant patted her veined and withered hand.

'I took ten thousand pounds from your safe in the Luxor,' McIver said. 'It was changed by a so-called bookmaker, Sammy. I met him at old Champion's bookshop in Paddington. I went back to see him again, by appointment, that night she died. He wasn't there. While I was away, someone killed the girl.'

Tarrant turned to his mother and then to the thin man with a look of despair. 'I don't know what to say to this young monkey, I really don't. Now you just listen, my son. You think I killed that girl? You're off your head. Still, you prove it if you can. If she was killed while you was supposed to be seein' this Sammy, he's a better spec for it than I am. And then there's the others that died. You think I killed two of my best friends and a young lady I'd put in films? Excuse my French, but what the fuck d'you think I am?'

McIver said evenly, 'A man who put fingers in vices and crushes them. A man who carves and stitches faces.'

Tarrant shook with mirth, smiling without laughter. 'Oh dear, my young friend. You got a lot to learn. Listen. I'm in business. Not a bad thing to be known as a hard man. Truth is, sight of blood makes me ill. I can't even eat tomato soup for the colour of it. You seen too many films, my friend. Read too much trash. Now put that thing away.'

McIver felt a rising desperation. 'When I get what I want,' he said.

175

Tarrant shook his head. 'You really goin' to shoot an old lady? You kill me, you'll have to kill us all, unless you fancy leavin' witnesses. And while you're shootin' one of us, what you reckon the other two'll be doin'? And, in case you hadn't noticed, that's got no barrel. You'd be lucky to hit the opposite wall, let alone one of us.'

'Where's Billy Blake? Tell me that.'

Tarrant made a gesture of impatience. 'No. You tell me. I never heard of 'im.'

McIver played his last card. He took the cigarette case from his pocket, pressed the catch, and flipped out the photograph of his shadow. He tossed it on the table beside Tarrant.

'Then why have I been followed by him? I suppose you don't know him.'

Tarrant picked up the photo. He looked at it, glanced at McIver and grinned at the other man. ''Ere, Foxy, catch hold of this and have a look.' Tarrant glanced at McIver again and bubbled with laughter. 'You don't know him?'

'He was acting like a CID officer outside the Luxor. He drove something like a squad car outside the Temple Court. Followed me down here.'

'CID officer!' Tarrant almost shouted with laughter. 'Squad car! Oh, that's rich, that is. You really don't know who this is?'

'I wouldn't ask if I knew,' McIver said grimly.

'Why, you poor fool, it's Jimmy Maxton the Moke! Hard man but not subtle. Runs half a dozen girls. Smacks when he has to. Puts on a show with one of 'em for small audiences. He once or twice squired that poor young lady that died. I seen them at it. Moke by name and moke by nature with the ladies. Savvy?'

'Why was he following me?'

Tarrant wiped away the moisture of laughter from one eye. 'You? P'raps he fancied you for variation. Or followin' because someone told him to. Not that much brain in his head for anythin' more. And don't ask if he worked for me. I can afford better. But you want to know who killed the young lady? I wouldn't put it past the Moke. If he had a guv'nor that made it worth his while, he wouldn't need tellin' twice.'

'It was Hallam that teamed him with the girl for private parties.'

'If you say so,' Tarrant smiled. 'Then you answered your own question.'

McIver sat in the chair opposite Tarrant. He lowered the metal weight of the revolver and let it lie in his lap. Tarrant got up and walked over to the sideboard, as if confident that McIver would make no effort to prevent him. He poured whisky and water into a glass without offering it to anyone else.

'I didn't kill her, my friend. You say you didn't. Still, someone's taken care to make it very likely you might swing for it. I'd say you're gettin' a smackin' for meddlin' where you never ought. Happens from time to time. Someone gets ambitious. Starts to meddle. Gets taught a lesson. As for the others, you think I had something to do with Sid Royce and Tom Foster goin' the way they did? You're wrong, my son. They weren't rivals to me. My right-hand men they were, both of 'em. That was done by someone who meant to wipe me out. See?'

McIver saw. 'Someone using Hallam and the Moke. Who's Sammy, for instance?'

Tarrant shrugged. 'You tell me.'

The lamps flickered as if the electricity supply had been affected briefly by a summer storm in the hot Channel sky.

'I want money,' McIver said.

'Don't we all?' Tarrant turned with his glass in his hand.

'Fifty pounds and you won't hear from me again.'

Tarrant looked at him and then turned to the thin man. 'Foxy. Give him fifty quid and take his gun off him.'

McIver took the gun in his hand again. Tarrant sat down.

'Listen, my friend,' he said, 'you turn out to have done me a favour by namin' Sammy. Who he might be, I'd have to guess. Whatever his real name is, he could be the reason Sid Royce, Tom Foster, and Latifa Noon aren't with us now. Right, then. I'm givin' you fifty quid for information received. But perhaps you were seen comin' here. Perhaps you told someone you was comin' here. For all I know, you could walk out of here and blow someone to bits with that thing, carryin' my money in your pocket. And if they catch you, it might look as if I'd paid you for doin' it. You want the money, you take the bullets out and leave that gun on the table.'

'No,' McIver said simply.

Tarrant sat down and clicked his tongue. 'You still got a lot to learn, my young friend. Over there, by the drinks, there's a little buzzer. Security. I pressed that just now. Couple of minutes and we'll have company up here. You don't believe me, you go over and look at the button yourself. But you make your mind up fast.

Foxy puts ten fivers on that table. You put the empty gun there, bullets beside it, and take your money. Don't think you can grab the cash and do a bunk. You'll meet our friends in the hall. Foxy'll see you right once you done as you're told. Now, you got about two minutes.'

The thin man held a slim wad of banknotes. He opened it and shed ten on the table. McIver listened for footsteps.

'You got the rope waitin' to go round your neck for Solitaire, my son. If you fancy wearin' it, that's your privilege.'

McIver placed the gun and cartridges on the table. He picked up the thin crisp paper of the banknotes and folded them into his pocket. To one side of him, the thin man moved towards the door. Tarrant looked up at him from the comfort of his chair.

'Yes, my friend,' he said thoughtfully, 'you're gettin' a smackin' from the big boys for meddlin' where you never should. And I'd say that the best bit of it is still to come.'

3

McIver stood in the darkness by the service entrance of the flats. The man whom Tarrant had called Foxy closed the double door and locked the inner bar in place. Now that it was too late, McIver wondered whether he should have called the bluff of the security button. But Tarrant was right. The penalty of misjudgement was an eight o'clock walk to the gallows. He had lost the Eley revolver. But what use was that to him? McIver felt the thin crisp paper of the fifty pounds in his pocket. He took the slim silver cigarette case from his breast pocket and folded the notes into it.

Something was missing from the case. The photograph. The large fair-skinned man whom Tarrant identified as Jimmy the Moke. McIver looked to see if he had dropped it on the ground and then remembered that he had left it in the apartment. What did it matter? That was Jimmy the Moke. Did the Moke kill her while Hallam watched? Maxton's 'private theatricals' with Solitaire would no more restrain him than a butcher who had nourished and raised the animals he slaughtered. McIver remembered the man who had followed him. It was the impassive, unblinking face of the slaughterman.

A light breeze stirred the pine trees in the darkness. McIver stepped forward and stumbled. He was tired and remembered drinking Louise's cherry brandy as well as his own. Cherry brandy and pale ale! He felt a slight nausea at the memory of it. On the asphalt crescent before the apartment block, he saw the Humber saloon. That was Tarrant's, surely.

He walked across to the sleek silver-grey car. The light from the plate-glass doors of the apartment lobby was reflected on to the braided leather of the car's upholstery. He cupped his hand against the driver's window and scanned the interior. Nothing. Only on this side, where a chauffeur might have sat, was there something on the shelf under the dashboard. Square white cardboard viewing glasses, one lens red and one lens green. A magazine with photographic images in blurred pink and emerald contours. *Folies Bergère in 3D.*

Hallam! Though the 3D glamour pictures might have belonged to any one of ten thousand men, McIver knew there was only one answer. It was too neat to be wrong.

And now Tarrant knew the rest. Hallam was surely in the apartment, concealed during McIver's visit. Was he now smiled on by his commander as a good soldier or sick with terror as his treachery over the safe combination-number was put to him? McIver glanced up at the black marble of the tall building. It seemed as secure as a prison and, like a hospital, it had the clinical air of a place of pain. He thought of Hallam and shivered. Then he turned and made his way across the car park to the road above the cliff.

179

11

MISSING PERSONS

1

McIver woke from his afternoon sleep and frowned at the ceiling of the hotel room. It was not like him to doze after lunch. He turned his head and saw that his cigarette had burnt to a finger of cold grey ash in the little dish on the bedside table. The curtains were filled with sunlight. A clatter of tea-plates came from downstairs. He closed his eyes against a mercurial glitter of the tide, and listened to Henry Hall's band relayed in another room by an old-fashioned cabinet radio.

Beyond the open window the air hung stagnant, the omen of a storm. McIver inhaled the hot nougat smell of candy-floss, the clean tang of tide-washed sand, the vinegar odours of fried fish. Recollections of the past few days gathered in his mind like shapes in a puzzle. He touched the hard thin edge of the silver cigarette case through the smooth cloth of his blazer and remembered Tarrant's fifty pounds.

After two or three minutes, he pulled himself up, straightened the counterpane, and used the silver-backed brushes on his hair. Standing before the mirror, debonair in blazer and flannels, he took the ten crisp banknotes from his cigarette case, counted them again, and put them back. With half a dozen cheques cashed in short order, he would have enough to see him all the way to the Cape.

The afternoon had gone and the little bar downstairs had just opened for business. Christ, McIver thought, he must have slept for about three hours. A broad-shouldered and dark-haired man in a hound's-tooth hacking jacket and grey flannels was talking to the woman behind the polished counter.

180

'Here he is,' she said, as McIver appeared at the foot of the stairs.

The broad-shouldered man turned, still smiling from his conversation with the woman. He was about forty, with the look of a sportsman, a safe wicket-keeper perhaps, and the dark hair was combed in separated strands over the height of his bald scalp.

'Mr Walker?' There was an eager, pleasant anticipation in his tone. 'Wing Commander Walker?'

McIver grinned and raised his hands, palms outwards.

'Guilty as charged,' he said amiably.

The man laughed and opened a small identity-folder.

'DS Abercrombie, Hampshire County Police. Could we have a word?'

The world went dead before his eyes as the smile left McIver's face. He heard himself mumble, 'Absolutely, old man. Absolutely.'

He was aware that the woman had tactfully left them alone. Abercrombie drew out two chairs at the window table. McIver had never expected it would come like this. What the hell was it? Not Solitaire. Not murder. They wouldn't send one man on his own to arrest a murderer. Tarrant? No. Tarrant had too much to lose by involving the law. Was it the Walker dodge? Well, he had a passport to prove he was Walker. And, thank God, he hadn't used the cheque-book yet. McIver knew he could face this one out.

'Drink, old boy?' he asked pleasantly.

'Better not,' Sergeant Abercrombie said with a grin, 'you'll get me in hot water.'

McIver laughed. His hand was half-way to his pocket for the cigarette case when he remembered the banknotes in it. He paused.

'Have one of mine,' Abercrombie said, pushing up the flap of a packet of Senior Service. He watched McIver thumb the lighter into flame and touched his own cigarette to it. 'I'm enquiring about Miss Allen.'

'Miss Allen?' McIver was caught between relief that this could have nothing to do with him and bewilderment as to why he was being asked. 'Don't get you, old boy.'

'Miss Louise Allen,' Abercrombie said.

'Louise! Yes, of course. Nothing up, is there?' Surely, McIver thought, the little fool wouldn't have gone to the police about her photographs?

181

'I'm afraid,' Abercrombie said, 'that the young lady has been reported missing.'

'Missing?' Without quite laughing, McIver indicated the absurdity of it. 'I don't think so, old man. I saw her two nights ago. We had dinner in this hotel.'

'That's why I'm here,' Abercrombie said. 'It wasn't until this morning that we were told. Her landlady at Boscombe knew that she hadn't been back on Sunday night. Still, there might be an easy explanation for that. Then she wasn't at rehearsal on Monday morning. By the afternoon, the theatre manager contacted Mrs Lyons, the landlady. No sign of her last night at the theatre nor at her digs. She hadn't stayed with any of the other girls. First thing this morning, the Hippodrome manager phoned us. Wherever she went, she took nothing with her. Seems the young lady said something to a friend about having a date here one evening. So we checked.'

'Dashed good thing you did,' said McIver earnestly, 'I walked her to the bus stop down the road on Sunday evening. She didn't want a taxi. I put her on the bus for Boscombe.'

'And came back here?' Mr Abercrombie asked.

'I took a walk along the front and then came back.'

Abercrombie sipped smoke from his cigarette. 'All well between you? No reason for her to be upset?'

'I should just about say not. I was hoping to see her again in a day or two.'

Abercrombie inclined his head a little. 'I have to ask, sir, because two witnesses saw you leave the hotel. They had the impression that there was a quarrel on the pavement outside. They didn't see her get on the bus.'

McIver was uneasy at being called 'sir'. 'They wouldn't see her get on the bus. You probably can't see the stop from here. Too far down the road. As for quarrelling, they're up the pole about it. The only difference of opinion was when I gave her some advice. I told her she should get a steady job with a dance company instead of traipsing round summer shows and pantomime. She thought it was none of my business. Perhaps she's right. I said it with the best intentions. But she didn't like it, so I shut up about it. That's all.'

'And you never saw her after she got on the bus?'

'Absolutely not.'

'No arrangement to meet again?'

'Not precisely,' McIver said, 'I was going to ring her at her digs.'

'And nothing said about her going away anywhere?'

'Not a dicky bird. She'd got rehearsals and performances.'

'Any witnesses when you put her on the bus? Anyone else waiting?'

'No.' McIver frowned. 'Not waiting for the bus. People walked by, of course.'

Abercrombie flipped shut a pad on which he had taken notes. 'What we'll need, Mr Walker, is a statement from you. Chances are, there's a simple explanation. Chances are, the young lady's perfectly all right. But you were the last person we know who saw her. And, you'll understand, we have to take a report of this kind seriously even when nothing serious has happened.'

'Good lord, yes,' said McIver eagerly, 'I should just about think so. I can't tell you how glad I am that you came to see me. She's a jolly nice girl, Louise is. A good little scout. Anything I can do, you just say the word.'

'I expect that's all.' Abercrombie sounded relieved. 'If you don't mind making a witness statement at the police station in an hour or so, I'll have Sergeant Thornton standing by to take it. The new police building in Madeira Road. Just ask at the desk. That's all.'

'Right,' McIver said, 'best foot forward. I'll see to it *tout de suite*. If you're going back to the cop-shop now, tell them to expect me in about an hour.'

When Abercrombie had gone, McIver went upstairs and closed the door of the room behind him. Alone again, he let out a long breath of relief. It was going to be all right. Louise's disappearance had come as a shock but he was in the clear. He had only to tell the truth, more or less. Best of all, he had a chance to establish the good intentions of Wing Commander Walker with the police. He saw a needle's eye of opportunity which could make him safe, completely and permanently. He stared from the window at the sea-front traffic, where a slow procession of motor-coaches packed with trippers moved glittering in the sun.

2

A piece of cake. With long, easy strides, McIver took the shallow steps two at a time in the evening light and pushed open the heavy glass door of the police station entrance. Sergeant Thornton shook his hand and led the way to a bare distempered office, two chairs either side of a stained wooden table and an olive-green filing cabinet to one side. As they sat down, McIver drew out the passport.

'I thought I'd better bring this,' he said pleasantly. 'I've never done anything of this sort before but I suppose you have to check that people are who they say they are. I've still got an RAF 950 identity card, if you want it. But this is more up to date.'

Thornton was a slight, clerkly man with rimless spectacles, a reject for military service, perhaps, who had spent the war as a policeman behind a desk. He glanced at the passport, thanked McIver, and handed it back. McIver recognized the form for the witness statement on the table.

'I'll write it,' he said helpfully, nodding at the paper.

Thornton turned the paper towards him, unsmiling. 'If you prefer. Just the facts as you told them to Sergeant Abercrombie.'

McIver began to write. He kept to those facts. He described Louise as 'known to me for several days'. Nothing about London, let alone the Copacabana. If they asked, he had only to transfer their first meeting to the stage-door of the Boscombe Hippodrome. He wrote carefully, avoiding each trap as it appeared. He read it through. There was nothing they could catch him on. After all, there was nothing to catch him for. Thornton went to the door and called a young uniformed constable. The young man reappeared presently with a mug of tea and two lumps of sugar. He put them down in front of McIver and stood back against the wall. Thornton picked up the statement.

'Good,' he said to McIver, 'I'm taking this down to Mr Abercrombie, while you drink your tea. Once he's given it the OK, we shan't need to bother you any more this evening.'

McIver drank hot tea and then put the mug down. He grinned at the young uniformed policeman.

'Bit of a sobersides, your Sergeant Thornton.'

'Is he?' the young man said indifferently.

'Not like Mr Abercrombie.'

'No?'

The young man looked away towards the window and McIver lit a cigarette. Ten minutes later, Abercrombie came back without Thornton. He sat down opposite McIver, still apparently reading the statement. Then he looked up. 'Fine in almost every respect,' he said gently. 'Just one thing. I don't like the end of it.'

'The end of it?'

'Here.' Abercrombie tapped the paper. 'You put the young lady on the bus. No one's seen her since. According to you, you went off for a walk about ten o'clock, after putting her on the bus. No witnesses.'

'I can't help that, old boy,' McIver said with an easy laugh.

'I wish you could. The last time anyone saw you, you were having a fight with this young lady outside the hotel. No one saw you come in before they locked up. That's rum. No one had to unlock for you. So far as the witnesses know, you were out of the hotel all night. Last seen having disagreement with a young lady who's not been sighted since.'

'All right,' McIver said, 'I got back from my walk later than I intended. They'd locked up. I did what we always did at Cambridge. Shinned up the drainpipe to my room.'

'And Miss Allen didn't shin up her drainpipe,' Abercrombie said thoughtfully, 'because she didn't get back at all.'

The young uniformed policeman turned on the light, a single bulb in a white china shade above the table. Between the metal slats of the Venetian blind, the first moths pattered against the dark window-glass. McIver lit another cigarette from the stub of the last. There was nothing for it. Tarrant. It had to be Tarrant. And Tarrant would never risk telling stories that might land him in the cart.

'If you must know,' McIver said wearily, 'I called on someone about business on my walk. That's what made me late. I was there within twenty minutes after the girl caught the bus. I don't like discussing my business affairs with you or anyone. I went to collect fifty pounds I'd lent him. He paid me.'

'And he has a name, does he?' Abercrombie asked quietly.

'Mr Tarrant. Albeira Court. Apartment 36.'

He saw with relief that the name meant nothing to them. Abercrombie looked up at the uniformed officer and the young man went out. McIver smoked and watched the moth at the window. It was Sergeant Thornton who came in next.

'Mr Tarrant was in the whole of Sunday evening. He had a

185

guest with him. Mr Fox. Mr Fox is with him now. Mr Tarrant's mother was there as well.'

'That's right,' McIver said.

'Mr Tarrant says that no one called on Sunday evening. Mr Fox confirms this. So does Mr Tarrant's mother who lives in the apartment and was also there all evening. Mr Tarrant didn't owe anyone fifty pounds and didn't pay it. He knows no one by the name of Wing Commander Walker.'

'Just a minute,' McIver said. He took out the slim silver cigarette case and sprung it open. 'Fifty pounds. See?'

'Yes,' said Abercrombie quietly, 'I see. But what bothers me is this. I mentioned Miss Allen to you this afternoon. I noticed that you almost took your cigarette case from your pocket. Then you stopped. Funny the way things like that stick in the mind. Well now. Suppose you'd had that money from Mr Tarrant, what would it matter? But suppose it came from the young lady that's not been seen since?'

'Where would a girl like that get fifty pounds from?' McIver said sharply.

'No,' said Abercrombie gently, 'the question is, Mr Walker, where would you get it from? Just put that cigarette case on the table, if you'd be so kind, and stand up.'

The swirls of cigarette smoke hung in the light of the white china shade.

'Why?' McIver asked.

'Because the sooner this is sorted out, the sooner we can all go home. Now, just take everything from your pockets and put it on the table with the case. Then turn the pockets inside out.'

'I'm a senior officer in the Royal Air Force,' said McIver firmly, 'and I'm here of my own free will.'

Abercrombie was still gentle with him. 'Then all you need do is turn out your pockets of your own free will. I'm not asking you to do anything else.'

Grudgingly McIver did as he was told. Abercrombie picked up the wallet. He took out the blue RAF 950 identification card with McIver's photograph and Walker's name on it. He picked up the pink return half of the railway ticket from Waterloo.

'Thank you,' he said. 'Put all this stuff back again.' Then he went out. McIver smoked and waited. Sergeant Thornton brought more tea and a plate of sandwiches.

'How much longer?' McIver demanded.

'As long as it takes,' Thornton said, 'that's what they always say. I'm sure Mr Abercrombie doesn't want to take up more of your time than he needs to.'

McIver glanced at his wristwatch and saw that it was half-past eleven. 'I want to go,' he said suddenly.

'When Mr Abercrombie gets back.'

Fifteen minutes later, Abercrombie returned. 'Right, Mr Walker. That's all we need. Just come through here.'

McIver got up, not understanding. But he was surely in the clear, no two ways. The door of the interview room was open. Ahead of him was the corridor. Beyond that the lobby and the glass door showed him the freedom of a wide avenue with street lights.

Abercrombie was walking behind him down the fluorescent-lit passageway when a woman turned the corner ahead of him.

Solitaire.

McIver stopped. She was coming towards him, dressed in a swagger-jacket and blue dress. Abercrombie blocked the way behind him. McIver was no coward. He walked slowly on but the sweat ran suddenly down his face and the muscles that drew breath seemed to be in spasm. He had seen her dead. The newspapers said that she was dead. But this was no trick, no waxwork imitation. The more subtle resemblance of features, the expression, the movement, the attitude. They were the image of Solitaire.

McIver trembled. It was not cowardice but a physical collapse that the mind could no longer control. She was older. He remembered a story in which the watchers by a coffin had seen the corpse age from youth to senility as death did its work in the night before burial. Was that it? But this was no corpse. He took one more step and then his feet would not move. Behind him he heard Abercrombie's voice.

'I'll be with you in one minute, Mrs Lever.'

Mrs Lever? McIver put his hand against the wall and shook, as the woman turned away. It was relief and laughter. Abercrombie took him by the arm.

'You don't look well, Mr McIver. Not well at all. You'd better come back and sit down again for a minute.'

McIver made no attempt to resist. He sat on the same chair at the same ink-stained and cigarette-charred table. 'You know who I am,' he said with a desperate attempt at anger. 'You've seen my passport.'

'I know who you are,' Abercrombie said, 'and I don't give a

fig for your passport. You are the man who travelled to Bournemouth with a first-class railway ticket from Waterloo, number 2964. I spent twenty minutes on the phone just now to Waterloo Station and Pickfords key-holder at their head-office. That ticket was issued by Pickfords branch in Regent Street ten days ago. Charged to the account of Mr Leonard Brown of Bournemouth for the use of his daughter Sally Brown who was to visit him this week. Understand?'

'No,' McIver said, improvising instinctively, 'I bought the ticket off a man at the World's End in Knightsbridge. He said his girlfriend had intended coming down here but decided not to. She needed the money and wanted to sell the ticket cheap. I fancied a trip to the sea, so I bought it.'

'And Miss Sally Brown had an elder sister,' Abercrombie went on quietly. 'Two years older but almost as like as a twin. I'm surprised you never knew they were a Bournemouth family. Mr Brown and his elder daughter were here in fifteen minutes after I called them. The sister had one or two photos of Sally and her friends – not the kind you take. You were in one of 'em. I recognized you straight off, when she showed it to me. And when she walked down that corridor towards you, you should have seen yourself. And that's all there is to it, Mr McIver.'

'There's going to be a lot more said when I get a lawyer here,' McIver snapped.

'Yes,' Abercrombie said quietly, 'I'm sure there is. Now, you're going to be charged presently with being concerned in the murder of one Sally Brown. And for that I'm afraid you're going to have to stand up again.'

3

McIver sat between the two burly officers in trench coats as the car skirted Hyde Park Corner and picked up speed down Grosvenor Place. Clouds of gunpowder grey, edged by pale copper, hung motionless as theatrical scenery in the warm summer dusk. Beyond the park trees, the lights of the Mall and the neon hotel signs of Piccadilly shone through the twilight, golden chains of streets, hung with splashes of red and green, blue and purple. No one had spoken in the last half-hour of the drive from Bournemouth. They crossed the front of Victoria Station with its advertisements for Dover, Paris and the Continent, then turned down the Vauxhall Bridge Road. McIver knew where they were going. Rochester Row divisional police station. He had been taken there once before, long ago in a world before the war. He stared at the back of the neck of the man called Rutter, next to the driver.

They brought food to his cell and let him sleep for several hours. McIver was surprised at this. With the girl missing, he had expected the questioning to continue without a break. It was early in the morning when they woke him with a cup of tea. Summer dawn had spread to a warm orange flush of sun.

'We'll make an early start, if you don't mind,' Rutter said quietly, 'there's a lot to be done.'

They stood over him while he shaved. They refused to return his tie. He was to be watched, protected, cherished, until the morning when they led him to the gallows. Rutter drank tea and watched him eat his breakfast on a tray. Then they went down to the interview room. It was little different to the last, the bare floor set out with wooden chairs, stained table, and filing cabinet.

Rutter sat down. 'Tell me again how Sally Brown died,' he said gently.

'I didn't kill her,' McIver said calmly. 'I wasn't there when she died. She was alive at nine o'clock when I left the hotel and dead before eleven when I got back.'

Rutter folded his hands. McIver, staring at them, noticed for the first time that they were the largest hands he had ever seen.

'No one else was seen going to that room nor coming from it.'

McIver gave a little grimace of impatience. 'If Hallam and this thug Maxton that they call the Moke did it for Tarrant or his friends, they wouldn't be seen, would they?'

Rutter nodded, as if he understood. 'But according to your statement, you saw Maxton driving a car in Paddington during this time.'

'So what? He could have got there in ten or fifteen minutes.'

'Yes,' Rutter said sympathetically. 'Our problem is that Mr Tarrant has been spoken to. He has never met Hallam, nor Maxton, nor you.'

'He's lying. Try Sammy as well.'

'Oh, we have done,' Rutter said. 'There is no licensed book-maker who fits the details you gave us. No one drew four and a half thousand pounds in cash at the bank you mention on the day you mentioned. Nor does this gentleman, if he exists, appear to be a member of the National Sporting Club.'

Caught in a grotesque labyrinth of circumstance, McIver made a bid for the truth. 'Talk sense, old man. They're not going to put the rope round their necks for Sally Brown and probably for Sid Royce and Tom Foster as well.'

Rutter shook his head. 'Tarrant was miles away with plenty of witnesses when all this happened.'

McIver saw a gap in the evidence and went for it. 'Then if the big boys reckon they never met Hallam nor Maxton, you know the reason why.'

'Do I?' Rutter rubbed his chin in thought. 'Hallam and Maxton have been running round London murdering people on behalf of their boss? Is that it?'

'I don't know,' McIver said bitterly. 'You tell me. They could be doing it for themselves.'

Rutter got up and went over to the uniformed policeman by the door. 'Ask Sergeant Brodie to come in. You'll find him in the next room.'

While the man was away, Rutter stood looking down at the prisoner. 'Your chances are running out fast, Johnny McIver. If you're ever going to tell the truth, you'd better start now. From now on, every word counts.'

'I've done nothing but tell the truth,' McIver said bitterly, 'I robbed Tarrant of ten thousand quid. That's what all this is about.'

Brodie came in, his red farmer's face matched by a tweed jacket and flannels. Rutter looked up at him. 'Find any evidence of a break-in at Temple Court, did we?'

'No.' Brodie took a bulky brown envelope from under his arm. 'Any complaint of a robbery from the Luxor Movie Palace?'

'Nothing.'

They sat down opposite McIver. Brodie drew a cellophane-wrapped shape from the large envelope. It bumped the table with its weight as he put it down. McIver saw the sawn-off stub of the Eley .455 revolver.

'This yours?' Rutter asked.

Without knowing the reason for the question, McIver could not guess which answer might save him and which would destroy him.

'Who says it is?' But even as he spoke, it sounded like an old lag's last stand.

Come on, son,' Brodie said gently. 'You can do better than that. Is it yours?'

'It's Tarrant's.'

'And how would you know that'.

190

'He had it that Sunday night when I went to see him at the Albeira Apartments. Lying on the table.'

'Three people were there overnight. They had no visitors.'

'I can't help that. It was there. Lying on the table.'

Presently they took him back to the cell and left him. McIver began to shake. They had him on a string, asking questions without letting him guess what they knew. He wasn't scared, he promised himself, not frightened of them. Just tired and rattled by it all. One gap in the cloud and he'd be away.

It was after lunch when they took him back again. He promised himself that he would talk his way out of it. Christ, McIver thought, it was what he was supposed to be an expert at. All he had to do was tell the truth. If you told the truth, you were all right. Hadn't they always said that? If he couldn't see off the pair of them, he deserved to get the chop. They were both there again, Rutter and Brodie, with another man, a senior officer in a suit, standing behind them and paying casual attention. This time, they explained themselves.

'I want you to consider your situation,' Rutter said, 'before we go any further. After your arrest, the disappearance of Louise Allen was taken very seriously indeed. For thirty-six hours, the wooded areas of the cliffs and chines west of your hotel were searched inch by inch. I think you should know that a body was found there yesterday afternoon and that the Eley revolver was recovered from undergrowth in the chines several hours later. They used a metal detector.'

McIver's protest came in a gasp. 'That's crazy! They never knew about her! They never had time to find out.'

Rutter stared at him and then understood. 'I'm not talking about the girl,' he said, 'Louise Allen walked into a magazine office in Fleet Street yesterday evening, trying to retrieve photographs of herself which she understood you had sent there. They had no such photographs.'

'Well, thank God she's all right.'

'The body,' Rutter said, 'was identified as that of Roderick Hallam. His neck had been broken. Quite expertly. He was probably killed somewhere else and dumped there. Like the gun. Preliminary examination suggests that he was killed on the night when you parted from Miss Allen at about ten and were not seen again in the hotel until the following morning.'

McIver let out a single breath of laughter. 'So I suppose you think I killed him as well? I wouldn't know how to break someone's neck.'

Rutter shook his head. 'Unless you did it. In that case, you knew how. Now, this weapon. No fingerprints on the gun. Not surprising. But it took only one bullet to do the job. Two cartridges still in the chambers. Prints on those. Your prints are in the Criminal Record Office files from Borstal training twelve years ago. And they're also on the cartridges.'

'Tarrant had that gun on that night!'

'I see,' Rutter said quietly. 'And you loaded it for him, did you?'

'All right,' McIver said wearily, 'it was my gun. I got it off Billy Blake a few weeks back. I took it with me when I went to see Tarrant that night. It was loaded before, in case I had to use it on him. He bought it off me for fifty quid.'

'Come on, my son,' Sergeant Brodie said gently, 'you'll have to do better than that. You just went there, sold him a gun. And Mr Tarrant was so pleased that he broke Hallam's neck, dumped him in the chines, and threw the gun away there. Is that it?'

McIver hit the table with the flat of his hand. He felt the sweat at his temples. 'I told him Hallam was shafting him.'

'Three people say you were never there,' Brodie said quietly, 'let alone telling him anything. You're not doing yourself much good this way, are you?'

'I don't care what they say. If Royce and Foster were his men, Hallam set them up for whoever it was killed them. And Hallam set up the robbery. He gave me the combination of the safe.'

'It wasn't robbed, though,' Brodie said, 'remember?'

'I did it, for Christ's sake! Can't you at least believe that? I told you the combination number of the safe.'

'So you did,' Brodie said. 'We tried it out, with Mr Tarrant's permission. And it doesn't work.'

'Well,' McIver said sullenly, 'anyone can change a combination. That's the whole point.'

'And three witnesses say you were never at Tarrant's apartment on the night Hallam died.'

'Of course they say that!' McIver snapped. 'They're lying. Can't you see it? I thought it was supposed to be your job to tell when people are lying!'

Rutter shook his head. 'That's the jury, not us. And just ask yourself this, Mr McIver. When you get up in court and say you were at Tarrant's and when three other people say you weren't, who's the jury going to believe? Give us a guess.'

McIver tried to come to terms. 'All right. Roddy Hallam was a vicious little tyke. Sure he was. But why the hell would I kill him? What's in that for me?'

Rutter shrugged. 'Sally Brown dies. According to you, it was the work of Hallam or Maxton or both. Maxton was in Paddington that night. You're his witness. No evidence he was ever in that hotel room. We found Hallam's body through a series of chances. If they'd both gone missing, this story of yours might have started to sound convincing. I'd say you had something to gain from keeping them quiet.'

'Then ask Tarrant about it!'

Rutter looked at him sadly. 'Before you get in deeper, Johnny McIver, I'll tell you this. Hallam's body was moved after he was killed. A dead weight. It was hidden behind bushes and covered with branches. Now, I've seen Tarrant. He's not in good enough shape to have done all that. But you might.'

They had stopped him on all sides. The brave resolution of talking his way past them had foundered in despair. McIver looked at the two men opposite him and the dark-suited man who was watching from the far wall.

'I'm not saying anything more to anyone,' he said wearily. 'Not until I've got a solicitor here. And probably not then either.'

12

WEST END CENTRAL

1

On the next morning, it was Marriot who began the interrogation. He stood against the light from the window with the air of a prosecution lawyer about to cross-examine a defendant. Rutter remembered being told that Marriot was one of the senior Scotland Yard officers who had been called to the bar in the 1930s. At the time, he thought it was no more than a story. Looking at him now, Rutter believed it. Under the cold interior light of the interview room, McIver was sitting at the table wearing his blazer and flannels, the shirt open at the neck.

'So far as I'm concerned,' Marriot was saying, 'you can have a whole courtroom of lawyers. For what good it will do you. How far do you think you'd get with a lawyer who didn't believe a word of your story? What you need, Mr McIver, isn't lawyers. You need friends. People who believe you. I'd like to believe you but you'd have to convince me. All you have to do, in that case, is to tell the truth.'

McIver gave an uneasy smile. 'I've done that.'

'Have you? Then let's see how this truth of yours is going to sound in court, shall we?'

McIver shrugged. 'If that's what you want,' he said sulkily.

Marriot stared at him for a moment. 'Though no one at the hotel saw you leave or return, you were conveniently out of the room at the time of Miss Brown's death? You would ask a jury to believe that?'

'Yes, sir,' McIver said smartly as if on parade.

'As an innocent man, then, your response to finding this young woman's body on your return was to run away and live under an assumed name in Bournemouth? Is that how innocent men usually behave?'

'I thought I'd been framed, sir.'

'And you thought running away would prove your innocence? You would ask a jury to believe that?'

'Yes. I needed time.'

'And everything you have told us about the young woman's death was the truth?'

'Yes, sir.'

'When you told the manager of the Bournemouth hotel that you were Wing Commander Walker, was that a lie?'

'It was, sir. But for a reason.'

'I do not doubt there was a reason for the lie. When you told several people there that you had been equerry to the Prince of Wales, was that a lie?'

'Yes, sir.'

'And what was the reason for that lie?'

'It was part of the story,' McIver said, as if puzzled by Marriot's slowness.

'I see. One lie to support another?'

'To make the character real. The two things went together.'

'Precisely. One lie to support another. If another lie had been needed to support the first two, you would presumably have told that as well?'

'It wasn't like that,' McIver said.

'Was it not? Let me put this to you,' Marriot said. 'Your story about being equerry to the Prince of Wales was quite unnecessary. It was believed that you were Walker. That was surely enough. I suggest that your second lie was superfluous. It was instinct, was it not? A matter of being a born liar?'

'That's absurd,' McIver said.

'Very well, Mr McIver. Let us go into it a little more. When you identified yourself to Sergeant Abercrombie at the hotel and to Sergeant Thornton at the police station, did you tell a lie on both occasions?'

'I gave the name Walker, sir.'

'And that was a lie.'

'I couldn't very well change a name, could I?'

'Because you had by then told a pack of lies, had you not? When you claimed to know nothing of Sally Brown, was that a lie?'

195

'It was part of the same thing,' McIver said desperately.

'Part of the same pack of lies?'

'If you want to put it that way.' McIver sounded like a sulky child.

'Is that not how one normally describes it when a man is guilty of deliberate and systematic falsehoods?'

'It might be.'

'It might be? So a deliberate falsehood might not be a lie, by your standards of behaviour?'

'It would be generally.'

Marriot paused to glance at Rutter and Brodie. 'When you promised Miss Louise Allen that you had a friend called Dicky Doyle who would place her photographs in *Lilliput* or *Men Only*, was that a lie?'

'I meant the photographs to go there. That was true. It was just a way of putting it.'

'That was not my question, with respect. Was it true that this man existed and that he could place the photographs?'

'No. The important thing was to get it done.'

'The lie then was unimportant? The lie by which you tricked this young woman into taking off her clothes and posing for you?'

'It could have helped her.'

'Could it?' Marriot surveyed him with distaste. 'Would it not have helped you? And when a thing will help you, Mr McIver, do you not lie as if to the manner born?'

'Of course not!' McIver snapped back. 'I told you the truth.'

Marriot picked up a sheet of paper and glanced at it. 'When you were at Bournemouth police station, when did you first tell the police the truth about your identity?'

'They found out for themselves.'

'So you only told the truth when they already knew it?'

'If you want to put it that way.'

'And when did you first admit to being involved with Miss Sally Brown?'

'You knew that from the letter I'd sent you after she died. Before I left London.'

'But you only admitted that to Sergeant Thornton, when he already knew it? You would have walked out of Bournemouth police station without saying a word about the dead girl, if you had been able to.'

'That's how it was.'

196

'Once again, Mr McIver, you told the truth only when you had to.'

'If you say so,' McIver said quickly, 'and one place where I've got to tell the truth, for my own sake, is now. And that's what I've done. Start to finish.'

'Mr McIver. You told Mr Rutter yesterday that you thought you had been implicated in Miss Brown's death as revenge for a robbery you committed at the Temple Court apartments in Knightsbridge during May?'

'I thought so.'

'No such robbery was reported. The premises showed no signs of a break-in, no fingerprints, nothing to substantiate your story. Who else knew of this?'

'Miss Brown, Hallam, and Blake.'

'Miss Brown is dead and you stand charged with her murder. Mr Hallam is dead and we may have more to say on that. Mr Blake is a fugitive. Are you not your sole witness? Worse still for you, are you not your sole witness as to your movements on the night of Miss Brown's death?'

'Champion and a bookmaker knew I was going to Paddington at ten.'

'Champion and the other man, if he exists, are not witnesses as to your movements on the night of her death. Does it not come to this, Mr McIver? We have only your word for the robbery. We have only your word for your visit to Mr Tarrant at Bournemouth, against that of three witnesses who say you were never there.'

'They're lying.'

'And you would have us believe that you would not tell a lie?'

McIver said nothing. There was no point. Marriot, who had been standing with one foot on a small wooden chair, leaning towards his victim, put his foot down and straightened up.

'Right,' he said, 'that's all. I've finished with you.'

'Meaning what?'

'Meaning, Mr McIver, that you'll be hanged bright and early one morning, a couple of months from now. I've got all that I need. Mr Rutter will go through the details with you.'

Marriot went out. Rutter dusted off the vacant chair and drew it up across the table from McIver.

'Come on,' he said gently, 'let's go through it again. You left the girl in the hotel at nine o'clock. You went down the back stairs and wedged the lock open with a cigarette packet. No one saw you?'

'Of course not,' McIver said sullenly, 'I didn't want to be seen with this chap watching from the opposite pavement.'

'Then you went by underground to Paddington. Neither of the booking-clerks remembers you, neither there nor at Paddington.'

'Well, they probably wouldn't remember one face in thousands,' McIver said helplessly.

'And all the time that you were in Paddington, you saw no one else.'

'Only that pimp they call the Moke. He was in a car at the Eastbourne Terrace traffic lights, coming up Spring Street.'

'You'll have to do better than that,' Rutter said quietly.

'He swerved across the road and nearly hit a cyclist. Someone must have seen that.'

'Does he have a name, this cyclist? Any way we could find him?'

'How should I know? He shouted after the driver. Something about taking his number and reporting him.'

There was a moment of stillness in the interview room. Rutter asked, 'How come you never mentioned this before?'

'I never thought of it. People say things like that. They don't usually bother to do them. I don't. Would you?'

Rutter turned to Brodie and nodded. Brodie got up and went out. Rutter turned to his prisoner again.

'You've had a busy morning, Mr McIver. What do you say we have an early lunch and come back nice and fresh at two o'clock?'

2

They kept him waiting. It was almost three o'clock when Rutter and Brodie entered the interview room again. Rutter sat down opposite him.

'Bit of bad news, Mr McIver. There was one incident of the kind you mention, in Paddington at about ten that evening. A car number was reported to the police. Unfortunately, that car was thirty miles away in Essex at the time. Someone must have got the wrong number.'

'But I told you it happened!' McIver said. 'How could I have known?'

'Gossip. Guesswork,' Rutter said. 'Now. Let's go on to the next thing. Stand up a minute. Back against that wall over there. Cross your fingers as tight as you know how.'

McIver obeyed. He stood against the wall, at right angles to the window. Brodie opened the door of the room and a thin man of about sixty took several steps into the room. He was holding a cap in his hand. Rutter turned to McIver.

'Have you seen this person before?'

'No,' McIver played for safety. 'Not that I know of.'

'And you, Mr Appleton?'

'Oh, yes,' the thin man said with a sniff, 'that's 'im. No two ways. He was dressed like that, in the blazer. Talking to the driver.'

Rutter thanked the stranger and Brodie saw him out. Rutter and McIver sat down again.

'You're a lucky man, Mr McIver. Not quite lucky enough, though. While you were having your lunch, Mr Brodie phoned every police station in the Paddington area. There was a complaint about a car that night but the car with that licence number was thirty miles away at the time. The complaint was not proceeded with. But Mr Appleton had left his name. He was the cyclist. He's a messenger at the Home Office. Only too willing to have an hour off work to come and take a look at you.'

McIver sat back and grinned. 'So that's it! I was in Paddington. I'm in the clear.'

Rutter shook his head and looked his prisoner in the eye. 'No, Mr McIver. You're not in the clear. You were back in the hotel room by eleven, when a phone call was put through from the desk. No one saw you again until a young lady sold you a ticket for the all-night News Theatre at about midnight. Miss Brown died somewhere between nine and twelve. What this does is to narrow down the time when you could have done it to about half an hour. Say, between eleven and half-past.'

3

'You think he'll still hang?' Brodie asked.

Rutter shrugged. 'All he's done so far is tighten the noose a little. Clarke reckoned she died between nine and twelve. If McIver was in Paddington at ten and at Victoria by midnight –

and in the room when the phone rang about eleven – he's still the man. All it does is to point the time of the murder to between eleven and half-past.'

A last flush of sun shone pink on Pimlico brick beyond the window.

'So what about all this Paddington stuff?' Brodie asked.

'We'll need to have it documented. Give you the car number that the cyclist thought he saw, did they?'

'TCY 14636.'

'Owner's name?'

'Mrs Wendy Worth, near Southend. Seems the car was home all evening.'

Rutter stared at him. 'Why the hell, Frankie, didn't you say so?'

'Say what? We ran the car number against vehicle crimes. Doesn't match anywhere. There's no criminal record for Mrs Worth.'

Rutter took a deep breath. 'All right, Frankie. It wasn't your case. Two years ago, when Hallam was driving a stolen car, they had to ram him near Earl's Court to stop him. He was done for dangerous driving. The charge of stealing the car was dropped, when the owner decided that she had given him permission after all. It was just a misunderstanding. She reported the car missing, not knowing that he had driven off in it. That was Mrs Gwendoline Worth.'

'Same car?'

'No, Frankie. Not the same car. Still, you and I are going to travel down to Southend tomorrow and have a look at the charming Mrs Worth.'

4

The lime trees were in pale leaf along the seaside avenue, shading the gardens of white flat-roofed houses. Through close-textured privet hedges there was a glimpse of lawns and swimming-pools, modernistic lounges with curved corner windows. It was a world of pre-war wealth: cocktail-cabinets and the moist rattle of ice before dinner, grand pianos and photographs in silver frames. Harrods found it worthwhile to send a delivery van forty miles from London once a week. Several of the gardens had the appearance of a small park. Walls and tall hedges of cypress or rhododendron gave privacy and silence.

Brodie stopped the car by gates of dove-grey steel which were set between dry-stone walls. Rutter uncoiled himself from the passenger seat, got out, then ducked his head back and spoke to the two men in the rear of the car.

'We'll call you, if we need you.'

He and Brodie passed through the open gates. The house was a white stucco building of the pre-war period with green tiles and modernistic lines. Raised above the level of the road, it was faced by windows of tinted glass. At the front, it looked out to the blue glimmer of sea. A sprinkler cast its rainbow arc of water over the deep green carpet of lawn. Rutter stopped. Though the white garage doors were closed, there was a long dark car parked in the driveway. It had the look of a recent arrival.

'Something tells me, Frankie boy, that we might be half an hour too late.'

'Too late for what?'

'To come between brother and sister, by the look of that limousine.'

They passed the parked car. Brodie read a supplier's label in the window. 'Brandon Garages. That's Tarrant.'

Rutter nodded. 'And Mrs Wendy Worth – she's Tarrant too. Born Wendy Tarrant. Married lucky Mr Worth twelve years ago.'

'Who told you, then?'

'Last night,' Rutter said grimly, 'while you were sleeping your life away, I read Tarrant's file for the Charlie Armstrong stabbing. Fifteen years back. His little sister Wendy gave evidence that put him somewhere else. Somerset House were very helpful. They turned up a marriage for Wendy Tarrant and John Worth, three years after the case. I hoped we might get here before him.'

'Watch your back!' Brodie said suddenly.

'Mr Rutter!' The call came across the lawn like a shouted rebuke rather than a welcome.

Tarrant carried his age and his weight grotesquely. At a distance, the piled grey-blond hair gave him the look of a weighty eighteenth-century footman. His newly cut suit had an old-fashioned look, as though designed for wing-collar and spats. He wore a black tie. Tarrant was in mourning again.

'Mr Rutter!'

He held out his hand and smiled as Rutter took it. But the eyes

201

were dead as burnt-out stars, though the bluff voice had a ring of confident and jovial insincerity, the patter of the racecourse tipster and the three-card trick.

'I'm here to see your sister, Mr Tarrant,' Rutter said, 'if you don't mind.'

Tarrant pressed a finger to his lips and led the way indoors. In the main lounge, the silver-grey curtains and pearl-tinted hangings made the reflections of the sun cool and neutral. Crystal pendants of a modern chandelier broke the aqueous light on ceiling and walls in shimmering lozenges of green and blue, red and violet. Beyond the glass tables and the cushioned chairs a Steinway grand stood polished like honey. Tarrant closed the door carefully, motioned Rutter and Brodie to armchairs, then sat down himself.

'She's been a fool to herself with that little bastard Hallam,' he said, 'though I shouldn't speak ill of the dead. She's upstairs now. Had something from the doctor to calm her down. I got here twenty minutes ago and had a talk with her. I can tell you what you want to know.'

'I'll need to talk to Mrs Worth,' Rutter said gently.

Tarrant lowered his eyelids in confidential understanding. 'Presently,' he said, 'when the doctor says so. You don't want to come heavy on her in her bereavement. She got it wrong about the car. That little toad Hallam had helped himself to it and drove off to town. Not for the first time. There was that fuss last year with the other car, the one the police rammed. He'd said nothing to her. She don't drive the car herself. She was on holiday that first time, come back and the car's gone. Course she thought it was pinched. Only thing come out of it all, I met this young lady, Solitaire. She was a bright spark, she was. Knew a trick or two and not shy about it neither!'

'So the present car was in London on the night of Solitaire's death?'

Tarrant shrugged. 'If you say so. Who knows? My poor sister can't really say where it was.'

'And how does Hallam come to be mixed up in her life?'

Tarrant held his hand up, as if for silence. 'Not through me, Mr Rutter. That's a promise. Poor old John Worth was called up two years after they married. Captain Worth, he was. Desert Rats. Copped it during the Salerno landings in the Italian campaign. My poor sister was the type that attracted all the wrong men after that. Then comes Sid Royce that was to die the same night as

202

Tom Foster and Latifa Noon. Dare say you've no cause to like 'im but he was one of nature's gems. Pure gold. You'd find his fingerprints all over the bedroom upstairs. They was to have been married this summer and I was to be his best man.'

'Sidney Royce?'

Tarrant nodded. 'Surprise you, does it, Mr Rutter? I know some of the dirt that's been spread about me. How I had Sid Royce killed and the others. You think I'd good as widow my own sister that's been through so much? Pardon my French, Mr Rutter, but what the fuck d'you think I am?'

'Hallam interests me at the moment,' Rutter said.

Tarrant opened his mouth in a silent O of comprehension.

'That little rat came from goodness knows where. One of 'em took him on part-time at the garages. Sid Royce very likely. Hallam knows a bit about motors and smarms his way in until he's let into the house here to fetch and carry and drive the car when called for. Rest of the time he's in London bein' a grease-monkey and movin' scenery in clubs durin' the evenin'. A year ago, when you rammed that car he was in, he took that vehicle from this house without a by-your-leave. And he'd got that young lady Solitaire in the passenger seat. He was a thief, Mr Rutter. Still, my sister, bein' soft-hearted, tells the law it was all a misunderstandin'. She'd meant 'im to have the car when he wanted it. Like hell she had! He took advantage of her, Mr Rutter. Soon as Sid Royce had his chips, that little wart Hallam was out the servants' quarters and up the stairs to bed.'

'Aid and comfort,' Rutter said thoughtfully.

'I'd have put the little bastard in need of aid and comfort all right!'

'And did you?'

'You're trying to rile me, ain't you, Mr Rutter? But I don't rile easy. Not over you. Not over any of you. Speak to my lawyer. He'll answer for me. You reckon a man of my age could break Hallam's neck clean then carry the man God knows how far and chuck him down a cliff? Not my style.'

Tarrant stood up. 'I got nothin' against you, Mr Rutter. Not personally, that is. When you're in town, you come over to the Temple Court one evening and have a drink. 'Ave a bite to eat with me and Mrs Tarrant. But don't come to me with rubbish about that little shit Hallam and how he died. Don't do that again. Will you, Mr Rutter?'

He killed his smile as easily as turning off a light switch.

Rutter remained seated. 'I wanted to ask you about the Temple Court. The safe and the combination lock.'

'What's that got to do with anythin'? I wasn't robbed. End of story.'

'I heard that you used your mother's date of birth as the combination.'

Tarrant paused. 'Did you? That's good. I used to put that about. I'm not so simple as to have a number that could be found out like that.'

'So, who knew the number?'

'Not many,' Tarrant said sourly, 'that's for sure.'

'Your sister?'

Tarrant looked at him in astonishment. 'Leave it out, Mr Rutter! I seen some of the men she thought were Sir Galahad. I couldn't take the risk.'

'Hallam?'

'You bein' serious?'

'The girl, Solitaire? Or Latifa Noon?'

'Course not. What would they need to know for?'

'Your mother?'

Tarrant shook his head mournfully. 'Poor old soul. She'd have forgotten two minutes after I told her.'

'Tom Foster?'

'Tom had a safe of his own. I had it put in for him.'

'Sidney Royce?'

'Look,' Tarrant said, 'this is playin' silly buggers. You've got no call to ask no more than I have to answer.'

But he had hesitated a fraction too long.

'Royce,' Rutter said again. 'Why Sidney Royce?'

Tarrant sighed. 'So long as it gets you off my back, there were keys that Royce had to use. Keys for the motor showrooms and the Luxor office. Anyone that knocked him over and took those could help themselves. Those keys needed to be somewhere safe but somewhere he could get them if I wasn't around. Someone else had to have that number apart from me. Sid Royce could have been my brother-in-law in a few months.'

'Simple as that,' Rutter said quietly.

Tarrant scowled at him. 'If you happen to have a simple mind.'

There was a movement outside the room and the unfastened door opened slowly. The two policemen got up. Wendy Worth was in a housecoat worn over pyjamas. Tarrant helped her to a chair. She was younger than Tarrant, a year or two short of forty. Her present appearance was a grotesque confusion of puffed and blubbered flesh with natural sensuality. There was a suggestive budlike pout to the lips, though the clumsily lipsticked mouth itself was too large for beauty. The cheekbones were rather flat, their points wide as the chin was narrow. The jaw was a little long and there was an openness to the blue eyes that somehow conveyed the opposite of innocence. Though her figure was not overweight, a band of slack flesh was gathering on her hips. Under the ravaged mask of grief, her face suggested bodily greed, desire, and stupidity combined.

'It's all right,' she said quietly, 'I'm all right. I know what I got to do.'

Tarrant hovered over her. 'I'm sorry to intrude like this, Mrs Worth,' Rutter said, sitting down again and leaning forward a little in her direction. 'There are certain things that I need to ask you.'

'I know.' She found a crumpled handkerchief and blew her nose bravely. 'I know.'

'I shall have to search this house.'

'Do what!' The explosion was Tarrant's but Rutter kept his eyes on the woman.

Rutter ignored him and kept his gaze on Wendy Worth. 'I need to search this house, Mrs Worth. The man who lived here has been murdered. Before that, I have reason to believe that he may have been implicated in a very serious crime. It has nothing to do with you. If he was innocent, then this will be the easiest way to prove it. If you wish, I will apply for a search warrant. In that case, I shall have to leave men here until it is obtained. It will not be possible for anyone to leave or enter the house. If you allow me, I will do it without a warrant. I have two men with me who will do it very quickly and with the least possible disruption.'

'You get a warrant,' Tarrant shouted. 'If you can. Meanwhile, I'm getting a brief in here!'

But Mrs Worth waved him to silence. 'Do what you have to. I want it done with. That's all. Please.'

Tarrant bowed over her.

'You just goin' to let them do it, Wen? Just like that?'

'It's my house,' she said weakly, 'I just want to be left alone here. That's all. I want it over and done with.'

Rutter motioned to Brodie, who got up and went out to the car. 'Thank you, Mrs Worth,' he said quietly. 'If you wish to be present in each room during the search, of course you may. In any case, everything will be put back in its place.'

While Tarrant and his sister sat in silence, Rutter heard footsteps in the other room and then overhead. The tell-tale sounds of a police search followed in sequence as they worked their way up through the house, leaving this room till last. He heard the rasp of a light aluminium ladder being expanded. They were inaudible after that.

'Sir!' It was one of the men from the car, now coming down the stairs. Rutter went out. The man was holding a package about a foot square and six inches high. It was wrapped in a piece of black mackintosh and bound with tape.

'Not very original,' he said to Rutter. 'Taped under the water-tank in the roof, between the rafters. Still, it wouldn't be found unless someone was looking.'

They went out to the car.

'What's the form?' Brodie asked.

'Open it now,' Rutter said. 'Carefully. I want to know what else we may be looking for.'

The man who had found it turned it on its back on the car bonnet, touching it as little as possible. He took the ends of the black insulating tape and peeled them away until the wrapping came free. There was an old biscuit-tin inside. Taking the lid in the tips of his fingers, he lifted it up. Inside the tin was a smaller wooden box and an object wrapped in flannel. The man lifted out the wrapped object and gently peeled the flannel back, revealing several small blotches of oil. He laid bare a child's toy, in size and appearance. It was a delicate silver shape with a pearl-coloured butt. A .22 target automatic, almost a plaything by the standards of armed crime.

The wooden box was opened. A strip of photographic negatives lay on top of folded paper. The paper was thin and crisp, printed with the black italic script of Bank of England notes.

'Looks like Mr Hallam was all set for a rainy day,' Brodie said wistfully.

Rutter shook his head. 'Not a rainy day, Frankie, more of a monsoon season. And it was a .22 automatic that said goodbye to Sidney Royce. You think that was some kind of coincidence?'

The next afternoon's sunlight dwindled to a sea-grey brilliance through the basement window behind Marriot's desk. Next to the superintendent sat Owen Johnson, legal adviser to Sir Harold Scott, Commissioner of Metropolitan Police. Rutter had met him once before, a man of forty with the tall shiny dome of intelligence, a gold watch-chain looped across the waistcoat of an expensive suit, and eyes that saw nothing. Owen Johnson, the legal brain of the commissioner's staff, had been blind for fifteen years.

Rutter and Brodie sat side by side, across the desk, like a pair of delinquent schoolboys. Marriot watched them with scepticism. 'Tell Mr Johnson what you told me last night,' he said gloomily.

Rutter took a deep breath.'We're investigating the wrong crime,' he said simply. 'I want the murder charges against McIver withdrawn. I don't think he killed Sally Brown. And I'm sure he didn't kill Roderick Hallam.'

'Go on,' Owen Johnson said quietly.

Rutter gestured towards the desk, the dainty silver shape of the .22 target automatic wrapped in cellophane, the wrapped banknotes, and the strip of negatives.

'The bullets that killed Sidney Royce were fired from that gun. The Science Lab at Hendon confirmed it this morning. The only fingerprints on the gun are Hallam's. The lab confirmed that too. He killed Royce. He must have done.'

'Why?' asked Marriot sceptically. 'You think he was so besotted with this sister of Tarrant's that he had to kill her fancy man? And then he killed Foster and Latifa Noon to make it look like some gangland massacre?'

Rutter shook his head. 'Nothing to do with Tarrant's sister. Royce was the only one apart from Tarrant who knew the number of the combination lock. If Hallam found out what it was, then Royce must have told him.'

Marriot sighed. 'So Hallam got the number. Then he killed three people to make it look like a professional job?'

Rutter shook his head again. 'Foster wasn't an innocent party. Nor was Royce. They were in it with Hallam. The group of them were going to collect Tarrant's illegal earnings. Royce and Foster set it up. Hallam took it over.'

'You can't know that,' Marriot said sharply. 'In any case, I don't see Hallam as a cat-burglar.'

Rutter looked at the gun. 'Hallam was a killer. He shot Royce. He didn't kill Foster and Latifa Noon on his own. Perhaps someone did it for him. But that's how he took over the operation.'

'You can't prove it,' Owen Johnson said reasonably, coming to Marriot's aid.

Rutter conceded the point. 'No. I don't have to. I can't prove that Hallam recruited McIver and set up the robbery as his own operation. I'm sure he did. Without Tarrant's co-operation I can't prove that McIver carried out a robbery. But again I'm sure he did. None of that is my business.'

'None of your business?' Marriot was looking at him with growing displeasure.

'With respect, sir, my business is the murder of Sally Brown. Long ago, I gave my opinion that it wasn't McIver's style. I still don't think it is. Of course, if he was in Paddington just after ten, he could still have got back and killed her between eleven and half-past. Except for the photographs.'

Marriot held up the cellophane sheath of negatives. 'These?'

Rutter took the envelope from a folder and shook four prints on to the desk. The first showed Wendy Worth smiling down at the camera from the half-landing of her staircase. She was dressed in the housecoat that Rutter had seen the previous day and she was looking at the camera with a self-conscious and uneasy smile. It was not a photograph she had wanted taken.

'Sergeant Brodie spoke to Mrs Worth on the telephone this morning,' Rutter said. 'She recalls the photograph being taken as a joke on the evening before Miss Brown was killed.'

'It's frame number twenty-seven on the roll of film, sir,' Brodie added helpfully.

'The strip of the film was cut at that point,' Rutter said, pointing it out. 'Nothing odd about that, except that most of frames twenty-eight and twenty-nine were cut out in the process. Now frame thirty. A flash-lit view of the Copacabana Club in South Kensington. A singer in a black dress on the stage. Anne Currie. She was booked there for a week and her last performance was about eleven o'clock that night. Just about when McIver was getting back to the hotel. This was Hallam's alibi for eleven o'clock. He was in the Copacabana Club, photographing the torch-singer. You'll see that the faces of several people at the tables are in it as well. He could have this timed and dated easily enough. Probably made sure everyone saw him.'

'Another thing,' Brodie said, 'the rest of the film is blank. Six exposures unused. Someone wanted it developed and printed too quick to bother about the rest.'

Marriot shrugged. 'All right. How does this help McIver?'

Like a man playing a hand of cards, Rutter laid down the last two prints. Most of the images on these two had been trimmed away when the film was cut into six-frame lengths. The prints were blank except for a vertical strip at one side extending over a quarter of the frame. It showed a surface of linen drawn into folds.

'I still don't see,' Marriot said patiently.

Rutter drew two smaller prints from his pocket. They showed Solitaire in a pair of silk pyjamas lying on a counterpane with her hands fastened behind her back.

'We found these among the photographs in her flat. The ones that McIver had taken. At the time, I thought the complete negatives had been printed. They hadn't. Someone had enlarged and cropped the view. Put them together and they match the remaining parts of the two missing images on Hallam's negatives. The texture of the linen, the direction and intensity of the light, the continuation of the folds and creases in the linen counterpane. Those prints were made and then the incriminating part of the negatives cut away.'

'I don't see the point,' Marriot said. 'Why leave these photographs for us to find?'

Rutter looked at the prints again. 'You can't see her face, of course. I reckon she could have been dead when these were taken. Accidentally or deliberately. Fastening her wrist to the pipes came later. But everyone knew she was McIver's model. Finding these prints, we were supposed to think that this sort of pose was part of McIver's photographic repertoire for the street trade. That was a bonus. Something to sink him once and for all. You think a jury would look at these and then acquit him?'

Marriot touched his lip and exhaled. He looked at the horizontal printed strip from a mutilated negative.

'There's a shadow on it. Just there.'

Rutter nodded. 'Between the light source and the bed. The lighting wasn't a camera flash. They could have used McIver's own photo-flood bulbs to stick the thing to him even tighter. I'm told it's probably cast by someone standing near the photographer. Someone else. Probably quite a large man. If she was dead when this was taken and then moved to the bathroom, that's probably more than Hallam could do on his own.'

'McIver?'

'The one person in the world it can't have been is McIver. He wouldn't have got back until about eleven. By that time, Hallam was in the Copacabana Club ostentatiously taking a flashlight photograph of the torch singer. He'd gone a long way to getting an alibi, supposing he ever needed one.'

'So where does this leave McIver?'

'I don't know,' Rutter said. 'You tell me how he could have done it.'

Marriot stood up. 'So who's the shadow-man? One of Hallam's friends? The elusive Billy Blake?'

'Maxton the Moke,' Rutter said quietly. 'A neck-breaker if ever I saw one. After the girl told them where the money was, they couldn't very well leave her to spill the beans to McIver. While she was tied up on the bed, I can see Maxton holding a cushion over her face until the struggles stopped. They reckon it takes sixty seconds if you've just breathed in and thirty seconds if you've just breathed out.'

'Hallam and Maxton?'

'They'd make a good team,' Brodie said. 'Hallam needed a big man when he went to see Foster that night. Someone to up-end him in the bath. When it came to Latifa Noon, Maxton could do the heavy stuff while Hallam doctored the car.'

'Suspicious circumstances,' Marriot said firmly. 'No proof of murder in those cases. You've got Royce and Sally Brown. And Hallam himself. Three clear murders.'

'What I fancy,' Rutter said, 'is thieves falling out. Maxton never got his money from Hallam. That's why he was in Bournemouth, watching McIver, watching Hallam, seeing if they'd arranged something on the side. In the end, he had it out with Hallam, lost his rag, and broke the little man's neck. Slung the body over his shoulder and dumped it in the bushes of the chines.'

'No,' said Marriot sadly. 'With Hallam dead, what you can prove against Maxton is almost nothing. Not for Royce, Foster, Latifa Noon, Sally Brown, nor Hallam himself.'

'I'd still like Maxton brought in,' Rutter said, 'I'm hoping someone else might do the proving for me.'

'What would they do that for?'

'About three and a half thousand pounds,' Rutter said innocently.

6

'Small world,' Brodie said.

In the dusty sunlight of the little street they stared from the windows of the parked cars at the little corner shop where Mr Champion had once carried on his trade.

'Mr Champion's got sensitive neck skin,' Rutter said. 'Rope brings it out in a rash. He didn't at all like the sound of accessory after the fact in the girl's murder. Those rooms above the shop get rented out apparently. Short-term but expensive to anyone who's shy of policemen.'

'He reckons they're both there?'

'Only Blake that he knows of. Maxton was round here the night of Sally Brown's murder, if you believe McIver. Champion reckons he's never seen him. McIver says he saw the Moke drive off from here about ten o'clock. He'd seen McIver arrive. So McIver reckons it was straight to Knightsbridge where the girl was alone in the hotel room.'

'Champion's an evil old scroat,' Brodie said casually, 'what's he say about the rest of this?'

Rutter shrugged. 'He knows McIver as a picture merchant. Artistic poses, Mr Champion calls them. Only knew Blake by sight. Never seen Maxton. Never heard of anyone called Sammy, certainly not a bookmaker. If McIver met a money-changer here, that's new to Mr Champion. They could have met in the public part of the shop, of course. They could have arranged to meet outside the shop, on the corner, at ten o'clock that night. Mr Champion wouldn't know. Seems he's suddenly got a very small circle of acquaintances.'

'He's a lying old ponce,' Brodie said philosophically.

'Not technically a ponce, Frankie. Still, he's a lot more scared of his friends than he is of us. He's not saying another word unless his lawyer tells him to.'

Rutter turned the evening paper and read the stop-press county cricket scores.

'We could be here all night,' Brodie said, 'supposing Blake hasn't given us the slip already.'

Rutter looked up. 'This is his only doorway in and out, Frankie. If he's in there, we've got him corked up. If not, we'll lift him as he goes in. Most of all, I want a good look round Billy Blake's little grey home in West Two. If there's no sign by the time we get the search warrant, we'll boot the door in for him.'

A slow half-hour passed at the end of the dusty afternoon. Beyond the Praed Street junction the grinding of gears and brakes dwindled as the homeward traffic grew thinner.

Rutter yawned. 'You know what Champion said? He reckons he's a college man. He rowed at Henley before the first war. Then it was school again. Real Mr Chips. Teaching the nation's future leaders.'

'So how the hell did he wind up like this?'

'Search me,' Rutter said. 'He says there's nothing wrong with any of it unless someone's got a dirty mind.'

Brodie snorted with laughter at the absurdity of it. 'If they hadn't got one they wouldn't be in his shop for a start . . . Watch it, Jack! There's a car pulled up behind.'

'Thank God for that!' Rutter said piously. 'They took their time about it.'

A heavily built man in a grey suit and trilby hat got out of the other car and walked forward. He tapped the window on Rutter's side and handed in an envelope containing a folded sheet of paper.

'Mr Rutter? With Mr Marriot's compliments. You can turn the place over as soon as you like.'

Rutter grunted. 'Right. You two sit in the car back there. See no one gets out of that doorway and arrest Blake if you see him going in. Mr Brodie and I need a bit of a scout around.'

With Brodie beside him, he went across to the street door beside Mr Champion's shop. He tried the handle and found it unlocked. 'Mr Blake could be at home after all, Frankie.'

They went silently up the narrow carpeted stairs to the door at the top. Rutter pressed against it and found it locked. He knocked on the door. 'Mr Blake?'

There was no reply. Rutter, listening hard, heard movements. 'Mr Blake? I'm a police officer. Inspector Rutter. I need to talk to you.' There was a pause.

'Mr Blake? You've nothing to be alarmed about. I need some information. That's all.'

From within the room there was an explosion and the smack of a projectile hitting the wall near the door. Rutter and Brodie instinctively pressed back on either side.

'Bloody hell!' Brodie said. 'The bugger's got a cannon in there!'

'If it is him, Frankie. I don't think he's shooting to kill. Not yet, anyway.'

But then they heard Blake's voice. He sounded close to tears. 'I don't want to hurt anyone. Just go away and leave me alone!'

'I can't do that, Mr Blake,' Rutter called. 'Don't make things worse. I only want to ask you some questions. I'm not here to charge you nor arrest you!'

'Then go away!'

Rutter looked across at Brodie. 'Get down to the cars, Frankie. Tell Marriot we might need firearms. I'll keep him talking.'

Brodie slid sideways down the far wall of the stairs.

'Mr Blake! There's no need for this. You're not in trouble. Put the gun down and come out. Or let me come in.'

This time there was no reply.

'Be sensible, Mr Blake! We're putting armed officers round the building!'

Still no reply. Rutter hesitated. The interior door was flimsy enough for him to kick it clear of its fastening. Then what? A fair chance of a bullet through the head. But surely Billy Blake was no killer . . .

'Mr Blake! It's Maxton we want, not you! He killed your girl, Solitaire. He probably killed Hallam to get three shares of the money. It's him we want, not you.'

There was no reply, no longer any sound of movement.

'Mr Rutter, sir!' It was one of the men from the second car, calling from the foot of the stairs. 'He's trying to get out the back window, above the yard. We can't get into the yard from here but DC Cuthill's got him under observation from a wall on the other side of the railway. He can't see any gun on him.'

'I hope you're right about that, my son!' Rutter said, too softly for the man at the foot of the stairs to hear. He drew back and kicked hard at the lock. The door gave a little but then held. He kicked again and listened. There was no sound. Rutter kicked a third time. The wood holding the lock splintered and the door flew back.

After the darkness of the narrow stairway, the sunlight in the flat dazzled him. The first room was furnished with a broken three-piece suite and a table. He ran through to the kitchen at the back, almost falling over a bucket of viscous dun-coloured plaster. The kitchen window was open and the air was full of slow bluebottle flies.

About ten feet below the window was the yard behind Mr Champion's shop with its high wall and the canyon of the underground railway beyond. Blake had fallen awkwardly and was picking himself up. He turned and ran for the wall. Rutter saw no gun. He straddled the window-ledge, lowered himself the full length of his arms with his face to the wall, his toes about four or five feet above the ground. He took a breath and dropped. There was a sudden pain in his ankle and he fell sideways, rolling on to hands and knees. He got up and saw that Blake had used a bin to get on top of the far wall. In shirt and trousers, the bulky man was half crawling and half stooping in his progress along the coping.

Rutter hobbled towards the wall. 'Don't be a bloody fool, Blake!' he shouted helplessly.

The man was mad with fear of something that Rutter could not begin to guess. Blake had had no part in murder, nor even in robbery, if Tarrant continued to insist it had not taken place. Despite Rutter's training, it was he who had twisted his ankle and Blake who had not. Using the bin, he pulled himself up painfully on to the high rear wall, the electric tracks in their canyon below him. Blake was far along the wall now, at the point where the iron access ladder ran down for maintenance of tracks and signalling gear. Where in hell were the rest of them? He saw Cuthill on the far wall beyond the railway. Much good was that going to do. There was no way down on that side.

Blake was going down the ladder in a flurry of hands and feet. Rutter felt a hopeless sympathy for the big frightened man, a child in the world of cruelty and treachery where Tarrant and his kind thrived. 'There's no need!' he shouted. But Blake could not hear him. At that moment, with a groan of electric acceleration, a train came out of the Paddington tunnel and clattered along the exposed length of track into darkness again. Blake, in the madness of escape, had little idea of what he was doing.

Rutter heard the bell of a squad car ringing. Then it stopped. Two men in suits and trilby hats were coming out through the rear door of the shop. A whistle blew. Uniforms from nowhere. Two sets of heavy boots crossing the yard. But Rutter's thoughts were with the clumsy bewildered man on the iron ladder down to the track. A train clattered past the other way into the underground station. Not another for a few minutes. Safe to run along the line after this one. Blake dropped to the gravel track. Crunch. The live conductor rail on its white insulating coils. Careful of that, for God's sake, Rutter thought on Blake's behalf. Easy to see which one it is, though. Heads looking over the wall above. Never catch him now. Billy Blake stumbling along the gravel towards the lit tunnel of the station. Platforms crowded either side. Perhaps a vision of Solitaire and Johnny McIver waving him on. McIver standing there with driving gauntlets on. The Chrysler Airflow parked in the street outside for a fast getaway. Tickets for the Cape. Come on, Billy! Come on! Not too close to the live rail! Watch out! Crack! White lightning . . .

'Poor bastard!' said a voice behind Rutter. 'Why the hell did he have to do that?'

Brodie and one of the others helped Rutter down from the wall. Someone had gone to the station manager at Paddington. Homeward-bound travellers would be late this evening. Current turned off. Recovery of a body from the track.

Rutter limped a little. 'Poor sod,' he said helplessly.

Brodie watched him hobble. 'If you can manage it, Jack, I think you'd better come and have a look upstairs.'

Rutter managed it, gasping once or twice at the sharpness of the pain. Entering the flat for a second time, he saw the gun discarded on the seat of an armchair, hidden from him by the chair-back on his first entry.

'Nine-millimetre Mauser, Parkes reckons,' Brodie told him. 'No wonder it sounded like a cannon. You could just about blow a hole through the wall of this building with it.'

Rutter hobbled a little more.

'What the hell was Blake doing with a Mauser?'

'Taking it off its owner and levelling the score,' Brodie said. 'This way.'

The kitchen. A bucket of plaster still wet. The smell of rotting food and the flies. Where the Victorian range and chimney place had been, the wall was smoothly boarded over. A rusty electric cooker was wired in beside a scrubbed pine table. The range and chimney had recently been unblocked, though the cooker and table were temporarily back in place. The boarding had been put back and one half had been plastered over. In another day or so, the job might have been finished and the wall repapered. At present, the boarding on one side was only lightly tacked in place. Brodie prised it away again and shone a torch through. He beckoned two uniformed constables.

'Thought Blake might have hidden in there somehow,' he said for Rutter's benefit. 'That's why we looked.'

The two men freed the plasterboard at the side and lifted it clear.

In the space behind it, sooty bricks and tiles, Maxton sat in a deck chair. He was dressed in shirt and trousers, staring ahead of him, like a man in deep thought. The shirt front had been blown to tatters of pink and rusty red. Rutter stared and saw with revulsion the white bluebottle larvae in the open wound.

'That's why Blake was running,' Brodie said simply. 'He hadn't quite finished the job of walling up the body. Another day or two and we could have been looking for Maxton until we gave up in six months' time.'

Rutter hobbled back into the other room and sat down. The pain in his ankle was making him feel sick.

'Call out the cavalry, Frankie,' he said feebly, 'I've had about enough for today.'

'And tell Mr Marriot what?' Brodie asked bleakly. He stopped and looked up as Cuthill came in.

'Reckon Blake went out like a light, sir. It threw him clear of the live rail and now there's a small security problem.'

'What's that?'

'His pockets are stuffed with fivers. Well over a thousand quid. No wonder he hadn't got room for a gun.'

'All right,' Rutter said. 'We'll get reinforcements.'

Cuthill went out.

'Any news for Mr Marriot?' Brodie asked.

Rutter winced. 'I'd say Hallam must have promised Maxton a share of the money they were going to get from the hotel when they killed the girl. But Hallam bilked him. Maxton went looking for him in Bournemouth, where he reckoned Hallam was being Tarrant's chauffeur or something of the sort. He didn't find Hallam at first, just McIver. Hence his interest in him. In the end he found the man he was looking for. Hallam hadn't got the money there. It was under the water-tank in Mrs Worth's roof. Maxton didn't believe him. There was an argument. A fight. Maxton could break Hallam's neck as easily as you or I could snap a candy bar.'

'And this lot?'

'You tell me, Frankie. Maxton moved in on Blake. The only one who still had money. He tried to take the money and got shot instead. He tried to blackmail Blake by threatening to tell us where he was. And all he got was shot.'

'And that's all?'

Rutter stared at the darkening sky beyond the window. 'Not quite, Frankie. I think Blake was a decent type. Perhaps he found out that Maxton helped Hallam to kill her. Perhaps he even discovered that Maxton was the one who held the pillow to her face. So he wiped out Maxton.'

'I don't see Blake suddenly committing murder for that.'

Rutter put his hand on his ankle and winced again. 'Tell you what, Frankie. Half of London was screwing her, pimping her, all the rest of it. I think Billy Blake did something that no one else did. Something there hasn't been a lot of in all this. People kill for it – even nice people. I think the poor bugger loved her.'

'All right,' Brodie said uneasily, 'I'll go and call the troops in.'

Rutter eased a shoe off. 'And while you're doing that, Frankie, tell Mr Marriot that I can't wiggle my toes any more. I think I've bust my bloody ankle.'

7

On the day of Chief Inspector Harold Gould's funeral, Rutter graduated from crutches to a walking stick. It was a humid and oppressive afternoon in late August, vapour almost condensing to droplets in the air. Following the coffin as it was carried out from the cemetery chapel, Rutter stared at it and was surprised that Gould had been so small. Perhaps death had shrunk him. He walked with Marriot behind the family and the flowers, between two rows of constables drawn up to attention in their ill-cut serge trousers, tunics, and tall helmets.

'It's a disgrace,' Marriot said quietly to Rutter from the corner of his mouth. 'Look at that turnout! More like Gilbert and Sullivan than a guard of honour!'

Rutter smiled complacently, a little embarrassed that Marriot's remark might have been overheard. But Marriot had not finished yet. He paused as they followed the untidy procession along the wide gravel path between the sentinel yew trees. Again the muttered remark came from the corner of the superintendent's mouth. It was a measure of his disillusionment that he used Rutter's Christian name.

'What a bloody summer, Jack! Royce and Foster wiped out. Latifa Noon and Sally Brown killed almost for the fun of the thing. Hallam and Maxton chopped. Then that poor devil Blake tops himself on the live rail at Paddington.'

'He's the one I feel sorry for,' Rutter said quietly. 'I reckon he was all right. Just out of his depth.'

They walked on to a space between two of the oval-shaped yew trees, where a grave had been dug in the summer clay.

'Funny thing,' Marriot said, as they got back into the car, 'I never knew his middle name before. Harold Shackleton Gould. They reckon his uncle was the explorer. Well, I suppose he's got different company now. Royce, Foster, Hallam, Maxton, and so on.'

'You're forgetting Solitaire and Latifa Noon,' Rutter said thoughtfully. 'And where does all this leave Pretty Boy McIver? Walking free?'

'Not on your life!' Marriot said. 'We're doing that bugger for everything we can. Attempting to conceal a death. Obstructing police officers in the investigation of a crime. Obtaining money by false pretences. Fraudulently obtaining a passport. Contravention of the Obscene Publications Act, 1857. That's just for a start. I don't think McIver's going to be fulfilling any social engagements for the next two or three years. He can count himself lucky not to have been strung up for murder.'

'How about robbing Tarrant's safe?'

The car moved off behind the others and Marriot shook his head. 'Tarrant says he wasn't robbed. Still, Tarrant's another matter.'

Rutter took advantage of the new intimacy with Marriot. 'According to Harold Gould, Tarrant hired a hit-artist to wipe out Royce and Foster because he was going straight and they knew too much about him. I never believed that. This isn't Chicago. Then it was supposed to be some other gang leader who wiped them out to take over Tarrant's operation. I never believed that either. Easier to buy them than kill them. Cheaper even.'

'You told us so,' Marriot said caustically.

'In the end, it could be something as simple as a little squirt like Hallam wanting Royce dead so he could get his leg over the gorgeous Wendy Worth. And, of course, help himself to Tarrant's safe. Good old-fashioned sexual jealousy and a taste for hard cash. Could be the same in almost any house in London. Nothing to do with gangs or hit-men. Just love and money.'

'And Tarrant,' Marriot said quietly.

'You still think he's worth the effort?'

They were travelling north now, through the shabby residential streets of Thornton Heath, on the way back to central London.

'Pass us the *Evening Standard* under the dashboard,' Marriot said.

Watching the road, Rutter drew out a folded sheet of newspaper with a banner headline.

SUSPECT'S BODY FOUND IN FLAT – GUNMAN DIES IN RAILWAY CHASE

'No,' Marriot said, 'not that one again. There's today's paper in there.'

Rutter found it and handed it over. 'Right,' Marriot said, 'pull in at the side of the road a minute and read this.'

It was nothing much, only three inches of a column at the bottom of an inside page devoted to financial news.

> Brandon Garages, motor retailing outlet of Tarrant Holdings, will enter into partnership with Samways Cars to form Brandon Cars, under an agreement announced yesterday. The development of three new sites by Brandon Cars is to be financed by Tarrant Holdings' disposal of its interest in the Luxor Movie Palace and the rationalization of all its funds in the new project. With the promise of eight garages and showrooms across South London, Brandon Cars bids to be one of the capital's major distributors. Mr Samways, shortly stepping down from active management, welcomed the merger and forecast a steady growth of business on the five existing sites and the three yet to be developed.

Rutter put the paper down. 'Samways?'

'Mr Sammy,' Marriot said, 'Mr Sammy is the friendly cartoon figure in the Samways Hire Cars advertisements. Played a good tune on the knuckle-duster too, in the old days.'

'You reckon he was McIver's friendly money-changer? Making peace with Tarrant?'

Marriot shrugged. 'You tell me, Jack. All we know is that McIver started off with ten thousand quid and ended up with four and a half. Tarrant got most of it back.'

Rutter started the car again.

'That's it, then,' he said philosophically. 'I can't see anything but grief in trying to nail those two now.'

Marriot let him filter out into the Lambeth traffic before he spoke. 'Then I should keep that black tie on, if I were you, Jack.

You're the one that's being sent out to get those two. Try not to come back without them this time. And let's avoid another massacre, if we can.'

The warm summer rain was falling like thin gauze as they crossed Westminster Bridge. Rutter drove in silence, consoling himself with the thought that no one was immortal. Not Royce nor Foster, not Latifa Noon nor Solitaire, not Hallam, Maxton, nor Blake. Not poor old Harold Gould. Not even Superintendent Marriot.